Wagner, Descending:

The Wrath of the Salmon Queen

Wagner, Descending:
The Wrath of the Salmon Queen

By Irving Warner

Warner, Irving
Wagner, Descending: The Wrath of the Salmon Queen
Irving Warner
ISBN: 1-929355-17-3
First printing

Library of Congress Control Number: 2003112885

Design and Composition by Lee Ryder
Printed in USA

Published by Pleasure Boat Studio: A Literary Press
201 W. 89th Street, #6F
New York, NY 10024
Tel: 212-362-8563
Fax: 888-810-5308
email: pleasboat@nyc.rr.com
URL: www.pbstudio.com

*"The little wheels of invention are set in motion
by the damp hand of melancholy."*— James Thurber

Pleasure Boat Studio: A Literary Press

Milepost 1
Escape

The hospital was astir. Even outraged. After the police left, Herr Direktor Horst Von Bracken paced angrily in his office. Dr. Emma Bokina fretted how she might have prevented the escape, for unfortunately she had been physician-in-charge. She looked appropriately hangdog. It worried her that those two, in particular, had escaped.

"Horst, are you aware that Professor Winslow, though long widowed, insists he's married and his wife is being unfaithful to him, and that Mr. Wagner has intermittent rage paroxysms about someone named Arbuckle?"

Herr Direktor stopped pacing long enough to glower once again at her, run a hand through a great shag-rug of graying hair and mutter, "They're both, of course, delusional."

Yes, but what she didn't know, was the why, for she'd only been on staff for a few weeks.

"Isn't it unusual for obesity patients to be delusional?"

Herr Direktor leaned towards her, and, knuckles pressed against desktop, he growled, "It's the hunger. It has them by the throat."

1

They shouldn't have snared Wagner in the first place, but now that he'd escaped, he swore it would be a cold day in Pago Pago before they'd nab him again, the sons-of-bitches. And to stay escaped, Wagner's instincts urged him to steer the truck off the I-95 corridor. The key to a successful escape, he knew, was along the North Carolina back roads.

It was a trivial drawback that he'd never been a free soul in North Carolina, and was completely ignorant of the countryside. Yes, Wagner's practiced skills at getting out of terrible pickles made him feel sure he could score on some goddamned clothes. Which would be tricky business.

Even after fifty-one days in St. Finn Barr's—loathingly called St. Finnys by patients—Wagner still was a tad over 430 pounds.

Of course, he credited The Fix for that.

With Herr Direktor—Dr. Von Bracken—and his toadies pumping syringes of Sodium Anhydroxaline into Wagner, they'd managed to sweat off almost a hundred pounds in fifty-one days, the fuckers.

But still, for an escapee of Wagner's physical stature, acquiring clothes on the run was going to present a challenge. Wagner indulged himself a Cheshire smirk, then took a lusty hold on the steering wheel of the Oh-So-Recently-Ripped-Off laundry truck.

It had been a brilliant improvisational escape—testifying to Wagner's vigilance and presence of mind. Certainly, it stuffed a deserved plate of crow down the gullets of St. Finny's staff, and of course the driver of the truck. Still, Wagner's drama was a long read from the third act and success—in fact, to be precise, 3,900 miles from his residence, a.k.a. "Swine Wallow," in Anchorage, Alaska. Well, the first hurdle was to get hell out of North Carolina's primitive jurisdiction where commitment laws were still medieval.

The Salmon Queen had used them well, goddamn her—his own mother.

He checked the rear view mirror, then pointed the box-shaped vehicle towards a narrow off-ramp. Bringing it from 85 down to 25 caused a thump, followed by a worrisome shifting of the truck's cargo. Yet Wagner held it tightly into the curve that whipped motorists around 120 degrees beneath an overpass. Though the techno-trash who engineered the off-ramp did so from professional angst—to promote ugly accidents—he managed the maneuver without mucking out. Stacking the damned truck up would definitely put a kink in his plans.

Wagner made it to be about an hour before dark, and he found himself navigating through terrain steeped in rural Gothic. It was cast in long shadows. On both sides of the road were sprawling stands of scrub pines and nothing more. One minute there had been concrete interstate, then *voila*, timbered wastes.

The road was new, yet narrowed to two lanes without shoulders. Wagner's editorial olfactories caught the scent of the politically rank: Somewhere close an influential politician owned a chicken plant, turpentine mill, or opium greenhouse. What else could explain the outlay of federal highway dollars for such a superfluous exit on I-95?

But until safe ground was reached, he could no longer be Eyes and Ears for the *Northern Socialist Review*, his brainchild that had made life miserable for fatcats and political parasites.

As an escapee from St. Finny's, what the hell did he care if some entrepreneurial maggot squandered taxpayer's money? For now, it suited Wagner's purposes to be cloaked in the North Carolina hullygullies—this obscure exit's presence was potent serendipitous medicine.

"Just go with it, Wagner; just go with it."

He sang this into the windshield as his escape grew stronger, and was working up a momentum hard to stop. He was miles from the broken down, wrought iron gate of St. Finny's. In fact, his intellectual curiosity, recovering from fifty-one days stunted by The Fix plus the frustration of involuntary commitment, was sprouting its usual rich crop of questions and ideas. Amongst other disciplines, Wagner was a student of regional folklore. He supposed this sylvan niche was peopled by genetic backcrosses heralding back to 1540.

After all, he wasn't in Alaska or even Washington State, where Euro-histories were comparatively infant. No, not at all. By contrast, Europeans along the eastern seaboard ran short of appropriate mates after six or seven generations of blood feuds and, when not making clandestine raids in the slave quarters, had fallen to intra-family humpings. By the time of the Revolutionary War, Wagner guessed that much of the present countryside was populated by people having extra body parts, and patches of hair growing from odd places.

But Wagner was concerned less about herds of abnorms as opposed to organized parties of cops, or, worse yet, Monarch Foods' corporate security thugs. Jesus Christ, yes! It would be only a few more hours until the Salmon Queen's hounds would be hot on her first-born's trail. And the Chief Hound would be Colonel Younghusband, a chartered, Limey public school shithead if there ever were one.

Wagner managed the hearty laugh of the traditional villain, and announced to the windshield, "Clothes or no clothes, I'm a long-gone 430-pound motherfucker now."

Oh God! Wagner was a foul-talking, foul-thinking slab of humanity. He'd long ago adopted this snippet of personality ambiance from his grandfather. Obscenities and profanities discombobulated the Salmon Queen's social pretenses and Orthodox sense of decorum—dirty talk as a partial defense against her intelligence and dark, oriental femininity. Goddamned rights—it worked for both grandfather and grandson.

During her initial visit to St. Finny's the Salmon Queen spent most of the time dabbing at her eyes with a handkerchief, musing on her eldest son's personality ironies and foibles. Of course, while doing this, she ignored the slight, semi-illegal detail (not to mention moral outrage) that she had directed Younghusband and his uncle/younger brother Oswald to deploy Monarch Food's security people to kidnap Wagner.

The corporate knuckle-draggers had surprised Wagner *en flagrante* with Crazy Sue in a Durham motel. Then the reptiles had stuffed him away in St. Finn Barr's Padded Rest Stop for the Magnificently Rich, Fat, and Fucked-Up.

She, of course, had denied using Crazy Sue as the lure to draw him into the legal sand trap that was North Carolina. Having dabbed all her mascara away, she reapplied it while lamenting, "One would never guess you had wonderful degrees in classics from Wanderlay College, the way you talk."

"Oh fuck Wanderlay. By the time anyone was a senior, half the goddamned faculty had sodomized them. A grand lot of buggers they were."

But that was fifty-two days ago, and Now was Now, and Then was Then, and fuck all.

Best to forget about the Then and get into this escape. And hell, while he was at it, he would do well to forget The Fix. Wagner would also forget about St. Finny's.

And forget about its staff.

Forget the sixty-plus moneyed abnorms who until just thirty minutes ago had been Wagner's co-sufferers, the poor miserable sots.

He brought the truck back up to a comfortable fifty mph along the humble secondary. Sunlight seeped through the stands of pines, filtering down to tawny stripes that painted narrow bands along the blacktop. He settled into the challenges ahead.

Wagner began with a list—a habit taught him during childhood, a part of all self-assessment activities. Lists clarified messy situations. "Why else had things like the Ten Commandments and the Seven Deadly Sins come about?" his grandfather the Salmon King had claimed. So, now was time for a hell of a list:

(1) He should find out where he was, at least more specifically than simply North Carolina, probably a map would suffice;

(2) Clothes. Something better than St. Finny's smocks for abnorms;

(3) Something to eat. He was hungry. He was really hungry.

Goddamn, he was hungry.

(4) Ditch the truck and score on less conspicuous transportation than a stolen 2-1/2-ton laundry truck with giant red letters proclaiming WHISTLER'S INDUSTRIAL LAUNDRY AND DRY CLEANERS on three sides.

(5) Activate Escape Plan.

(6) Check on Lulu.

Wagner was getting into rearranging his list for maximum efficiency when the service door to the cargo bay slid open with a loud and abrupt WALLOOOOSSSP! and Winslow whirled into the front compartment semi-free fall style. His still huge body slapped against the right hand double-door and ricocheted with a sickening "THWAP," causing even the huge vehicle to shudder.

Goddamn! Wagner had almost forgotten about Winslow, the poor, miserable bastard!

The unfortunate man gulped at the air like a goldfish thrown out of its bowl. He grabbed at his pale, fleshy throat.

"Jesus, I'm going to be sick! Stop!"

Winslow slid the right-hand service door open before the truck rolled to a stop and hucked copiously onto the State of North Carolina's immaculate road. Wagner winced as he listened to the ghastly retchings.

Wagner amended and rearranged his list to read:

(1) *Get rid of Winslow*, with the rest following in as yet undecided order. Wagner's eyes narrowed as he noted Winslow's halfway-in/halfway-out position in the door. Hell, the answer to the Winslow question was close at hand.

"Winslow, you inconsiderate asshole, be sick completely out of the truck. Don't do things half-assed."

But Winslow clung to the handle, swaying back inside, gasping. "You'd leave me."

"And why the hell not?"

Wagner took off with a brutal jolt, sending Winslow on a bone-brutal return trip into the cargo area where Wagner hoped he'd brain himself swan diving into the truck's iron chassis. Wagner shouted over his shoulder in the direction of his recently departed rider, "Winslow, you sorry fuck! It was my escape and you screwed up the purity of it. At the first opportunity, you're out, O-U-T, OUT, you understand?"

He heard Winslow wallowing, trying to regain his footing then his weak predictable rejoinder—a pathetic whine. The lucky bastard had soft-landed in the laundry.

"But it's my money."

After fifty-one days of The Fix on alternate days, plus being fed little more than would keep a pair of gerbil healthy, Wagner was in no mood for cloudy thinking. His shout took on a definite menace.

"You *loaned* me the twenty-seven G's, motherfucker. When you loan somebody money, it is theirs, not yours. Understand? Or has The Fix sapped every solitary speck of gray matter from what's left of your confectionized brain?"

Winslow's mental degradation was a sad truth; Wagner should be more tolerant. The Fix frequently did heavy things to patient's mental faculties, and of all people at Finny's, Winslow had been there the longest—173 days. Allegedly, this pharmaceutical scrambling was temporary. But temporary or otherwise—upon checking in, Winslow had a Ph.D. in Particle Physics and weighed in at seven hundred pounds. Now the infirm bastard came in just under four hundred, but couldn't add, subtract nor recall with any reliability the names of his three children.

But sympathy and reflection had no place in what essentially was combat. Kindnesses meant nothing. What did convey meaning was that the hundreds and fifties in the cloth poke around Wagner's neck were his, not Winslow's. Wagner's innocuous looking pendant was access to Freedom From Want: A return north to the editorial offices of the *Northern Socialist Review*, and not inconsequentially Kokanee Joe's Special Denali Fried Chicken and Biscuit Superbucket anytime he felt like it.

Wagner had freedom in his sights, and goddamnit he wasn't about ready to allow a blob of mentally mangled humanity like Winslow to get in the way.

Milepost 15.0
The Pursuit is Born

Dr. Von Bracken answered the urgent call from Mrs. Wagner after steeling his courage by tossing back a half-water tumbler of schnapps. It was going to be tough, but mollifying the old bird would be a matter of tricky transactional techniques. Also, it didn't hurt having coupled with her during the Wagner Foundation's annual meeting in Seattle. This liaison had surely expedited St. Finn Barr's $700,000 grant application. That, and agreeing to committing her loathsome eldest son, truly one of the most puerile, vituperative men ever brought forth upon the planet. Now, bedding the old girl would have survival benefits, as well.

Jesus, Oh God Almighty! If any of his colleagues knew he'd humped a 68-year-old woman, professional mockery would be heaped upon him. He was both a biochemist and endocrinologist—either profession had honored traditions of preying on far younger women—preferably graduate students or student nurses.

Then, there was Herr Direktor's wife Greta. If she knew, there would be only a minimum of understanding for the sacrifice he'd made. And this, despite the fact that within thirty minutes of the moneys being deposited from the Wagner Foundation, his wife had nailed the malls harder than the day after Thanksgiving.

How in hell did she think—with 127 applicants for only two one-time grants at the foundation—that he'd prevailed? Because of the scientific merit of St. Finn Barr's grant!?

As his executive assistant routed in Mrs. Wagner's call, Von Bracken again recalled that he'd found the sixty-seven-year-old woman rather good sport, with extensive gifts in navigating the male body—an art which age had surely done nothing to diminish.

Birth of The Salmon Queen

She had begun life on Attu Island in 1933, daughter of Innokenty and Fervyovnia Prazoloff, both Aleuts of the far western language group in the Aleutian Islands of Alaska. She had actually been born on nearby Agattu Island in late winter of that year while mother and father took part in the annual fox trapping expedition. Actually, the evening of her birth, the eager and proud father had been kept away by bad weather, and the future Salmon Queen was escorted into the world during a foul, Aleutian winter storm sweeping in from the west, northwest.

Her grandmother Aliciaoff had been midwife, coming along to winter trapping grounds with daughter Fervyovinia for that specific purpose. Since both parents had agreed on names for either gender, the girl child, destined to become one of the wealthiest women in the United States, was named Anna Perescovia Prazoloff.

2

Wagner cruised by the bubba tavern cautiously. It was twilight and the rural citadel's lights were the nucleus of a tiny road settlement that was a garage and a half dozen semi-rundown mobile homes perched on cinderblock foundations.

'Perfection'!

Yes it was a kick-ass jerkwater icon set amongst the scrub pine. He could wander anywhere in Alaska or the Pacific Northwest and locate an identical cultural pit. So, despite his marooning in this Dixie backwater, he felt at home.

It was a weekday evening and a dozen pickups replete with capacious toolboxes aft of the cabs were parked in front. Several had giant antennae sprouting from rooftops. There was one shiny-new SUV with no-see windows.

Probably a drug dealer slumming, Wagner guessed.

A quarter mile down the road he pulled off and considered his situation. On cue with his reflections, Winslow wheezed and oofed his way from the cargo area back into the cab, fracturing Wagner's train of thought.

"Where are we?"

Wagner had to pee like nothing he could ever recall—the excitement of the escape was subsiding, and The Fix's notorious grip on his kidneys returned in force. He had stuffed all 430 pounds of himself behind the wheel in the heat of his escape, and the lower part of the steering wheel pressed down on the layer of lard over his bladder.

He concentrated on wiggling from under and behind the wheel, and not peeing himself in the process. No easy task.

"Where are we?"

Wagner's buttocks, too much for the hospital gown to cover in a sitting position, had allowed bare skin to paste against the vinyl seat cover. So, in addition to the urgency to urinate, and Winslow's incessant whine, Wagner winced in pain as the vinyl—stuck with great stubbornness—relinquished its adhesive hold on the epidermis of his posterior. Wagner howled as if a two-foot-long bandage were being ripped from a wound.

"Oh, cocksucker!"

Though getting in and out from behind a steering wheel was a routine physical act for normally proportioned people, with behemoths like Wagner, it could be dangerous and painful. Even the chowder-headed Winslow, a veteran Gigantic, grunted in vague sympathy.

"Wow, that musta' hurt, huh? Where are we?"

Wagner snapped his head back, and in the last few seconds of his skin coming free of the seat snarled hoarsely, "In the middle of fucking nowhere, now shut the fuck up!"

And at that moment, he slid free and out the open side driver's door. When his great weight settled to earth, there was the usual ominous snapping and semi-buckling of joints, vertebrae, and connective tissue as his still oppressive mass nestled in for the ride on his frame. His heart lub-dubbed a dozen of so beats of protest until it too adjusted to the burden.

It was yet another grim Wagner encounter with gravity. He sighed, peeing copiously into the night.

All around, the pine forest was rich with insects calling out in vast networks of languages; the resins reeked from the pine. There was a weird stillness to the air—it hung thick and suspended around the truck. Wagner, born and raised amongst the forests of the north and northwest, sniffed tentatively, listened to each call—for this seemed a foreign zone, where Wagner should never have been.

Hearing Winslow performing an identical duty on the opposite side of the vehicle, Wagner resisted a certain-to-be-fruitless attempt to heave himself back in and bugger off. But he knew he wouldn't make it; furthermore, a plan occurred to him that would make fair use of his stowaway. He altered his voice while crawling back in, allowing it become somewhat convivial.

"Winslow, you sad, burned-out slab of humanity, you are fucking everything up. But, you can make amends—become part of the team, so to speak."

"How can I do that?"

"A good start, would be to fetch me a piece of linen from in back. I must have torn off a square foot of skin on this goddamned seat."

While fishing around for something, Winslow whined, "I must get home. My wife is sleeping with one of my colleagues from the department. You can't believe how humiliating that is."

It was Winslow's wearisome refrain. As they always did, Winslow's martial problems—real or imagined—brought Wagner to the point of mayhem. Yet he had to be tolerant! If his scheme worked, it would make wise tactical use of Winslow. And then he'd ditch the bastard. For now, he had to make his passenger gain a sense of camaraderie.

"Winslow, put a lid on the shit about your goddamned wife for a second and listen: I'm going to drive back down the road and stop in front of that tavern. I'll give you a fifty, OK? Go in, get change. Then make a phone call, and tell who answers that I've escaped."

Still in back, Winslow paused in his shufflings for a requested seat cover. Wagner knew the poor sap was doing his best to think it through, but hopefully, he'd never manage it.

"Did you hear Winslow old boy? Do this without fucking up, and you're part of the team, OK? We'll be officially teamed up in this enterprise."

"But I don't know the number."

Wagner knew the tone: it betrayed a hoped-for flaw; so despite mental infirmity, the cowardly worm was trying to weasel into the deal for little as possible.

"You half-wit! I'll provide you with the fucking number!"

"Oh."

There was a bit more shuffling, then Winslow appeared with a meager specimen of linen in an extended paw. Wagner took it, demonstrating powerful restraint in saying nothing. While slapping together his makeshift seat cover, it occurred to Wagner that Winslow wasn't wearing his glasses.

"Damnit all, Winslow, can you work a phone without your glasses?"

"Oh, yes. Clear enough. But why don't you go in? You'll leave me. I know you will. But I won't leave you. I want to see my wife. She's having an affair with a colleague. He's not even tenured."

An incredible wrath, seemingly unimpeded by any limit, erupted—dragon's teeth from a soul already steeped in angst: Wagner reached over and grabbed Winslow by his gown, a big generous knot of it.

Though Wagner's arms were coated with inches of blubber, hidden beneath were muscles inured to the daily tasks of hefting five or six hundred pounds up from a chair or davenport or pulling his vast weight up stairwell handrails. It was the sort of daily workout requisite of super-heavyweight Olympic power lifters.

So, on the grab, Wagner reeled in Winslow as he might a box of dried mackerel. Then, with a couple of shakes, he quieted Winslow and pulled his face up to his. The physicist emitted rodent-like squeaks before this furnace of Wagner's sudden rage.

"Did you know—I SAID, YOU IGNORANT PILE OF SHIT— did you know, that in his final days, Fatty Arbuckle had to wear padding to *pretend* he was fat. That in his—GODDAMNIT, LISTEN AND QUIT SQUEAKING YOU LITTLE FUCK—last days, his fans made fun of him because he wasn't *Fatty* Arbuckle any more, but instead *Skinny* Arbuckle. And during his funeral, it was closed casket because his friends were ashamed to admit he was no longer their great, magnificent sonofabitching Fatty Arbuckle anymore! Did you know this in amongst all those equations and laws and neutrinos and shit that's coiled up in your miserable brain-pan?"

Winslow shook his head, and Wagner pushed him away in disgust. He struggled to cram his bulk behind the wheel.

"OK. You go in the bar, do what I tell you. If anyone says anything, you tell them about Fatty Arbuckle, goddamnit. You tell them."

Wagner looked around for a pen. No pen. He looked around for a piece of paper. No paper. He was breathing heavily, and his arms ached. A tremendous throbbing began in his head. Winslow gazed at him as if he'd suddenly become a dervish and had whirled off across the treetops.

"Wagner, The Fix got hold of you again. You're scary when that happens. The nurses used to hide."

Wagner's lapse seemed to have passed, and he tried to restrain laughing at Winslow's statement.

"Oh bullshit. The Fix doesn't phase me one goddamned bit. Now hang on!"

Entering the Pine Jack Tavern parking lot, Wagner enjoyed the neat crunching sound made by his rear wheels as they passed over the crushed oyster shell surface. He hated oysters, and the sound mollified. It reminded him that he was further obliterating the former homes of seven or eight thousand of the vile-tasting bivalves. Furthermore, their single purpose on this planet was relegated to preventing the boots of arriving Pine Jack hominoids from muddying up.

Wagner stopped the truck near the door.

Ordinarily, if either of them could have walked more than seventy feet, he would have attempted to park the twenty-six-foot-long vehicle out of view. But they would be lucky to make the door from here—less than thirty feet.

There was a flash of headlights from somebody pulling up, and in that moment, Wagner saw a compartment at the base of the truck's gearshift handle—in it was a ball-point.

When Wagner took Winslow's hand, he drew back, still scared from the recent bombast.

"Give me your hand back! I've got to write the number on something, goddamnit."

When Wagner looked out the windshield, he was holding Winslow's hand, having just completed writing the number on his palm. He found himself staring directly into the porcine eyes of Pine Jack's most recent arrival.

He wore soiled Levi's and the obligatory billed hat. Even from where Wagner sat, he could see the outline of a snoose can through the worn, blue material of the shirt's single arrow-shaped pocket. A fist-sized wad of keys hung from his belt. His upper lip bulged with snoose, and his eyes were fixed on the two oversized men who held hands inside the truck.

He shook his head and walked into Pine Jack's with a faster-than-normal pace—to report the weird sighting to his beer-sotted comrades. Wagner guessed that Winslow's entry onto the premises would provide this testicled primitive with his warm-up act. Something like a whine seeped from Winslow's thin lips—evidently a sign of him struggling for voice.

"Wagner, I don't remember why, but places like this scare me."

There was, Wagner knew, an issue of Winslow's simple survival in a cesspool like Pine Jack's. But better him than Wagner, for Winslow's gown at least extended down almost to his ankles. In backwater rat holes like this, appearances were everything, but Wagner rationalized that Pine Jack's clientele could conceivably mistake a St. Finny's gown for baptismal clothes. Now if Wagner had walked in, even chromosomal misfires like them would recognize him for what he was, a phenomenally obese man with folds of lard hanging down front and back, wearing garb that barely reached halfway to what at one time had been knees.

No, it had to be Winslow, and God help the poor bastard.

Without taking eyes from the tavern entrance, Wagner took his poke from around his neck, peeled off a fifty and stuffed it in Winslow's mitt.

"Here. Call the number collect I've written on your hand, and tell them I'm out. It is a special number. The call will activate my entire plan, Winslow. Remember that—just tell them 'Wagner's out.' Repeat it."

"Wagner's out."

"Right! You're really getting into this Winslow. I'm fucking proud of you. Now, afterwards, buy about as many of those bar sandwiches and snacks you can. I'm hungry, aren't you?"

"Oh, yes, very much."

"Damned rights. Those cocksuckers at St. Finny's have been feeding us on eighteen cents a day. Oh, and a jar or two of those sausage snacks too. Don't worry about liquids. There's a vending machine across the street, and we can empty that som'bitch—flush the fucking Fix out of us. Now go for it. We're a phone call from liberty, Winslow."

For the first time Winslow smiled and nodded—this primordial glow of enthusiasm caused a surge of un-Wagner-like optimism. Food had clinched it—the absolute carrot!

With renewed resolve, Winslow slid open the passenger side door, holding on gamely to the fifty. He waddled towards the entrance, but even before he labored up the two low steps into the place, leering faces came into view—bobbing Punch and Judy style between beer and tobacco signs. The occupants were clearly anticipating their movable freak show with high spirits.

Wagner knew that, ultimately, everything rested upon the Shoulders of the Gods.

Milepost 36.1
The Hound and Fox

Colonel Younghusband, Director of Security and Logistics for Monarch Enterprises International (M.E.I.) preceded the Salmon Queen by seven hours into Raleigh/Durham. He brought two impact teams with him, just to get started. He was confident which priority this situation rated.

Younghusband knew that in matters of business and personal conduct, Mrs. Wagner (whom he always thought of simply as 'Herself'), above all else, was endlessly practical and cunning. But, her single weak spot—the only weak spot—in this amazing woman, was the living eyesore and bane to her existence—and certainly Younghusband's—her eldest son, Vidar, referred to always as simply "Wagner."

She would do anything to help him, and she had over 18.5 billion dollars with which to do it as well as the multi-national corporate resources of M.E.I.

Securing the north wing of the Planter's Inn in downtown Raleigh/Durham—and the presidential suite for Herself and her youngest son Oswald—Younghusband went to work. He chartered two choppers, three Cessna 206's, and a mobile communications truck; and he made damned sure fresh croissants, unsalted butter and Russian tea was available promptly at 8:00 a.m. for Herself.

"I'm not sure if we have Russian tea, Colonel," worried the supervising concierge.

"I'm sure you will. Her brand is Troika Black Leaf. By 8:00 a.m. tomorrow, in fact, I know you will."

The basics accomplished, he settled down for his daily respite—to maintain body and soul. Unlike his missus, he missed England. So Younghusband took a late supper while reading a London Times. He checked into the mess developing between the Labor backbenchers and the scandal regards turf accountants fixing dog races. An outrage like that had Labor cronyism written all over it, of course.

HISTORICAL LANDMARK #2
The Admiral and the Salmon Queen

The Salmon Queen was eight years old when the Japanese invaded Chichigof Village on Attu in June 1942 and discovered nothing but forty-two Aleuts, a school teacher and her slow-witted husband. The Aleuts, to arriving officers, looked virtually Japanese. Militarily, there were no U.S. Marines, no U.S. Army, and no U.S. Navy.

"Quite surprising," Admiral Kuchihora was recorded as declaring, "so, what is there, then?"

A simple question, and when informed there were a few families of Japanese on the island, and two white Americans, the Admiral directed some of these alleged Japanese be brought to him.

By evening a family of these Japanese stood trembling before him on his flagship. In fact, the three were the Salmon Queen, her mother, and her father—examples of male, female and a child.

The Admiral asked them how long they had lived on Attu in Japanese, but they babbled on in a language none of his officers could understand.

He then tried Korean, Cantonese, a bit of Portuguese he'd picked up on leave in Macao, and finally, an American English salutation he'd memorized from a book while on liberty in Honolulu during the late 1920's which came out as, "Do you suck pineapples from trees?"

And they didn't understand that. The Admiral concluded they were some sort of quasi-Japanese, a half step between the hairy Ainu and true Japanese. They were meager pickings to result from an entire invasion.

3

Not surprisingly, Winslow made a complete mess of things.

Wagner slowed to fifty several miles from Pine Jack's, feeling somewhat guilty about abandoning Winslow and worried about committing a felony vehicular assault. But, no matter, his lawyer Moynahan would handle that. The man had a legal mind that was absolutely unchallengable.

Minutes before, Wagner watched the ugly episode in the tavern unfold, and it became wicked rapidly. He had closed his eyes, lowering his head to the cold rim of the steering wheel. Clearly, Winslow wasn't up to the task.

The rough stuff began within sixty seconds after Winslow entered. Through the semi-dark window, between beer signs and lottery posters, Wagner watched in horror as Winslow's white hospital gown levitated into view, then began ghost-like spasm of jerks and drops in mid-air, evidently, sans Winslow. It took the simplest of deductive efforts to conclude it had been torn off and now was being tossed back and forth like a rag doll by playful terriers. Even from inside the truck, raucous HEE HAWWWWs and HOT DAMNs were audible.

No doubt about it—Winslow was screwed.

Wagner saw beyond the simple violence of the scene and appreciated the basic misfortune of it all. In view of the time elapsed between Winslow's entrance and being pounced on by Pine Jack's troop of australopithecines, there was no time for a phone call.

But the game of toss-the-gown lasted less than a half minute. Then the door exploded outwards and a naked Winslow cartwheeled Bump-Ta-Bump-Bump down the steps—a human truck tire, deflated and headed for the trash heap. Doing the shoving were three Good Ol' Boys having a Helluva Good Ol' Time. This was their toy, and they were making an evening of it. A fourth sportsman emerged, holding Winslow's gown aloft—the gold medal of the evening.

A scaly duo of Stand-By-Your-Man Bubbettes sauntered out the door, hips akimbo, ample butts swelling out worn designer Jeans. Beers-in-hand, they looked on. One tendered minimal disapproval by closing her eyes momentarily, though her partner looked on with a harder, I-could-do-a-fuck-of-a-lot-better smirk.

And there was yet a fifth participant. It was the recently arrived messenger figure. Wagner recognized the knot of keys bouncing in time to his excited dance. He ran from the door with a pool cue. Taking care to avoid being hit by a flying leg or arm, he danced about the fallen Winslow, attempting to tweak his shrunken member with his makeshift probe.

Ancient school ground memories hurtled Wagner into action.

A fierce, abrasive sound caused Pine Jack's habitués to freeze-frame, looking away from Winslow, now curled embryo style. What they saw rendered them slack-jawed. The truck's rear wheels spat back oyster-shell fragments thirty feet when Wagner floored the son-of-a-bitch. Fishtailing slightly to the right, he caught the wielder of the pool cue with the fender, launching him buttocks first into the night. It was a solid ten-point hit Wagner felt clear through the steering column. But his next two strikes, including the celebrant holding the gown, were glancing, lacking the satisfying thunk of the first. By expert steering, Wagner missed Winslow's right leg by inches. He truly would have liked to take another pass, but getting the hell gone took precedence.

Instead, since the driver's side window was down, Wagner yowled to those left standing, "Eat shit, you Bohunk Dickheads!"

Mile 40.4
Point of Interest
Lulu

In court briefs Wagner's lawyer, Mac Moynahan, maintained that Lulu was not a Canadian Lynx but a Mottled Macedonian, a rare and expensive breed of domestic cat. Fish and Game authorities claimed Lulu was obviously a Northern Lynx who'd been given a fancy grooming job; therefore, Alaska state law required a permit for Wagner to have her, and they did not issue such permits for lynx cats.

"Simply put, your honor, the animal's a public menace."

Lulu did have unresolved issues regards domesticity: She liked no one but Wagner (though tolerated Leggy Peggy, her occasional Nanny). She'd skinnied by with minor neighborhood infractions until sadly the line was crossed. Lulu killed, then sampled a bit of, a State Senator's eight-year-old Lesser Schnauzer who'd made the mistake of chasing her.

"She was in her own yard," Wagner had defended. But the problem grew to a controversy, until even Moynahan's legal talents were hard pressed. Ultimately, the only way out was doing something few would have thought the founder of The Northern Institute for Social Reprisal would do—he bribed a magistrate.

The following day, Lulu was legally declared a Mottled Macedonian house cat. "Fucking cat," groused Wagner to the staff at the journal and Institute, "she cost me $75,000 dollars." But it was a small expense for a person who made such sums in bank interest per forty-eight-hour period.

Milepost 40.9
A Flank Move

The urgent message from Peggy came in while Moynahan watched his client Boris deliver the final forty lines of his "I Am Innocent" soliloquy: Boris wept, eulogized his Mother in Omsk, and lamented both his drug-addicted sister in Tashkent and his legless brother's humiliation at the hands of the Russian Mafia.

The Asst. U.S. Attorney for Alaska and his associates watched placidly. Drained of all further hope, Boris's head sank to the table and he wept. Moynahan had to admire his client—with each delivery the improvement was obvious.

So when Moynahan's pager went off, he gladly excused himself, for it not only added to the dramatic effect of Boris's emotional collapse, but it broke the boredom.

On the phone in the outer office, a breathless Peggy explained, "The North Carolina State Police called. Mr. Wagner's escaped. They got the phone number from his hostage's hand! My God, do you think they'll shoot on sight? I mean, down there, they might do anything. And hostages! Mr. Wagner has never taken a hostage; he's non-violent. What in earth has happened?"

Moynahan quieted Peggy and told her to activate Wagner's Plan A—car, money, and clothes to be left at Dulles International. She stuttered nervously while noting details, and Moynahan realized the wisdom of Wagner's plans: Excitable by nature and inextricably Wagner's devoted administrative assistant, Peggy formed a leaky and naive vessel regards caution and security. All strategies—especially duplicity—had to be utilized in getting hell out of North Carolina and their primitive commitment laws.

Wagner had thereby decided to employ her for an ingenious feint: For now, pending definite contact from Wagner, Moynahan would activate the secondary plan, put in place weeks before. Another getaway car and necessities, including Moynahan, would be waiting at the Spartanburg, South Carolina, air terminal! "The stupid fucks," Wagner had chortled, "will never anticipate a southerly escape, plus they will tumble like slug halibut for my decoy. Get ready. When I get over the border, it's party time for lawsuits, sabotage, and other forms of vengeful mayhem on all these dirty bastards!"

Moynahan was about to return to the Boris Show when he thought that since he would soon be flying south to attend this serious, stressful business, might he not partake in a brief stop at an old friend's place in Florida? Wagner was more than equal to handling the hour-to-hour logistics of an escape.

The Emperor and the Salmon Queen

When Emperor Hirohito heard the news of the successful capture of American territory and the liberation of the tiny village
of strange Japanese, he was interested. A marine biologist, he
immediately thought of their academic significance. "We will
bring the village in total to Japan, to protect and study it."

The 90-year-old Archduke, uncle of Hirohito and brother of
the former Emperor, looked with sadistic mirth at the confused
faces of the three military Commandants. At the completion of
the audience in the Royal antechamber, they bowed to the
Archduke and asked, "Did the Emperor mean the entire village,
including buildings and belongings?" The Archduke knew they
wanted shut of this silliness and depended on him to finesse the
matter. In mitigating royal whim, he usually complied.

But not this time! Of late, they'd annoyed the Archduke. 'A
scheming lot of soapmakers they are!' It was about time they
were ordered to do something completely stupid. Humility was
an important thing in service to the Emperor.

"The Emperor's words were clear."

And they were dismissed.

So, in 1942, late summer, the Salmon Queen, her parents and
the thirty-nine other Aleuts were loaded on board a Japanese
coal carrier and brought to the island of Hokkaido. By that time,
of course, the Emperor had moved on to other matters and
never asked about them again.

4

Capture seemed likely, and Wagner knew it was Winslow's fault. This was a low point of the year, perhaps the decade. Things were coming up bullshit: He was now an escapee from what, technically speaking, was a mental institution. He'd visited vehicular mayhem on fun-loving North Carolinians. Oh, yes! Wagner's public profile was increasing by the hour.

He sped along like someone possessed until he saw the small, welcoming verdant hiatus in the flood of his high beams.

He stopped—then backed into this glen, feeling temporary peace when, in the rear view mirror, he saw it was a narrow cul-de-sac affording cover from the main road. Thick shrubbery scraped against the truck, and as he backed farther in, branches snapped back to conceal the vehicle even more.

With lights out, he withdrew into a lurking mode.

Twice in thirty minutes, police cars sped by, ignorant of their prey's proximity. Wagner marveled at how their emergency lights transformed the surrounding pine forest into a kaleido-scopic montage.

He took time to assess this setback:

Wagner was hungry, thirsty and dressed like a gigantic cocktail waitress in the middle of a dark, hostile forest. He winced, imagin-ing the text of the All Points Bulletin being flashed on all comput-er police nets: MAMMOTH MADMAN ON THE LOOSE! SCANT-ILY CLAD! HEIGHT, 6 FEET, WEIGHT INCALCULABLE. LAST SEEN ARMED WITH A 2-1/2 TON STOLEN LAUNDRY TRUCK. SHOOT THE MOTHERFUCKER ON SIGHT! $150,000 REWARD COLLECTED IN 25-CENT CONTRIBUTIONS FROM ALL HIS ENEMIES.

Wagner lamented his sinking fortunes with a sigh, then leaned his head against the back of the seat. It was true—stealing a truck, Winslow's stowing away, running over three people and enjoying it—these were all unforeseen wrinkles. But he should go easy on himself: With improvisational escapes, necessity and free form decisions produced troublesome offspring. One had to do one's best.

But there was this insane asylum angle, and it bothered Wagner even more.

St. Finny's, prior to Von Bracken's Swiss-based takeover, had been a mental institution for genuine screamers, wall-climbers, self-mutilators, ductwork brachiators, and other diverse lunatics. Despite the State of North Carolina's sale of the facility—all a part of greed-motivated downsizing—it was still classified as an institution for the criminally deranged.

From such confines, self-furloughing was a topic worrisome to North Carolina citizenry.

Wagner's arrogance began to swirl wastewater style into a depression, best counteracted by Kokanee Joe's extra-sized family bucket of fried chicken and jo-jo's. Wagner's mind wandered back to better times: Kokanee Joe's fried chicken had that extra jolt of batter that was supercharged with grease and salt. Each juicy piece (especially the dark-meat sections!) delivered the necessary balm to Wagner during hard times.

Yes, things were quickly sinking into a vast pool of misery with this escape business. And make no doubt of it, any substantial hit of food right now would do the job, somehow compensate for the fact that he was—officially speaking—an escaped lunatic.

Plus, he occupied a state where, most likely, the landed elite still toured asylums—amusing themselves by tossing stale biscuits and molasses candy to inmates just to see the crazy bastards fight it out.

Only Foodheads knew how a major blast of kilocalories could flatten out a major depression, enabling its victim to get a grip on things—to manage the old recovery. Food made veritable kiddie-toys out of Prozac, Zoloft, Well-fucking-butrin, or any of those joy-popping pharmaceutical wall hangings.

But out here, hunkered down sow-bug style in the North Carolina hinterlands, there wasn't even a decent vending machine, let alone a fast food drive-thru. No, if Wagner were to survive this bit of emotional low-pressure area, he'd have to resort to a list. Lists were the things of discipline.

So, struggling, Wagner sat up bravely, and decided on composing a List of Things Totally Fucked Up, knowing this would be one of his more sobering compositions:

(1) He had committed two, possibly three counts of vehicular assault before a pack of locals—assuming the rear duels hadn't run over a fourth or even fifth upon departure;

(2) Wagner committed Grand Theft before sixty or seventy witnesses, and in the unlikely event they were afflicted with group blindness and/or amnesia, security cameras videotaped it all. As a walk-off for his Small Screen Bad Boy performance, he'd crashed the truck through the security gate at St. Finny's—an elaborate (or formerly elaborate) electronic affair;

(3) He had enough Sodium Anhydroxaline leaping from corpuscle to corpuscle to eliminate hunger response in a herd of dairy cattle. Without water to flush his system liberally for the next seventy-two hours, the drug would cause the meltdown of several body systems (Note: Strange behavioral aberrations were a possibility in most patients, especially the weaker variety like Winslow.);

(4) He had no idea where he was; and. . .

The list had begun working its magic, and Wagner's mind was being elevated with list-making when the opposite entry door rolled back revealing two dark, rawboned men. Wagner's euphoria was yanked into the present so brutally his bowels nearly failed him.

They played a flashlight over Wagner with clear astonishment. The taller of the pair's mouth dropped open, but remained mute. The other found voice—words dripped with North Carolinian diphthongs and bilabial finctives: "Hot damn, jes' look at you!"

When he scratched a sodden, scraggled mustache with not a finger but a pistol barrel, Wagner knew worse times lay ahead. The man moved the menacing blue object back and forth over his hairy upper lip, blinking slowly and moving his semi-oblong cranium side to side in marvel. While so absorbed, his companion shuffled around to the driver's side and opened the door to have a closer look. In one hand he played the flashlight over Wagner's body; in the other, he held the greasy stock of a worn, single-barreled shotgun.

Wagner's heart catapulted into the highest ranges of frantic pumping. Guessing the urgency of the next few minutes, he remembered the long-deceased Salmon King's steadying words when events spun orbital: "Steady-as-she-goes, Grandson. Think or sink."

His visitor holding the pistol stepped into the cab and allowed, "You the fattest ol' thang I ever saw. Damn!"

Wagner was relieved when he stuffed the pistol into a wide leather belt. This was adorned with a massive brass cougar-head buckle with embedded greenstone eyes that glittered in the illumination of the flashlight. Finally, the man with the flashlight found voice.

"Assahgoodssombitchenmufukantruckannoshat."

For a second, Wagner thought he'd erupted into Scythian or Double Dutch—but no, it was vowels and consonants greased by generations of fried chitluns and red-eye gravy. Thick. Very thick.

His more articulate partner nodded in wise agreement, looking around approvingly at the truck. He hooked his thumb in his spiffy belt a few inches away from the pistol.

"Damned straight it is."

He put down the jump seat and sat with clear relief, allowing a second to gather what might be thoughts. He gestured towards the woods.

"Ezra, bes' fetch a shovel—hell, two shovels—then tell Wanda to git a thermos of coffee together an' such. I'll stay here, so gimmie the torch—and oh yeah, have her come 'long too cause of needin' the other truck to be drove back."

A brief oozing of language communicated sufficiently to the Man-in-Charge to cause a scowl. Taking the proffered flashlight in his free hand, he rested the other on the pistol handle.

"Ezra, I'll tell ya: Wanda give ya any shee'yat, tell 'er I'll come back and keek her fat ass from beehind that computer. Ah'm sorry ah ever stole the dayam thang anyhow."

At that, Ezra vaporized into the night-shrouded undergrowth. Wagner's sentinel lifted up a bit, passed a generous amount of wind and shook his head.

"'Scuse me. Ah gots this wife fixin' me these foreign victuals alla' time. Goddamn, gives me the gut wind sumpin' awful."

Wagner's new co-pilot might be, like himself, an escapee, but not from a high security fat farm. Instead, from the page-bound confines of a Flannery O'Conner short story. But this tad of literary musing paled compared to the request for a shovel—not one, but two. It was definite foreshadowing.

Wagner knew he was flat-fucked unless he salvaged a trick move from his storage vault of Trick-Moves-Past. In fact, he might have to come up with something entirely new.

Keeping the flashlight on, his captor rested it on his lap, and maintained a disappointingly steady eye on Wagner. He allowed a chuckle, and again gestured outside.

"Heard 'bout all your problems down at Pine Jack's on ma po'leece scanner. An' a figured raht'ly youdda' be hid-out 'long this stretch. Ah've always been handy secon'- guessin' thangs."

Wagner endured a bit of hate for the retail outlet that allowed primitives like this to buy scanners and other corporate garbage. And the pistol, he mustn't forget the pistol.

Though the mustached rustic might be a murderer, this was after all the Deep South, the heartgirth of hospitality, so his captor leaned back, warming to conversation and general conviviality.

"Me an' ma brother, we, ahhh," he dropped his chin a bit, and suppressed a bit of a smile—the archetypal naughty boy, "got ourselbes an op'raytion over yonder. An' boy, thees here rig is a'gonna make ah helluva shine truck, soon as it cools down a tad and we toss a batch a paint o'er it."

At the moment, Wagner wished himself back at St. Finny's, even knowing that Von Bracken would now despise him even more— maybe doubling-up doses of The Fix. Oddly, more than his premature death at fifty-two, Wagner resented the possibility these human flea traps would posthumously come into a small fortune, when—like true carrion creatures—they stripped his body before rolling him into whatever grave they would excavate.

His life now hinged on pure Wagner wit—and it had to be now.

"What your name? Mine's Wagner."

His newly made comrade lifted the flashlight a bit, thought, then made an 'Oh, what-the-hell, I'm going to kill the fucker anyway,' shrug prior to answering. Wagner's eyes fixed on the flashlight—a lightweight scrap of junk.

"Name's Taft. But mos' calls me Taffer." He again bobbed his chin into his chest, blinking self-consciously. "My Momma started callin' me tha'yat, and it kinda stuck."

"OK, Taffer. So, other than blind half the county and murder strangers, what else do you shitheads do around here except fuck your sisters and blow each other?"

Taffer's face dropped into a mask of outrage, and quick as a serpent, brought the flashlight over Wagner's skull while hissing an expletive that would pass muster even with Wagner.

The cheesy flashlight burst, spewing batteries and parts against the windshield and floor. Though Taffer was thrown into darkness, Wagner experienced a synaptic light show of yellows and fluorescent purples, but struggled to remain conscious, and, most vitally, mobile.

And he did.

Taffer now had the strategical misfortune of occupying a small space in sooty darkness with a desperate animal almost four times his size—thus being within easy reach.

Wagner latched onto Taffer with both hands, and the force of this grab caused an audible whoosh followed by an immediate OOOOOOF! as the gunman's lungs expelled what air they'd held.

On the first stroke of this extraordinarily violent shaking, Taffer's skull bashed into Wagner's—already numbed by the flashlight. On the second stroke—the outgoing, as it were—his clothing began to rip, and his cervical vertebrae rattled and snapped. Wagner knew his captor was now his captee, the rotten swine!

On the next six or seven shakes, Wagner topped off the job. The pistol clattered onto the metal floor, followed by a spray of pocket change and other contents. Taffer did not manage an outcry prior to passing out and slumping to one side.

When Wagner released him, Taffer thunked hard onto the floor, emitting a satisfying death-groan. As Wagner's grandfather the Salmon King used to say, the chump was 'Out for the Fucking Count.'

The downside to his risky tactic was that the cab became rank with feces and urine. Turning on the cab light and fielding the pistol, Wagner determined it was his urine and Taffer's feces. As the topping to this violent horrific, a set of dentures was poised atop the dash as neatly as if placed there. They smiled inanely at Wagner.

This portable dentition and Taffer's bowel contents were minor dues compared to providing operating capital and a vehicle for Taffer's business activities. Also, the humiliation of peeing himself, along with Wagner's mammoth goose egg and cut forehead, were infinitely better alternatives to being dead.

For being dead was no sort of being at all.

Milepost 48.3
Royal Guilt; Royal Angst

The Salmon Queen stared out the window of her private jet. Her dark Asiatic eyes reflected the despondency she'd felt since learning of Wagner's escape and subsequent escapades. Oswald, her next-to-the-eldest, which she and only she called Ozzie, sat across the aisle nursing a Bombay Tonic and getting financial runs off his laptop. He was, as always, an ardent dependable son. How unfortunate Oswald had come to hate his brother Wagner so intensely—or was it that Wagner had initially hated Oswald?

She sighed. What did it matter? Oswald had only been too eager, along with the Colonel, to design and execute the plan to ensnare Wagner, thereby committing him to St. Finn Barr's Sanitarium. She had given the go-ahead; she had known, of all people, what involuntary confinement meant. Yet the Salmon Queen's motive was different from Oswald's and surely Colonel Younghusband's, who also—like almost everyone else—found Wagner despicable.

She had listened in dread months before when the cardiologist told her, "Mrs. Wagner, at 598 pounds and fifty-one years of age, your son is every hour in peril of his life. This heart attack, well, it is amazing it has not happened years prior to this." It was a mother's despair that made her instruct her lawyers to look into a mother committing a son—and there had been no doubt regards the results: The only state where a mother could still do so was North Carolina.

She concocted her plan, and using that despicable tart as bait, the Salmon Queen had betrayed her best friend and most desperately loved son. People saw Wagner differently than she did, of course. Anytime there were problems with Wagner, memories swept all else aside. They went back fifty-odd years, when just a few days into her fourteenth year she'd given birth to her first born.

With an age difference more like big sister and brother than mother and son, it followed that these two people would always be interwoven absolutely within the same fabric.

On her first visit to St. Finn Barr's he'd called her a Medea, a Messalina, and finally, for the first time, other less historical things. She wept. Then he wept. She had not seen him weep since childhood. Wagner weeping would have astounded and rendered jubilant hundreds of his enemies. But it did not her. For in this insane world, where all loyalty and meaning seemed—like old rain gear—to have been yanked inside out, the Salmon Queen loved and cared for her preposterous son Wagner first, always, and forever.

HISTORICAL LANDMARK #4
Captivity and the Salmon Queen

By late summer of 1945, everyone had forgotten the surviving twenty-eight Aleuts in their tiny hut in Otaru, Hokkaido prefecture. The Salmon Queen's mother and father had died of starvation, and her uncle and aunt had too, along with assorted cousins. The civilians could not have guessed or cared why these strange foreigners were here. They had to be coerced to do the most simple, civilized things: regularly bathe in a bath house, work for the war effort in the claymines, deal with the money, learn and speak even the most rudimentary Japanese, eat properly (though this last point was often moot), and on and on.

So, when Police Constable Hikito Sayamura once again escorted this woebegone and now tiny group of people to the bathhouse, he fixed his gaze on the wispy thirteen-year-old girl, now parentless. Whoever the imbecile was that decided these primitives should be put under his charge had caused him no end of problems.

His wife had quite inconveniently starved to death, and his job overseeing the Aleuts' semi-house arrest had become short on perks. It was time to remedy that. No matter that starvation had reduced her to bones and delayed any semblance of physical maturity.

But . . . she had pluck.

Despite being weak from starvation, the young girl clambered into the overhead lattice work of the bathhouse, and forced Police Constable Sayamura to finish off his risen lust manually while she looked down from the rafter—occasionally giggling—in a mixture of mirth and wonderment. For the future Salmon Queen, it was a strange yet sullied introduction to male sexuality.

5

Wagner's arms still hurt from literally shaking the crap out of Taffer. Yet his spirits were on the ascent. Having immediately fled from the area of his attempted abduction and murder, he'd driven like, well, like a madman, until coming across a construction site. A bit of a turn followed by a jog brought the laundry truck out of view ofF the highway.

While Wagner plotted his next dramatic act of the evening, he pressed the forty-five against the tip of Taffer's nose while he revived.

When he was convinced Taffer was awake, Wagner barked, "OK, now clean up the goddamned mess you caused."

While overseeing Taffer's cleaning duties, Wagner went through his wallet, finding nearly eighty dollars in small bills and even some coins. The former would be good for drive-thru window food purchases, where fifties and hundreds might be awkward, and the coins—excellent for upcoming, strategic phone calls.

Also, Taffer had six or seven driver's licenses and credit cards in various names. And it got better! The licenses had a wide range of descriptions and ages.

These, by Jove and Big Bill Haywood, lifted Wagner's spirits even further, almost more than a batch of bar-b-que ribs. What in hell difference did it make if the descriptions were a bit off—anybody could gain two or three hundred pounds during the legal life span of a goddamned driver's license—hell, Wagner had done it a half dozen times.

Wagner selected one closest in height and age and decided He was Him.

Using a corner of Taffer's shirt, he picked up the dentures. These were an additional leverage to warranty Taffer's cooperation. Right away, the sap had asked for them, alerting Wagner to their potential. And it made sense in this Be-Beautiful-or-Be-Screwed culture. Certainly being toothless was beyond the pale—like weighing four, five, or six hundred pounds.

And Wagner had learned hard lessons in existing beyond the pale. After all, it didn't get much more beyond the goddamned pale than having one's butt shut up in St. Finny's.

Wagner reflected how things had a natural way of working out if poetry and righteousness were on your side. This was his hidden side, the romantic in him.

Milepost 48.8
A Point of Interest – Peggy

Peggy Rothstein was the administrative heartbeat of both the Northern Socialist Review and The Northern Institute for Social Reprisal. She made them tick. She was the daughter of Max Rothstein and Erma Gilderbeck, and the granddaughter of Bomber Rothstein, an icon of the American radical movement. Peggy moved north to Anchorage when just out of Radcliffe to work for social justice on behalf of Alaska natives. In view of her cause, she straight-away partnered with an Inipuit (In those days they were called Eskimos, if they were lucky) named Chalkline Moxie. It was 1976.

Chalkline was the beginning of a long line of male attachments who variously spent all her money, stole her credit cards, invited half their village into town to freeload for the winter, impregnated her, ran her car into ditches and snowbanks, pawned her belongings, told everyone she was a lousy fuck, screwed diverse women in her bed, infected her with crabs, cankers, herpes, clap, syphilis, and Hepatitis-B, and gave her countless black eyes; and would absolutely never put the toilet seat down after peeing and/or puking.

Peggy Rothstein was tall, slender—all in all quite crane-like—seemingly all legs. Never attractive nor wise in the way of dress and cosmetics, she only managed an intimate life when, in the early Alaska years, the Anchorage single-male-to-single-female ratio was little better than a 19th-century British man-of-war. As the sixties changed into the seventies, and then the eighties, and this imbalance became history, Peggy's romantic life grew thankfully semi-dormant.

She was devoted to Wagner and to causes of the Institute and continued viability of the journal. She even baby-sat Lulu when Wagner was out of town. Contributors and benefactees called her Ms. Rothstein, her few friends and associates called her Peggy, but only Wagner called her "Leggy Peggy." She hated that. But when Moynahan or others instructed, "Just tell the boorish, sexist asshole to stop calling you that—he needs you, for Christ sakes," she would demure.

Wagner, after all, had his ways.

6

Wagner watched with pleasure while Taffer tiptoed, naked as Adam, between crane trucks, backhoes and bulldozers. Taffer's assignment: to inspect a half dozen pickups parked just beyond the heavy equipment, then use his ample criminal skills to boost one for their use. Wagner felt no pity for the rat-brained turd.

The Tarheel's skin, having forever been sheltered from sunlight by clothes, save for the neck area, shone milk white in the rising quarter moon. While keeping one eye on Taffer—and the pistol close at hand—Wagner struggled to push a foot into one of Taffer's boots. Any footwear was better than these goddamned hospital slippers. Expert at getting shoes on without bending, he managed to stuff each foot in a boot.

That was better.

Now Wagner could remain focused on maintaining lousy working conditions for Taffer. Minutes before, he'd begun this project by demanding that his erstwhile murderer venture forth on his mission sans clothes.

"Naked, I know you won't run off, you homicidal pile of crow bait."

Taffer—now wearing maroon hospital scrubs scavenged from the truck—set his jaw obstinately with prideful, male resolve.

"Ah ha'int gonna' steal no goddamn truck buck-ass naked, so go ahead and shoot."

And Wagner did, the bullet striking within an inch of its former owner's left foot, punching through the floor as effortlessly as if it were warm fudge. The muzzle blast deafened both, but despite this, Wagner knew the frantic workings of Taffer's mouth signaled unbridled cooperation. Taffer stripped off clothes so recently put on, keeping a worried eye on the pistol. To help the chap maintain focus, Wagner slowly brought back the hammer and aimed the ugly barrel at Taffer's genitals.

"Now, I require something with a crew cab. That way the seat will be back far enough to accommodate my bulk."

So, it was on this note of authority that Wagner and Taffer began their new relationship.

As Taffer prowled, Wagner watched. In one of the pickups Wagner saw, at last, a glimmer of dash lights, then heard freedom's call in the sound of the engine starting.

When Taffer drove up with his prize, Wagner wasn't appreciative. It spewed exhaust, the rear window was broken, and the chassis seemed twisted. Lastly, it sported a greasy pile of uncovered junk in the bed—an invitation to any state trooper looking for a cheap stop.

"This'un was the onliest with a crew cab. Now I'd be wantin' my clothes back—and ma teef."

"No teeth, Taffer. First, empty all that shit out of the back. And the son-of-a-bitch is three feet off the ground. Get me something to step up on."

Muttering, Taffer went about completing his duties, and when Wagner stuffed himself behind the wheel, he admitted the truck might work. Taffer stood below him, and once again there were mewings about clothing and teeth.

"No teeth. Not until we eat. Speaking of which, where's the closest fast-food drive-thru. And don't bullshit me, or I'll kneecap your miserable tarheel ass. And keep those hands clamped behind your wretched fucking neck, too."

"But damn, Ah'm freezin'. I need clothes, goddamnit."

"Then answer my question."

Taffer reluctantly switched from wrapping his arms around his torso, to locking hands-behind-neck, Hollywood badass style. In amongst the other pocket contents had been spare forty-five cartridges, and Taffer looked on as Wagner cranked open the revolver, reloaded and locked it shut. Taffer raised his eyebrows.

"Not everyun' knows how them hawg-legs work. They're a might of a unique weapon, that kind is."

Wagner gave the cylinder a malicious spin, and eyed Taffer. The Salmon King had been a primo gun nut, and taught his grandson well. Wagner felt no need to tell this scum that—just keep him guessing. Instead, he used the pistol to motion first left, then right.

"OK, shithead, which way is food?"

"Tha'yat be in Elizabethtown—thatta' way. Cain't miss'er—eet's about nine miles. Now I'll be requirin' my clothes, teef and other possibles. I kin' unnerstan' you needin' the hogleg. Yer welcome to it."

A sense of common justice dictated that Wagner leave Taffer naked, toothless, and at the scene of his latest crime. But a canny thought reminded him that in North Carolina, every humanoid wearing a star and gun was looking for one mammoth man in a laundry truck—but not two men in a pickup. Wagner was in control here—he made the plans.

"Taffer, I'll be frank with you. Your plans to kill and bury me have resulted in my harboring ill-will against your miserable carcass."

A ripple of emotional anguish came over Taffer.

"What!? Now I was gonna' do no such th'ang. We was gonna' use them shovels to dig up shine. Ahm' a night runner, not no assassin," he shook his head at the horror of such a misunderstanding, "an' a man given to Christian thank'ing."

"Taffer, get in, you lying wad of spit. From here on in, you are my guide."

Taffer risked unlocking his hands, and pointing towards the heavens.

"Now I done raht by you in boostin' this here truck. An' iffa' ya pardon ma sayin' so, you're a bad spell of luck lookin' to happen, an' I had my share. The State of Nawth Carolina got itself a Three-Times-an'-Yer-Out law, and ah'm pushing raht at it."

Wagner allowed the barrel of the pistol to lower.

"Taffer, I could care less. Now get the hell in the truck or I'll blow your miserable right leg off."

Wagner rumbled down the highway steering with one hand while cradling the pistol in his lap. Taffer struggled back into his scavenged hospital scrubs while opining (half to himself and half to the Gods) about his recent turn of ill-fortune. But Wagner's thoughts centered not on luck, but sustenance. It was time to do some serious eating, for as The Fix wore off, his hunger came on all the stronger. He was hungry; Jesus, Mary and Joseph he was fucking hungry!

Despite weeks at St. Finny's, Wagner's formidable digestive apparatus was rising untethered from its enforced idleness. Images of french fries, hamburgers and two or three hogsheads of pop ('Easy on the Ice, please!') pranced through his consciousness like polka dot reindeer.

The fact he was shod in field boots and wore something approximating a tutu paled in comparison to the food and drink situation. Yes! This took priority over the minor problem of clothing and fleeing from six or seven hundred cops supplemented by, he knew oh-so-well, a dedicated force of Colonel Younghusband's security hounds. It was the latter Wagner worried about—almost more than this goddamned, unyielding hunger.

Milepost 51.2
Chains of Command

Colonel Younghusband watched placidly while the Commandant of the North Carolina State Patrol arm-wrestled the owner of Pine Jack's Tavern to a standstill. Then, emitting a backcountry whoop that made Younghusband wince, the Commandant nailed his opponent's hirsute forearm flat to the bar.

Outside, square in the middle of the highway, a tribe of rural primitives admired the Commandant's red and white chopper while being kept beyond touching distance by the nervous pilot.

Mr. Picket Witterveen once again told the harrowing story of being run over by Wagner to the reporters who accompanied the Colonel and the Commandant—how Witterveen and fellow Pine Jack patrons had risked everything to free Wagner's hostage, the poor, unwitting Professor What's-His-Face.

"The po' ol' som'bitch was scared speetless by bein' obdockted from thet loony bin."

Witterveen, amazingly enough, had only a broken shoulder, some scrapes and abrasions resulting from his jousting match with Wagner's stolen truck. There were other issues: Next was the matter of one Ezra Taft's claim to the $35,000 reward put up by Monarch Enterprises. Mr. Taft awaited them, along with three State Patrolmen, at the precise sylvan locale where Wagner had kidnapped his older sibling. The Commandant spoke warily about the locals.

"In this part of Nawth Carolina, Colonel, we've got some almighty tough and wily customers."

Of course, Younghusband knew the entire lot of them were beer-guzzling, incest-ridden liars with as much credibility as tobacco executives. This included the Commandant, who had months earlier been bribed to a more-than-adequate degree of cooperation to set up Wagner's original ensnarement and abduction. As the Colonel belted into the backseat of the chopper, he sighed, anticipating the Commandant would require additional inducement now that the miserable Wagner had buggered off—committing seven or eight felonies in the process.

Thank goodness Younghusband's Dirt-Stoats had nosed out the Commandant's fruitful coupling with a fifteen-year-old black babysitter, Now hidden back west with her grade-school-age Commandantette, Younghusband knew bribing this leather-brained fornicator was no longer an issue. No, tomorrow the Commandant would receive a letter from the wronged party, and the Colonel would be there to make it all go away for his friend, the Herr Commandant.

Afterwards, the Commandant would become lickspittle grateful and obedient—or he jolly well better be! He'll need to perform serious redemption—do any favor for his colleague Younghusband. Who knows what might be required to bag the odious Wagner before he slipped over the state line?

Wagner!

Oh, indeed, it would be a banner day when Younghusband nabbed that endlessly arrogant glutton and stuffed him back in St. Finn Barr's. But until then, the Colonel would have to keep himself amused by putting the hard-cheese to this uniform-clad bag of southern hot air.

Now dealing with Herself, that was different.

Explaining what had all gone wrong would be far trickier. He would, of course, hang her youngest son out to dry along with that greedy fool Von Bracken. It would be something of a crib, but it could be done.

As they lifted off from Pine Jack's, Younghusband took in the Commandant's manly and authoritative air with an ironic sigh. Regardless of how many times he'd deflated bags of pomposity like the Commandant, the Colonel had never lost his taste for it.

The Salmon Queen and the Administrator

Donald Foster, Director of the Alaska Territorial Native Service, was semi- to fully pissed off at his staff. Why was it that when it came to taking half-truths and weaving them into plausible full truths did it require his personal intervention? His staff weren't the ones to have kissed congressmen's and senators' butts to secure their 1946-47 budget.

"For Christ's sake, rebuilding Attu Village would cost twenty times what our new administrative and housing facility in Anchorage will. You want us all to live in Quonset huts for another fucking winter?"

For Foster, dealing with the twenty-five surviving Attuans, who until two months back everyone thought had been executed by the Japs, was a cakewalk. In fact, he would work it into a teaching opportunity.

"OK, show them in. And watch. Learn."

When he'd finished and the smallish, shy Attuans threaded their way over to a nearby buffet line, he noticed something unnerving: Staring at him was a strange young girl, her intense black eyes locked on his. She frowned and, Foster was to later think, shook her head.

How could Foster have known, much less anticipated, that the future Salmon Queen's instincts for detecting double-dealing piss-ants had already grown strong. They would become much stronger.

Except for lapses caused by matters of the heart, it would be an instinct that would serve her faithfully. In just another twenty years, the Salmon Queen would cut apart tinhorns like Foster over croissants and tea—before the business day had even begun.

7

The eighteen-piece tub of Dixie Charlie's Deep Fried Chicken was Wagner's first fried poultry in seventy-eight days. He was about to rip into his next piece, but Taffer's incessant yakking fucked him up. Initially, Wagner understood and respected his prisoner's motives in discussing his wife Wanda's obesity problems. It was a primitive but potentially effective ruse to distract him, possibly enabling Taffer, despite being tethered at the wrists, to snatch the fire extinguisher from its rack and knock Wagner senseless.

A desire for freedom, after all, was something Wagner understood. But it was Taffer who became distracted and instead was drawn into his own rhetorical net.

Ironically, Wagner once again was the captive. This was why he always ate alone, except with close friends—which meant Moynahan. There were many chronic problems that went along with being like Wagner, that is from two to five times normal sized, or in medical parlance, *morbidly obese*. Actually, the more graphic and less jargonesque *stupendously fat* said it better.

But no matter—an insidious social torment accompanying this most visual of afflictions was serving as sounding board to every obesity problem, every diet idea, every cockeyed bit of advice Anyone Anywhere had ever concocted or conceived of, regards the situation of fatness extraordinaire.

And now Taffer was following in this long, dreary column of sorry-ass motherfuckers who were an unparalleled plague to Wagner. And almost invariably, whoever the imbecile was who would serve up their medicinal palaver would choose to do it during meal times.

So having Taffer sitting there dribbling on about Mrs. Whoever's obesity problems spoiled hell out of doing a proper job, both physically and aesthetically, on Chicken Charlie's finest.

Wagner had also scored on several pounds of crinkle-fries and of course two Jumbo-Sized pops, though his usual was only one.

(After all, Wagner had to be careful concerning his overall cellular balance in view of weeks on the goddamned Fix. He needed the extra liquid.)

But now this nonsense—wasn't he in control here?

Taffer held a single chicken leg in the air—both hands together—rather like using a tiny baseball bat to conduct his monologue. He had taken one bite from it, while Wagner was on his sixth piece, and well into the fries.

Jesus Wagner was hungry. The Fix must have about run its course. But Fix or no, Taffer's conduct astounded: How could anyone hold one succulent piece of fried chicken aloft and not eat it?

He'd watched people talking ceaseless rot over plates half- or fully ladened with food—with no more notice taken of their plates than one might note lint on the floor.

It was behavior that mystified Wagner ever since childhood, for he could never recall not having a powerhouse appetite. Oh, but Taffer's voice marched on—and the chicken leg waved back and forth in cadence to oily Tarheel vowels and consonants.

"My Wanda was a mighty pretty gal. But when she and I got hitched, that woman shore gained weight. An' she's miserable 'cause of eet. I can forgive her, but she cain't forgive herself. Read myself a book about tha'yat."

To Wagner, discussing anything when devouring blissfully greasy and super-caloric food was like discussing Kant or the Age of Enlightenment while getting a blow job. He'd had enough.

"Taffer, shut the fuck up. I don't care how goddamned fat your wife is. I'm eating. Now, am I going to have to gag as well as hog tie you?"

Taffer shrugged, and took his second bite of chicken, chewing thoughtfully. The chicken began to execute a tuck and whirl in Wagner's digestive system. He couldn't tell if it was lack of being in Eating Shape, or a result of the conversation.

Most likely the latter.

Taffer allowed a respectful pause, then held the drumstick aloft again and declared, "I apologize for disturbin' your supper, but ah' love that girl dearly, ah'm shorely sorry for her. Ta see her miser'ble, wal, it pains me."

Wagner felt a little guilty—true, though Taffer had intended to kill him, by rights, he should show some sympathy—fatness was an affliction he understood. The purity of his long anticipated pigout was ruined anyway. Problem was, he was habitually suspicious when a friend or relative complained about obesity—usually the problem was one of culinary dilettantism, at most a paltry fifty or sixty pounds over one's desired weight.

"How much does she weigh, or do you know?"

"Shore I do. Two hunnert an' eighty pounds now, but last yeer she went onna diet, lost a lot. But she has a piece to go."

Wagner respected that number. It wasn't some half-fucked cosmetic problem of a frustrated orgasmless female addicted to afternoon sloptalk TV. No, two hundred and eighty was edging into Bullshit City, even for a man. But for a woman, such a weight was the Hiroshima and Nagasaki of body images.

Yet Taffer's credibility enjoyed no improvement, and before tossing the skeletal remains of a breast into the pile, Wagner aimed it at Taffer.

"As I recall, this Wanda, whom you so dearly love, was the same woman whose fat ass you were going to kick from behind the computer."

Taffer suddenly found the chicken very eatable, and nibbled at it, chewing, even looking at it fondly. Taffer's neglected drumstick offered an easier escape than to answer the unanswerable.

Somehow, this contradiction annoyed Wagner more than Taffer's designs to murder him. He brushed away six or seven ounces of Dixie Charlie's standard crispy recipe from his hospital gown and struggled to remain composed.

They'd parked the truck in a tree-cloistered glen just outside the city limits. At a nearby intersection, seen through branches of weeping willows, were two mobile homes. Wagner, for the third time in an hour, struggled from the truck to flush further toxins from his body, causing him to silently curse. 'Oh, that goddamned Fix!'

While doing so, he noticed that behind them was an ancient cemetery, thick with deep bending trees. Most of the headstones—massive affairs outlined against distant town lights—were moderate, but some towered, topped with angels or crosses.

Well, it was good place to park and hide. His prisoner and guide knew his turf. Still, Taffer's hypocritical oral ballad entitled "Fat People I Know but Love and Feel Sorry For" shoved Wagner into dark mental recesses.

This mental nose-dive could possibly be the heaviness of the chicken, but more likely it was his insufferable, albeit involuntary, company. He looked into the cab at Taffer who had become indifferent again with eating, and in fact had put the drumstick aside.

"Taffer, you troglodytic, hypocritical fuck, did you ever hear of Fatty Arbuckle?"

Taffer pondered this while Wagner reached in, gripped the steering wheel and hefted himself back inside—feeling the vehicle sag noticeably to port in the process.

Wagner no longer considered motivation; fuck it, just let expression rise organically. Get it out there! He was in charge here.

"Taffer, I find it singularly astounding, that you, a murderer, liar, moonshiner and close to three-times-and-you're-out scumsucker, would have the unparalleled nerve to forgive someone for being fat. Now, have you figured out who in hell Fatty Arbuckle is yet?"

Taffer had not, so instead concentrated on an imaginary point on the windshield. Wagner's voice sharpened and rose in volume.

"Don't bother thinking much longer, Taffer. You don't know who Fatty Arbuckle is, but I do, you understand, you MISERABLE MOTHERFUCKER." Wagner pointed his massive arm at Taffer; his voice increased, "And did you know that Fatty Arbuckle was a millionaire by 1919, and yet got hundreds of letters from devoted fans and they'd invariably start their WRETCHED PUNY FUCKING LETTERS with 'Dear Fatty'?"

Wagner's voice began an unsettling canter, alternating between musical hoots and extraordinarily loud shouts. Concluding each shout, he slapped the steering wheel with such force, the entire dash quaked. More alarming, with his free hand he began whirling the pistol overhead.

"So [hoot], they did not begin [shout] as, I repeat, *not*, 'Dear Fucking Roscoe'; [strikes dash—wham!] [switches to a hoot] which was his real fucking name, not even . . ."

Taffer looked at the door then back at the pistol; escape and sound health were not in the same picture. Wagner took umbrage at Taffer's lack of attention; his voice switched entirely to that of shouts—continuing its ascent, until it attained banshee levels.

Wagner worked the pistol in increasingly erratic patterns; fully incensed, he waved it in circles like a demented Cossack. His prisoner shrank against the cargo door, looking on in abject horror.

"HEY, TAFFER, YOU PIECE OF SHIT! YOU LISTENING? YOU DON'T KNOW JACK SHIT ABOUT FATTY ARBUCKLE, SO BY CHRIST, BUDDHA, AND MARY BAKER EDDY YOU'RE FINDING OUT! SO LISTEN UP, OR SO HELP ME I'LL FUCK-ING SHOOT YOU THROUGH YOUR BLACK MURDERING GOAT-HUMPING COUSIN-COUPLING TRISOMY HEART. YOU HEAR??!!"

Wagner had attained full vocal Nirvana—the Great Caruso himself would have envied him: He emitted a rapid sequence of hybrid whoops, bellows, and hoots, and Taffer's already belabored and humiliated anal sphincter tightened into a tiny knot when Wagner hooked his thumb over the hammer, and cranked it back two clicks.

The end was at hand!

"So, one day, Arbuckle wrote back—NOW GET THIS, GOD-DAMNIT—and he was fucked-up drunk, and he wrote several dozen of these unparalleled piss-ant fans. Yes, he wrote all sorts of neat obscene shit to them. Like how their relatives, friends and neighbors copulated with dogs, orangatangs, anteaters . . . ." Wagner fell into a spasm of laughter, coughed up a stray bit of phlegm, but spitting it clear, raged on. "NOW GET THIS, BECAUSE HERE COMES THE GODDAMNED PUNCH LINE— Arbuckle referred to Jesus Christ, the Twelve Apostles, the Holy

Ghost, and the Almighty himself in the fucking past progressive participle. GET IT, TAFFER—GODDAMNIT, I'M ASKING YOU, DO YOU GET THAT!"

Another spasm struck—this one consumed Wagner with demonic cackling, and who knows what might have eventually developed if, at that moment, the pistol had not discharged, sending the projectile through the truck roof. This deafening apex to Wagner's ranting was finalized by Taffer himself, who cried out, "Great Balls of Fire!"

Silence.

And a strange silence it was. Wagner looked around, saw Taffer cowering against the door—saw and heard at the same moment a small dog running across the road from one of the mobile homes where lights were coming on. Wagner looked at the pistol he still held aloft, staring dumbly at it, momentarily confused as to how it went off.

Two people rushed from one of the mobile homes, looking fearfully in all directions.

Wagner knew what was next: He started the truck and backed out, causing an earsplitting gnashing in the gear case as he crashed into first and got hell out of there. Taffer shouted directions. Wagner grasped the problem; the goddamned pistol was a menace.

"Jesus Christ, Taffer. Only an asshole files a trigger so. . . ."

Yet his voice was strangely fuzzy, and his throat hurt—raw. Taffer belted in, and looking to their rear with a veteran eye advised, "Goddamn, you gets raht cranked up 'bout that Arbuckle fellah. But slow down! You'll scare up a John Law shore and neither of us is a-wantin' tha'yat. Go left up hea'yah."

As directed, Wagner pulled into a narrow road that went between rows of barn-like structures. Now they were fully in the country, and the sylvan ambiance pacified. Pulling inside one of the barns and shutting off the engine, Wagner welcomed the return of silence, save for the engine. It crackled away as it cooled, and Taffer's respectful gaze said it all regards an assessment of his captor's mental togetherness.

"What you say they had you in tha'yat place for?"

Sweat seeped through Wagner's gown; his buttocks stuck again to the seat. He looked up to examine the pooched-out exit hole in the roof—the force of impact created a shiny crater where the paint and rust was blown clear. He looked slyly at Taffer.

"In point-of-fact, I didn't say."

Right at this minute, Wagner wasn't completely sure what had happened, but at least he would salvage the element of fear from it. A reptile like Taffer understood violent unpredictability. Despite his pride regards the strength of his constitution, Wagner had no choice but to reappraise the effect of The Fix on his system. It had definitely seeped into and fouled his ordinarily clockwork-smooth nervous system.

Milepost 51.2
Abrupt curve; slow to 5 mph

The Northern Institute for Social Reprisal
14568 Hayward
Eagle River, AK 99508

To: Mr. Mark Storham,
Asst. Deputy Secretary of State for Non-Governmental Agencies
Department of State
Washington, DC 20002

From: Vidar Wagner, Director
Northern Institute for Social Reprisal
14568 Haywood
Eagle River, AK 99508
Re: Funding issues, ELF, & Flying Vegetables

The Institute for Northern Reprisal has indeed funded the Ecuadorian Labor Front's (ELF) campaign for social justice via a $125K grant (on file, your office). But the Institute, though not condoning ELF's opposition to the profiteering swine of Pan American Floral (PAF), does not condemn it either. The Institute's legal firm (Moynahan, Moynahan and Glump) has established our position, i.e. that the provisos of our grant to ELF are standard NGA contractual inclusionaries.

Now, if ELF uses funds to develop and deploy a steam-driven catapult capable of bombarding PAF's commercial greenhouses with non-violent projectiles such as squashes and melons, the Institute commends them. Our thoughts: Better melons and squashes than artillery rounds. If PAF treated their 3,450 Ecuadorian employees as well (i.e. not kill and maim them when they attempt to negotiate better conditions) as they did the long-stemmed roses they lovingly pack onto chartered 747s, it would not have this situation.

Regards your section's threat of declaring our Institute terrorist affiliated: If you do so I shall instruct Moynahan, Moynahan and Glump to whip an injunction on your section's assortment of shelldrakes and puppy humpers. Then, after making a horse's ass out of you personally, we'll go global with the story on CNN like the last time you tried that shit. Personally, during my past dealings with you, I find you the sort of political bottom feeder whose forte is shaking down monks and the terminally ill for campaign funds. Humanitarian stuff? From you? Mark Baby, I would no more expect that than I would your fellow toadies at the State Department moving off their dead asses and working for a living.

Wagner

Milepost 51.3
A Status Report

Colonel Younghusband had spent his life dealing with powerful people, and Mrs. Anna Wagner was no different save for her uncanny allure. And age didn't seem to impede. Herself sorted the needed and wanted from unneeded and unwanted and quietly got on with it.

Younghusband admired that.

And in Herself's presence he felt that allure: A tiny woman just barely five feet, and of an ethnicity that was a matter of mystery: Was she of Korean/European origins, Chinese-Uzbeckastanian—or something more ordinary, such as Japanese-American?

No one knew; no one asked, in fact. It was his job to find out if anyone was poking around trying to find out such things. But still, even Younghusband wondered on occasion. Genetics yielded no clue: First off, there was that fat lout Wagner, her first born. He looked entirely European, save for dark hair and eyes. But, Oswald, her youngest son: As each year passed, he looked more Oriental.

"I think she's a bloody Wog. That's what I think."

His assistant Teddy had voiced such to Younghusband on many occasions. But that was just Teddy, who thought anyone not alabaster-white was a wog. The 48th Fusiliers were always a bigoted lot anyway.

Yet on this early morning in Raleigh, North Carolina, when Younghusband sat before Mrs. Anna Wagner and delivered his "sitrep," he once again found himself wondering.

Dressed in a simple silk lounging gown, she sat, legs folded beneath her, listening and sipping tea; her faithful maid Katrina fussed about the suite's sunroom. After his report, Herself pushed the cup a tad with a delicate fingertip, and with that same quiet no-nonsense cadence (Was there an accent?), declared, "Fine, Colonel. Rewards are useful, but let everyone know that if the slightest harm comes to Wagner, the only reward they'll receive is ruination."

As he was leaving the suite, with Katrina tut-tutting about Wagner's activities at his elbow, Herself added, "I'll deal with Dr. Von Bracken early this afternoon."

In the entryway, he checked in with Stromboli, Herself and Oswald's personal security man, determining what Oswald was into or out of that day, then exited. Stromboli was a good chap——strong as a draught horse, quick as a leopard. And discreet. With influential and wealthy people, you absolutely needed discretion.

As Younghusband walked down the corridor to the elevator, he grimaced. He would not enjoy being in Von Bracken's situation, not at all. Von Bracken's status had shifted most definitely from the needed to the unneeded.

The Salmon Queen Meets Junior

It was 1947, and "Junior" Wagner, only son of the Salmon King, was given Wicked Harbor Cannery for graduation from college. Though the titular superintendent of the wilderness operation, he cared nothing about canning salmon and knew less.

So when the thirteen-year-old Salmon Queen stepped off the amphibious aircraft with other native girls, Junior was there fielding the fairest and finest for the summer.

And he got first dibs!

Second choice went to the Asst. Superintendent (who really did know how to can salmon), then the plant engineer (vital to making the ancient machinery work), and after that, it was absolutely forbidden for male workers to fraternize with females. The Monarch label stood for wholesome family foods.

Because of his special status Junior took two of the girls instead of the more egalitarian one. His football brawn had already begun to creep to lard, for since graduation the previous year he'd done nothing but screw, eat, drink, and sleep. And occasionally he needed to sign something.

In the summer of 1947, the Salmon Queen was his second pick, mostly because she had tiny breasts—and Junior did like breasts. "She'll be my housekeeper," he allowed, for even at thirteen, she was a pretty little thing. Even the Asst. Superintendent and Engineer had been eyeing her keenly.

So, on the second day at Wicked Bay Cannery, the future Salmon Queen ran room to room from Junior, eventually hiding in the lower drawer of a white-oak bureau. But Junior was diligent.

"Aha! Shy, are you!"

Junior reached in and grabbed her by a leg as easily as he might a joint of lamb. Later, the Salmon Queen made it a point never to tell Wagner what an absolute pig his father really was.

8

After the fourth North Carolina State patrol cruiser whisked by, even Taffer began to be curious.

"Mah God, boy! What'yah do back tha'yar at Pine Jack's, kill a couple a guys? Didn't say so on the scanner."

Wagner let Taffer keep guessing—what the hell, it was good for morale, gave him a sense of comaradie to think he was in the company of someone also with homicidal abilities. Kindred spirit and all that shit.

"Taffer, this isn't much of a casino."

Through the thicket of maples, directly off Wagner's port bow, squatted Big Wampum's 24-Hour Indian Casino, on the outer edge of the Alsonquahila Indian Reservation.

"Hee'yits only a small tribe of blanket-butts, but they do raht good by it, I reckon."

Wagner allowed a smile—his real ethnicity known by only him and the Salmon Queen, it always gave him secret pleasure to hear unkind monikers for diverse sorts of American Natives. This was probably similar to the secret pleasure a CIA mole took in the old Soviet Union when party goons ran down American military items, but moonlighted by peddling their daughters' and mothers' bodies for Camel and Chesterfield cigarettes.

Wagner had parked the truck between a line of thick-leafed trees and a column of defunct stores. The town's core area had long since cashed out, regards the American Dream, giving way to acre-happy Walmarts and Dead Fred's.

A chest-high wire fence was between the trees and the casino's parking lot. Parked were perhaps fifty cars and a few RV's. Wagner was disappointed with this lack of variety. He'd hoped for a richer pick.

"Taffer, I need a cell phone. But I want to be fair, even with a shithead like you. So, if I allow you to do this, clothes on, and you come back with a functioning phone, I'll give you a thousand dollars cash-on-the-barrel-head. I don't believe in slave labor, even for a murdering hunk of gristle like yourself."

Taffer began to defend his previous motives, but Wagner stopped him by raising the pistol.

"Don't give me any bullshit, just tell me your decision. If you don't come back, I'm not much worse off than I was before."

"Ah'd like to see the color of yo' money, fu'st. Ol' Taffer is a-riskin' his butt out the'yah, and fo' all I know, you could jes' take the phone and shoot me day'yead. Plus, the'yas John Law everywhere."

Wagner removed the poke from under his gown, put the pistol in his lap, opened the phone with a touch of drama and took out Winslow's wad. Taffer's eyes glowed with reptilian fervor. Wagner nodded—then allowed a sadistic chuckle.

"If you would have searched my body before burying me, this would have been all yours, but ultimately, fuck you. Now asshole, what do you say?"

"Two thousand, is what I say."

"Fifteen hundred is what I say back."

"You're on. Ol' Taffer will get you a raht' good phone for fifteen-hunnert skins."

"OK. Give me your teeth."

There was a volley of complaints about the teeth, but Wagner wanted a little edge to strengthen his newest employee's devotion. Just before Taffer was about to embark, Wagner gestured to the teeth and pointed ominously at Taffer.

"And Taffer, I warn you. I'm aware that you might find a piece in one of those cars. When you come back to the truck, do so in full view and both hands empty."

"Da'yam! How do'ya 'spec' me to hold the phone?"

"Clench the motherfucker in your gums! But know this: If I don't see both hands—you're fucking ventilated, you got that? But be straight, and the fifteen oysters are yours."

The muzzle of the pistol lowered, tapping the top of the steering wheel.

"You got a raht 'spicious natch'ure on you."

And with that he was off, over the fence like a hound, threading his way into the parking lot. Wagner readied himself for a rapid escape. He'd taken a chance, but he needed a phone to call Moynahan, so Wagner had to do some risk-management.

This escape business was tricky at best, and trusting an utter criminal like Taffer was even trickier. Wagner fingered the ignition switch nervously—and, of course, he had to pee. God! The Fix poured out of him—it had probably turned his kidneys into high-pressured pumps and his liver to half-digested *fois gras*. The god-damned Von Bracken occupied first item on Wagner's To-Be-Fucked-Over list when he crossed into South Carolina.

But outside, suspense ruled the moment:

While Taffer sneaked by one of the RV's, Wagner watched as it came alive with interior lights. Like a wisp of steam, Taffer vaporized behind a large sedan just as the door of the RV opened. A man stepped out and exhaled luxuriously—as he might exiting an outhouse, or . . . . Wagner smirked familiarly.

'So, a little parking lot push-push,' he said to himself.

The pleased man adjusted his tie, gave a port side hitch to his suit coat and going to a nearby SUV with vanity plates reading "STUDLEY," got in and drove off.

Taffer stayed put. Wagner stayed put.

The RV door swung open again, the light went out, and a tall black woman exited, her attire leaving nothing to guesswork regards presence, purpose, and mode.

Handbag swinging at her side, she sashayed off towards the Casino in search of further financial reward. Taffer reappeared, went off into the lot—stooped low, and went out of view.

Though Wagner didn't know how much money that goddamned Younghusband had put on his head, it was more than the amount in his poke. If Taffer now knew how much Wagner was worth, he would gallop off like a hyena with blood in its nose. And, of course, he would rat out his erstwhile murder victim to the closest John Law. Odd how things worked.

So, keeping Taffer ignorant was Wagner's only workable tactic.

Taffer popped up from behind a classic Mercedes sedan. With the smoothness of a weasel, he came fast towards Wagner, climbing back over the fence. Then, true to instruction, held his hands out, each empty; in his mouth, he held a tiny cell phone. *Ah yes,* thought Wagner, *Eureka! Rover has come home.*

Wagner motioned him in, and taking the cell phone he couldn't help but admire Taffer's efficiency while, for the sake of hygiene, giving the phone a swipe on his gown.

"That was damned fast, Taffer. You're a real pro. Here."

He used the fifteen-hundred dollars as a napkin to return the teeth. Without pause Taffer pocketed the cash and clumped the latter in place, clacking them with a satisfied grunt.

"Hay'aint nothing to eet when you know the tricks."

Wagner, to satisfy his own curiosity about Taffer's potential for betrayal and deceit, pressed the re-dial button. A woman answered, and when Wagner asked for Taffer, she explained in thick dialect that her husband was a might busy, but could she take a message? For some reason, she seemed anxious to get off the line.

Wagner clicked off, aimed the pistol at Taffer's chest, and extended his hand the same instant he thumbed the hammer back a double-click. Taffer's eyes shut in remorse.

"Taffer, don't trifle with your betters. That was a fifteen-hundred-dollar phone call. Now, hand over my money, you double-dealing pile of sewage. Now!"

Mile 51.4
Scenic Viewpoint Ahead, 1 Mile
Oswald

It wasn't easy being named Oswald, even if your last name was Wagner and your mother was worth $13.7 billion. It also wasn't easy having a half brother who was more like a three-quarters brother and who—though ten years your elder—was your nephew. That was hard.

It was difficult having a father whose wife's first sort-of-husband was her second husband's deceased son therefore presenting Oswald with a half brother who was his mother's first husband. All of this wasn't easy.

What could you tell people? And look at what you had better not tell people. They would not understand.

Also, it was awkward not knowing who or what to order in for sex. Sometimes men were nice, other times women. And then, there were days when both would be good. Then, at other more equivocal occasions, he desired something different, but he didn't know what.

Sexuality wasn't easy for Oswald.

And when his father found out he wasn't a red-blooded boy who liked to hunt, talk tough, and behave even tougher, he didn't bother with him anymore. Barely talked to him.

It was hard having a father who didn't talk to him, and who died before Oswald could get on with life and make his father out to be the asshole he truly was.

And his mother didn't love him. Oh, she said she did, but she didn't. Not the way she loved Wagner, who was as horrible a nephew as he was a three-quarters brother.

Life wasn't simple when your brother was your nephew and made fun of you because you looked Chinese. Or Korean.

It wasn't easy not knowing why on earth you looked Chinese. Or Korean, or possibly Japanese.

9

Wagner acknowledged begrudgingly that Taffer's shortcomings and skills were making this escape into what it was—a scrappy, take-no-shit-from-any-som'bitch escape. In short, the kind of escape he respected.

Wagner was stuffed pimento-in-an-olive style behind the wheel of the hooker's dilapidated RV. He admired the stolen cell phone, but the stolen RV had a negative: it stank like a cheap roadside bordello, which until twenty minutes before it had been. But no longer! With Taffer's touchy firearm pressed against the Tarheel's double-dealing spine, hammer back, it presented sufficient emphasis for him to liberate it from the casino parking lot.

But the cell phone—oh, now that was something!

It was one of the spiffier models he'd seen—and he knew them well. Wagner went through at least one a month via such attrition as sitting on them, or flushing them down toilets (only the smallest models made it past the bend)—and the standard of dashing the buggers against a wall when conversations didn't go well.

"Taffer, this phone is one damned fine piece of technology."

Wagner spoke before remembering he'd locked Taffer, bound hand and foot, in the tiny, windowless toilet/shower of their crib-on-wheels. This cruel confinement was warranted in view of Taffer's breach of good fellowship regards the phone call to his wife.

Subsequent to buggering off from the casino, he'd driven about to get the feel of his new transport, then doubled back, parking a few blocks north. The RV fit snugly beneath an expansive overhead trellis at the rear of a First Revelation Church. The building was overwhelmed with an assault of thick vines—and shaded with a half dozen broadleaf trees. All this thick, eastern seaboard vegetation was exotic to Wagner, bringing to mind Gothic horror tales by Hawthorne or Poe. The cross atop the bell tower was akimbo, and Wagner wondered if this wasn't a Last Revelation Church.

The cell phone was put to immediate use.

Employing his thickest Russian accent, he left two messages for Moynahan, one at his office and the other at home. To anyone overhearing, they would be simple queries about legal advice. Moynahan would know what they meant, though: the activation of "Plan Blue," i.e., leaving a second car, clothes, and necessaries at the Spartanburg Air Terminal, with Moynahan himself stationed close by, ready for lift-off.

Plan Blue completed Wagner's artful feint, and his gullible pursuers would gobble up this bait like trout do juicy mayflies.

Younghusband was such a British, predictable piss ant when it came to original thinking. And of course, state and local cops were the usual array of agency abnorms and neurological lunkheads.

Leggy Peggy would spill the Dulles International plant to everyone, probably even the fry cooks at Kokanne Joe's, not to mention the diverse ferrets Younghusband would affix firmly to her scrawny posterior.

Now Moynahan—he would be quite another matter. He'd be more careful—far more. He'd take all sorts of evasive measures, and that was the joy in Plan Blue. Even if Younghusband's ferrets became mediaeval, and tossed him against a wall a half dozen times, Moynahan would divulge nothing. What else was friendship for?

When Moynahan focused on issues, he became more locked, tracked, and centered than an allied tanker in the range finder of an archetypal U-boat captain. And Moynahan could be just as diabolical!

Yes. Craftiness was Wagner's exit visa out of North Carolina.

With the acquisition of the RV, his basic equipment regards managing hour-to-hour logistics was beginning to have possibilities. To begin with, it was debatable whether the hooker would even report the RV as stolen, so he probably had time—at least until daylight, and by then Wagner could orient himself geographically.

In the RV, he'd scrounged up a good wristwatch, another cell phone, and, first and foremost, the RV had an am/fm and CB radio. Best to be in touch with the world.

Then, regards creature comforts—a good-sized plastic garbage bucket to pee into (Wagner, of course, could not fit in the toilet, even if Taffer were not occupying it. Also, frequently squeezing out the RV door would itself empty his bladder, or at least cause serious leakage.)

Then the RV came with provisions: Three two-liter bottles of Tom Collins mix in the frig and six large cans of Chef-Boy-R-Dee's ravioli—and a can opener, which would save on ammunition. Clearly, the hooker admired Italian cuisine.

And in fact, with the fried chicken wearing off—and his metabolism in high gear—Wagner took time out from his escape for a ravioli repast. He wisely opened only three of the cans (best to use moderation and keep three in reserve); then he unstoppered one of the Tom Collins and drank deeply. Fluid in, Fix out. That was the old pepper-upper!

Wagner tuned through a brainless array of late-night talk radio before giving up.

"Ee'yat stanks in hea'yeah, goddamnit!"

It was like Taffer to intrude into his repast. The man was turning into a constant complainer.

"Keep your voice down, Taffer. We're in hiding here."

And it gave Wagner cheer knowing Taffer didn't know where "here" was. A good field commander kept everyone ignorant and guessing.

"But ee'yat stanks awful."

Wagner struggled from the driver seat, and opened the toilet and switched on the ventilator fan. Leaving the door open a crack, he returned to his meal. There were no candles, fine music or wine—so what the hell, might as well make a bit of light conversation.

"Taffer, what in fuck did you tell your wife?"

"Ah' tol' ya—Ah jes' was checkin' in. I know'd she'd be raht worried."

"And what did she tell you?"

"Zee-ro. Ah's jes' checkin' een."

"You're a thief, liar, murderer, and wife beater, and you probably steal and sell children into servitude. So don't give me any bullshit about caring enough to check in with anybody. Just tell me what you told your wife; otherwise I'll close that door, and turn that switch off."

"Jes' what Ah say'yad."

Taffer had become sullen, and Wagner could understand that. The last eight hours had gone poorly for him.

Tossing aside one spent can of ravioli and diving into another, he pointed back at the casino with his fork. He'd fill in the blanks for old Taffer.

"Odds are, your little woman called a covey of your reptilian kinfolk. They then oozed from under their rocks and slithered to your aid within minutes." Wagner sighed while presenting his line of analysis. "Your observation regards my money poke would provide the fuel for their enthusiasm. In the event we left the casino prior to their arrival, you would have cunningly told them what we were driving, and where you hoped to guide me, which is why I changed horses, so to speak. How'd I do?"

Silence.

Well then, fuck him, and Wagner reached over between mouths full of Chef's best, switched off the light and fan and closed the door. Why waste power if Taffer insisted on being obstinate—refusing to recognize how thoroughly outwitted he'd been?

This was paydirt time, regards Wagner's decoy. While his pursuers chased their own tails and just generally jerked themselves off, time was on Wagner's side. There was a good eight hours until daylight.

Being an aficionado of submarine movies, Wagner knew it was time to run deep and lie on the bottom. Thus ensconced, one kept low until the hounds either wrote you off or moved on to bark up an endless array of wrong trees.

Yes! Craftiness.

When Wagner got on top of a situation, things like escapes became matters of simple technique.

Milepost 51.8
The Truth Shall Set You Free

It was breakfast at Dixie Charlie's Chicken Shack. Sheriff Laughton Fairchild of Wellington County and the Commandant of the North Carolina State Patrol came together in what began as a battlefield meeting between senior officers. But, at the invite of Dixie Charlie, it turned into a power breakfast.

They struggled red-faced, wolfing down chicken sausage and gravy slathered over giant breakfast biscuits. Both men cranked away at mugs filled with steaming coffee touched lightly with Wild Turkey, thus abating the bitterness of the Charlie's over-strong brew. They were surrounded by the proprietor's Rotary Club and Lion's Club trophies, and, not insignificantly, Charlie's vintage collection of Joplin Hardware girly calendars. Occasionally, the two would pause to admire one or more of the calendars.

Sheriff Laughton, called "Lawty" by intimates and simply "LF" by underlings and voters, aired such questions as: 'Who in hell did this limey som'bitch Youngfellow think he was, telling me how to run my county?' And also: 'Just who is this fat fucker that's worth so much goddamned money?' And: 'How in hell did this aforementioned fat fucker get to North Carolina from Alaska?'

The Commandant mustered patience.

He was into the second day of Wagner's escape and hadn't slept. Plus, effective with this morning's express mail, he was getting squeezed by that "goddamned colored babysitter" who bought comic books and Nintendo games with his hush-money payments. Now, she had kicked up the stakes, and the Commandant hadn't become the Commandant by being a dumb shit. That goddamned Younghusband was, of course, behind it all.

The Commandant frankly didn't give a shit about Lawty's county at this present time.

"Lawty, you dumb som'bitch. The name is Younghusband, and he's Monarch Food's security man. They got influence going all the way up to the fuckin' White House, and sure as hell to the Governor's office. So with Younghusband and this colored girl business, well, it's getting tight for me."

Lawty and the Commandant's friendship went back to their supply sergeant days in Vietnam. They were comfortable with each other. Yet Lawty reflected that it wasn't his fault the Commandant served at the pleasure of the Governor, who was dumber than a can of worms. Fuck the Governor. Lawty's was an elected office. His brow furrowed while he cornered a stubborn puddle of gravy with a biscuit. Then a word tugged at him, and he became confused.

"What in hell you talkin' 'bout? A nigger girl? Where's she enter into this business, goddamnit?"

"The one I knocked up! What happened to your recollective faculties, Bubba?! Remember? When Etta tossed my ass out, I stayed out at your place at the lake? And she got herself that mean motherfucker from Charlotte for a lawyer. What I'm saying, goddamnit, is that the limey som'bitch put that colored girl up to blackmailing my ass, and he's got me by the balls."

Lawty frowned, this seemed a minor ailment compared to someone ripping off one of the eight RV/whorehouses his department oversaw in the interests of hygiene, order, and overall morale for his forty-five deputies. The RV's and their income were sort of an in-house cost-of-living allowance. Lawty waved his hand before him as if warding off a small insect.

"Oh, shee'yet! What ol' boy hasn't knocked up a nigger girl 'round 'chere. Jes' do a throw down, and send her up the river. Then keek that Limey's ass back to England. What about my goddamned RV? The fat som' bitch Vogner shorely was the fucker that stole it. My boys found a B-and-B Construction truck next to eet, and goddamnit, he stole that som' bitch too. Plus, he run down my quail huntin' partner! I tell ya, the cocksucker is a plague on my county!"

The Commandant criticized his friend's outdated choice of words, not to mention thinking, wondering aloud, where the Sheriff had his head inserted for the last thirty years. Both men paused for deep draughts of coffee, and the Commandant took the opportunity to rise and remove one of the calendars, leafing familiarly through it.

"Would you look at Miss Ju-Lie here. She's my no-bullshit favorite: Got nipples on her the size of Chevy lugbolts! See thay'yat. Goddamned oriental, too."

There was something in the photo that reminded Lawty of times past. The old friends had flogged this Wagner business ragged; after all, in the end, they were men of action. So what in hell could they accomplish talking about it? They shared lascivious glances. The Sheriff picked up his coffee, gesturing to the well-endowed Miss July with it.

"You remember that Filipino girl in Saigon—at Missy Kit-Kat's?—she'd pick up a full bottle of VO with her snatch. Damn! Can you believe that shee'yit!"

Lawty and the Commandant laughed, reflecting back on the cozy old times of their youth. They sat, leaned back, satiated with Dixie Charlie's best breakfast—which of course would be on the house.

Lawty shook his head and wondered, "What gets me is how that fat som' bitch could'ah got the jump on Taffer. Ol' Charlie here said when that guy Vogner pulled through here last night, he bought enough chicken to oil down the innards of a fuckin' grizzly bear. And Taffer was a makin' faces at Charlie's nephew who was on the drive-thru window." Despite the seriousness of it all, Lawty couldn't suppress a chuckle. "Ol' Taffer was tied up like Hogan's goat!"

Again, they couldn't resist sharing a laugh over this image. Then Lawty shook his head.

"Well, lahk it or not, tha'yat no-'count jailbird Taffer's my big sister's boy; otherwise, I wouldn't give a shee'yit."

The Commandant nodded, for he understood. A political office was important; responsibilities to high officials were also important; but the Commandant understood family. In the end, family was bedrock.

HISTORICAL LANDMARK #8
The Salmon Queen & The Birth of Wagner

To Mrs. Erma Hadden, Headmistress of the Mission River School for Native Girls, Anna Perescovia Prazoloff's pregnancy was another case of a poor simple-hearted native girl corrupted by ethnic cross-fertilization. Furthermore, the girl refused to consider adoption. "Give her time, Mother," consoled the Reverend Mr. Hadden, the school chaplain and Superintendent.

And the pregnancy was not easy; Anna was tiny, and the baby weighed ten pounds, nine ounces, and she nearly died. Mrs. Hadden explained to the new mother that the school's contract with the Alaska Territorial Native Service did not include mothers with children. If Anna kept the baby, her schooling would end, and, "My dear, who would take of a child with an illegitimate child?"

Still, Anna would not sign adoption papers.

In a rare bow to ethnicity, the Haddens called in Father Plopitch, the Orthodox Priest. In badly accented Aleut, then Old Slavonic, he lectured on mortal sin. Still, she would not sign adoption papers. With growing impatience—in a diatribe of English—arms waving about over his bearded head, Father Plopitch suggested eternal hell.

But she would still not sign adoption papers. She simply kept demanding her baby.

No one had seen such obstinacy.

The staff at Mission River School weren't seers; they could not know they were dealing with the future Salmon Queen. Even at age fourteen, and under duress, our precocious young heroine recognized the Haddens and their minions for the brainless muttonheads they truly were.

In fact, anticipating events, she made plans.

Months prior to the birth, she hid all her cannery earnings not pocketed by the school. And during a late night in May of 1948, Mission River School saw the last of the future CEO of Monarch Foods International and, of course, the infant Wagner.

Early on she'd visualized a target, and Junior occupied its bulls eye.

10

Wagner concentrated on sorting through the RV's pathetic excuse for a first aid kit. His torn fingernail required treatment. Next up for attention was a gouge on his forehead. Both injuries hurt like hell.

Minutes before, there had been a spat between himself and Taffer about the grossly unfair treatment Fatty Arbuckle received during his infamous 1923 rape trial. And Wagner had to admit his temper got the best of him. But this was not the whole story.

Quite arm weary, Wagner rested on the RV's kitchen couchette that was now without a table; its upright floor post did remain, with chards of tabletop clinging to the bolts. The table's yellow Formica top protruded halfway out of the smashed side-panorama window, or halfway in, depending on one's perspective.

Maybe that's how I gouged my head—getting that goddamned thing through the window, thought Wagner as he dabbed on iodine.

On the floor an extra-large jar of Love Lubricant lay open, most of its pink contents spread Jackson Pollack-style over the front of the refrigerator and stove. Wagner reflected that his impromptu mural seemed inconsistent with an argument over Fatty Arbuckle's rape trial. But straying was common when tempers flared.

Flour coated everything, including himself and Taffer; Wagner had found a sack of it, and remembered spraying it about during a particular voluble point about Arbuckle.

On the floor, a rainbow of pink, turquoise, purple and dayglow red condoms lay scattered from stem to stern; their presence was more understandable. During his lapse in composure, Wagner remembered uprooting a drawer packed with them. He couldn't remember where—or was it when?

Feeling something dangling alongside his left temple, Wagner became flustered to find one of the more ornate French Tickler models attached to his ear. He plucked it away quickly, grateful his unlikely choice of earring had gone unappreciated.

The wires and bits of plastic hanging from the RV's now naked steering post momentarily confused him. But then Wagner recalled an urgent need for a substantial bludgeon by which to smash down the RV's tiny toilet/shower door and to intimidate Taffer. Fearing his end was at hand, the wretch bleated sheep-like cries for mercy. The man was a hopeless coward!

Wagner had no pity for him.

For Taffer still cowered there, wedged incongruously between the tiny toilet and bulkhead, holding the bent remains of the uprooted steering wheel before him—a pathetic attempt to ward off possible death blows.

His voice had long before lost its good ol' boy strength, becoming instead a plaintiff croak, thick with emotional exhaustion.

"Ah swear to Almighty God on High, Mr. Wagner, if'n you let me go, Ah'll not tell a soul—and not claim no ree-ward. For the love of God, man, don't be talkin' no more about that god-damned Arbuckle fellow."

A CB's microphone and cord were wrapped around Taffer's neck—the cord then passed down to his ankles hog tying him absolutely. Yes, the CB was central to the situation: Finding the RV's CB had led directly to the present state of the vehicle's interior and Taffer's crisis. When it came to betrayal and craft, Wagner's memory was virtual bioelectrical flypaper. Yes, he remembered all!

It is best to fall back thirty minutes or so to more peaceful times:

While cruising the channels on the CB, Wagner learned that Taffer's choice of Dixie Charlie's Fried Chicken Drive-Thru had been no coincidence—a long ways from it. Wagner listened with humiliating dismay while two chicken ranchers gabbed about Dixie Charlie's newfound fortune. It seemed Charlie'd spotted the 'escaped Fat Crazy Man' and was 'shorely comin' inta the $75,000 ree-ward.'

They had a good laugh at the expense of Sheriff Lawty, whose nephew Taffer had somehow ended up as the lunatic's hostage. Oh, this led to other hayseed Marconis joining in. And a horrified

Wagner gleaned more bits of dismal information from this chicken-feathered grapevine.

Most notable and depressing: The probable theft of Wagner's present mobile abode was anything but unreported. In fact, it was now established local history.

Wagner realized time was not on his side, and his newfound intelligence launched him into the payback phase for the devious Taffer! Somewhere at this point, memories of Arbuckle's own tragedy regards betrayal were jarred loose from Wagner's already aggrieved mind.

His brew of *aquas vituperatis* shot past boiling temperature and catapulted immediately to vaporlock in the erstwhile bordello.

So, at 3:45 a.m., when Wagner uprooted the steering wheel and smashed down the RV's toilet door to discuss this business of deception with his guest, he was in no mood for quiet discussion.

"You miserable turd! I'm going to beat your fucking head flat."

Anyhow, now that Wagner thought about it, his loss of temper was a bit more understandable, even justified, despite the ruin he'd made of the RV.

The vehicle's use in his escape, of course, was at best limited to the briefest of jaunts—probably between midnight and 12:04 a.m. on national holidays.

Truth was, Wagner's freedom was now measured in hours, and not many hours at that. Suddenly, amidst the ruin of his renewed momentum, it struck Wagner how once again he'd been ground-sluiced by his lifelong unyielding appetite. Since birth, his hunger had always exceeded others'—usually by a factor of five or six.

So even such a meager lower primate as Taffer had been able to hoodwink Wagner via his heedless quest for food, and especially fried chicken.

Even the Salmon King had questioned his appetite, though always tolerating it—fighting off the Salmon Queen's concerns. "And after all," he'd say with a great sigh, "what in hell could we do about it? Strong appetites run in my family and make us Wagners what we are."

Oh, what a miserable wretch Wagner was—once again hurled into the Pooped-on-by-Fate department. He'd need a goddamned rocket launcher to get out of North Carolina. But just at this moment—on the cusp of primal despair, Wagner remembered that he must compose himself—*Don't become overwrought, old man.*

He had to begin conducting himself with his usual precision-like the clear and original thinker he truly was.

It was that goddamned Fix—that's what was precipitating his fucking lapses. He had to make allowances—cut himself slack as a result of Von Bracken's insidious chemical cocktails.

Securing a Band-Aid across the gouge on his forehead, he waddled over to Taffer, and grunted with exertion while untying him. Time to do something unexpected.

"Taffer, get the fuck out of here. But, I will naturally keep your clothes, your teeth—oh, of course, I'm wearing your boots—and that goddamned outlandish firearm of yours, and your wallet and its contents. So, that said: Goodbye. So long. Vamoose. Adios. Sayo-fuckin'-nara. To wit: take a goddamned powder."

Taffer looked up and shook his head, grasping the bare reality of Wagner's words.

"Ya' mean, Ah can go?"

"Well, how much plainer can I make it, you bacon-grease-sotted lump? Your lack of good fellowship fucked up my escape; hence, your reptilian frame is no longer of any use to me whatsoever."

Though Taffer, while stripping, volunteered cursory whines about being cast upon society naked and without teeth, he kept the complaints to a minimum. After all, Taffer was appreciative regards his simple continuance on planet earth. In a way, Taffer was experiencing a second birth, embarking in the same guise he'd worn for his original debut on this vast and mysterious orb.

Milepost 56.6
Washout! Proceed With Caution

Dr. Von Bracken: Von Bracken applied his best aftershave lotion, and dressed wisely. With older women, one dressed for maturity not youth. It made them more comfortable. At medical and scientific conferences, Von Bracken enjoyed a distinct masculine mystique, and it served him well, as it had in Seattle with Mrs. Wagner.

Ah, Anna! Great anticipatory wantonness took hold.

When Stromboli admitted him into the suite, the midmorning sun backlighted her, and by Jove, man, she did look good for sixty-seven years of age. Especially in that light. But when she turned—perhaps she'd been in something of a reverie, Von Bracken knew his mystique had just splashed down into the channel.

Her ebony-black eyes fixed on him with unnerving intensity, and instead of leaving, Stromboli stayed, hands clasped behind his back, vigilant. She sat, and pushed daintily at a corner of a printout with red letters warning, "CONFIDENTIAL"; then she said, "Before we get to your resignation in lieu of prosecuting you for various offenses, I want to know what sordid concoction you've poisoned my son with?"

During the interval when Von Bracken realized the ceiling was falling, he heard Stromboli humming a snippet of Verdi. Despite the catastrophe of the moment, Von Bracken wondered, 'Gottenhimmel! Where would a mammoth creature like him be exposed to opera?'

Seeing his hesitancy, Mrs. Wagner drew up a cup and sipped, lowering it just enough to gaze squarely at him.

"I'm waiting, Doctor."

Von Bracken knew that rhetoric wasn't going to get him out of this one. He was squarely and absolutely screwed.

11

Wagner was working fiendishly to reattach the steering wheel to its original fixture so he could get gone when he heard a tapping at the door.

'Oh, Jesus, now what?!'

Picking up the pistol, he waited. The tapping persisted. But it wasn't an obnoxious, testicle-heavy cop-style tapping, but a light rap, almost shy.

It went on, and a trickle of angst molecules oozed forth from Wagner's copious gall bladder into a yet overheated bloodstream.

He had the momentary, albeit reckless idea, of putting a bullet through the door. If he aimed high, he wouldn't hit anyone unless they were eight feet tall, or someone riding piggyback upon another. It would, though, encourage whoever it was to depart; hence, yield time enough for Wagner to reattach the steering wheel and flee to another hideout.

But he steeled himself. It had only been a few minutes since Taffer padded away from the church. It would take the rotten bastard at least an hour to get clothes, and talk his way into a position where anybody would even listen to a nude man without teeth.

The tapping stopped.

Wagner eased his bulk over to the window—the side of the RV/bordello without the table protruding from it. When he moved the curtain aside a few inches, he saw an ancient man peeing into the nearby shrubbery.

Beside him sat an equally ancient dog, very fat, sitting straddle-legged, waiting with endless canine patience for his master to finish, which he did, buttoning up clumsily, then leaning back and offering, "Praise the Lord," an odd conclusionary declaration at such a time.

A cane swung into view, and the ancient turned, looking again at the RV. He was so old and heavily lined, Wagner could not tell if he was white or black until he stood before the door again. Peeking out from beneath an old straw hat was the snow-white hair of an extremely aged black man.

Again, the tapping. Wagner pushed back the curtain, and slid the window open. His honeyed tongue jumped eagerly into the vernacular of lies and excuses—Wagner's home idiom.

"The driver walked to town to get help. We broke down."

The Ancient looked up at Wagner, back at the road, down at the dog—then back to Wagner. He wore huge, thick-lensed glasses, and Wagner hoped for a second he might be blind, but behind the glasses the eyes looked able, even keen.

"Well Suh, you should've told the poor fella to put some britches on. He was naked as Adam last time I saw him." He then reached down, instinctively patting the dog. Wagner looked for signs of levity—or anything, but there were none. The Ancient said something reassuring to his dog, then looked back up.

"I was wonderin' if you could donate some whitenin' fer mah coffee. Mrs. Leggers is on the coast, and mah weakness is whitenin' for my coffee, sir. Jus' anythin' would do me fine, thank you, sir."

Wagner felt the advent of a Lucky Break—this walking petroglyph was surely senile; oh yes, sighted perhaps, but hopefully baffle-brained. Best to go with developing events—'Don't paddle upcurrent,' as the Salmon King was wont to say.

While Wagner labored to get the refrigerator door open despite all the Love Lotion smeared on it, the Gods returned their beneficence to Wagner when it opened and a squat pint of coffee whitener sat there smiling at him.

But there was still the conundrum of showing his unique and certainly widely advertised physical appearance, so a crib would be to hand it through the window, which necessitated pushing the screen out. This done, he reached through, whitener in hand.

"God bless you, pilgrim. But mah goodness, it appea'yahs you discombobulated yo' screen; the bugs will 'et yah alive, latah in the yea'ah."

He executed a 180-degree turn with an awkward shuffle, but the dog remained, looking blankly at the RV; the Ancient muttered a

"Come on, boy," and the animal hobbled off, more fragile and uncertain than his owner. Wagner was about to return to his escape labors, when the old man paused, and turned, "Yew' awl are surely welcome to share mawnin' coffee, Sir. Plus, I have sea-biscuits, praise-the-Lord."

And then he continued, threading his way along the badly overgrown path until out of sight. Wagner sighed the traditional tribal sigh of the Recently-Lucky.

Oh, I'll praise the Lord, all fucking right, cackled Wagner, returning to the RV's steering problems with renewed vengeance. He was sweating, thankful it was still mid-spring. My God! This cursed land would be a rice cooker in a few weeks!

He was just making forward momentum when a cell phone twittered. He turned: Goddamn! Which one was it? The cheap piece of swap-meet junk in the RV, or the spiffy model Taffer liberated at the casino? The sound seemed ventriloquil.

Damnit, was there such a thing as peace in this world?

Wagner was a compulsive phone answerer; he could no more allow a phone to go unanswered than allow a half package of delicious cream-filled cookies go uneaten.'*By God Man,* he reminded his stealthier half, *those insidious little chirpers transmit the second you answer them. Your enemies will nose you out like hounds.*

Finally, reaching under Taffer's trousers, themselves littered with flour and dozens of unused condom packets, he found the guilty gizmo. Ah, yes! It was the stolen casino phone, faithfully chirping its mating call.

Remember, Wagner old boy, precision. Let it go, he reminded himself. But it pained him. It really hurt. The very least he could do would be to click on and tell whoever it was that the owner had been killed in a head-on, or some-such frothy bit of tom-foolery.

But Wagner recognized one intractable truth: Sometimes, to negotiate an increasingly complex escape, one had to pass up choice moments for comedy relief. After all, he had more immediate problems.

Gathering all his resolve, he powered off the offending phone, then worked on. God! That took strength!

And now? God help him! More problems.

Nature just didn't call, it bellowed—Jesus Christ, it worked arpeggios in his lower intestine.

This was no body function fit for an inside bucket.

Wagner looked askance at the narrow door on the RV. This was another dimensional challenge, and an urgent one at that.

Milepost 56.9
Road Advisory, Rough Road Ahead, Next .1 mile

His colleagues rammed Abe into the gym's medicine bag, once for losing the cell phone, and the second time for sneaking out of authorized embassy territory—and doing so with his girlfriend from the Chinese delegation.

Then, hell, the two Israeli agents rammed Abe into the bag once more because they didn't like Abe much, anyway.

He lay on the floor of the Embassy gym listening as the agents rained scorn and derision on him—something Hebrew was particular suited for.

Major Lena Beinhorn entered, sat down primly, took out a cell phone and quickly keyed in a number, crossing her legs.

God, Abe couldn't help eyeing those legs, despite the fact that her ostentatious orthodoxy disallowed her shaving them. He moaned when a great pain passed down his spinal column. Probably three or four compression fractures.

One of her agents looked over and asked, "Who are you calling, Major?"

She looked with patience at the fellow, and answered in English—for benefit of Abe, whose formal Hebrew was never that good.

"I'm calling Abraham's cell phone." She glared at him. "You know, the one with twenty-seven contact numbers of our most confidential diplomatic and industrial sources in its rather considerable memory." She softened a bit, looking down at Abe. "Is that right, Abraham. It was twenty-seven?"

Being unable to talk, he nodded. It was definitely twenty-seven. She rang off, put the phone away, and said, "So, surprise, surprise. No answer." She leaned over, her generous breasts almost touching him, and half whispered, "Abraham, if the Chinese have that phone, you will be given a court martial, then—I assume—shot."

She and her people then left. Abe moaned. His collapse of willpower had been the Chinese girl. She liked gambling, sex, and cable television available in all American motels. What man would have been stupid enough to ask why she liked such things?! That she did was enough.

Milepost 57.0
Family Matters

Even though it was the second day, Colonel Younghusband was feeling worn by this Wagner business. So it was damned good getting the message from Teddy that morning.

Teddy rather melted out of the woodwork, in the classic style, and they had a high time of it, talking up the old M3 days. They talked family: Teddy's old neighborhood back home, then Younghusband's on Seattle Mercer Island.

Since moving to Seattle, his missus became "American-Struck," as Younghusband put it to his sympathetic listener. Ironic when he remembered how she'd sniffed and poo-poo'd her disapproval at him taking the Monarch Foods situation. Now, damned if she wasn't hinting they should retire here. In the States! God help him, retirement was only nine months distant.

Sixty-five years of age.

Younghusband didn't look it, though. Yet, as Teddy said, being Nanny to the Wagner family—especially that walrus of a son—seemed a pity, regards the overall scheme of things.

That's how Teddy put it—'the overall scheme of things.' Quite the euphemism for private industry—and yanks, at that. Yet Teddy was the sort of chap who would never accept how extraordinary an employer Herself was.

"So, Younghusband, you old nab, if your Fat Chap has that Israeli cell phone—not saying he does, mind you, but if he does, our technical ferrets need just a few minutes, as you well know."

And of course, Younghusband agreed—Queen and country, and all that. "With the proviso, Teddy old man, that the interests of my present employer be maintained."

And Teddy went along of course—why not?! His chaps would get loads from the phone. Suddenly, Younghusband's bad mood returned.

What a tedious snarl this damnable Wagner was causing. During his recent briefing, Herself had put aside the portfolio of the North Carolina packing company's MEI was nudging off the field, and, trying to disregard Oswald's obvious enjoyment of Wagner's burgeoning problems, asked,

"Colonel, do you think he has that cell phone?"

"It's probable, Marm,"

Then Younghusband explained how M3 would try their best to embarrass the Israelis in front of their friends, the U.S., concerning the Chinese.

Alone in his room, napping after afternoon tea, Younghusband mused nostalgic about the old days.

Oh yes! Knocking about in Beirut, Tunis, Islamabad—the entire Middle East beat. Now those were days when a fellow was up against it—daily challenges with substance. All the major players fished in Middle East waters, of course. A day didn't pass when the old bone wouldn't be passed about, with everybody wanting a go at it.

Now, it was industrial espionage and this Fat Chap business. Was that all his thirty-five-odd years of intelligence background amounted to? Which is what Teddy meant by the old backhanded, 'the overall scheme of things.'

They'd both been silly and idealistic when they'd been recruited out of St. Matthew's.

Making the old difference, and all that.

But in the end, all of it was a job. And, as the missus pointed out, after they retired into a six-figure income, "Teddy and Barbara will be still renting that sordid little flat in Vauxhall, dear."

But Younghusband's feeling of selling his talents somewhat downstairs persisted: Corrupt commandants with gravy stains on their uniforms, greedy sheriffs whose only allegiance was to football clubs. Then, sordid criminals like this Taft family—mundane beyond belief.

Grandfather Younghusband had single-handedly changed world events—had been knighted by King George. Then father had made an ass out of himself (and sullied the Younghusband name) in that humiliating dirigible scheme.

"You must struggle to recover my husband's good offices, Blinky," as his grandmother gently admonished when she'd arranged for his admissions to St. Matthew.

Younghusband reminded himself that once he'd had a bit of rest, these present maudlin reflections would fade. Nine months simply was not a long time, and after that, his Fat Chap could go to the blazes, and have done with it.

HISTORICAL LANDMARK #11
The Salmon Queen's Revenge

She would have killed Junior where he stood if it had not been for his lawyer—present that a.m. at the Seattle family mansion. Ironically the counselor had been negotiating Junior out of another potentially fruitful *affaire d'amour*.

The maid showed the tiny Asiatic girl carrying her baby into the front room, and when Junior strode annoyedly into the hallway to see who in hell it was, the Salmon Queen set her baby carefully on a nearby couch, removed the weapon from its blanket, took quick aim at Junior's frivolous heart. The lawyer, for reasons purely professional, knocked the girl's hand downward. So, her mortal shot was not to be.

The melodrama resulted in Junior getting off with a .38 caliber bullet grazing his lower leg, and the future Salmon Queen being booked for assault with intent to kill, rather than murder in the first degree. Seattle newspapers had inky orgasms of sex-schlock over thousands of printed pages. It was the "Salmon Shooting," the "Eskimo Escapade," or the "Salmon King's Castle Hassle."

It all resulted in the Salmon King himself flying home from Washington, D.C., despite unresolved contract talks regarding a canned salmon pact with the U.S. Army. The Monarch label needed the military contract, and the Salmon King was not happy with Junior—or anybody.

On the flight west, he made a list of items to fully resolve: (1) Who in the son-of-a-bitching-hell was this girl? (2) Was her child indeed Junior's? (3) Why in hell did Katrina let her in the house? (4) Was it in the Monarch label's interest to allow the whole goddamned greasy smear to continue in the courts? and (5) What in fuck was he going to do with Junior?

He'd have precise answers or hides would be nailed firmly to the deck and scrubbed down, as only the Salmon King could do.

12

Wagner watched the ants circle before him excitedly. They were undoubtedly scouts, and would return to their colony exultant, reporting the largest food-find in the history of their colony—possibly all antdom.

Wagner's carcass would last them through several years, especially if, like all ants, they were frugal, and stored even the most inconsequential morsel in underground larders.

To end one's life as ant food: it was a goddamned outrage, actually. But there were worst things, Wagner concluded. Now that his escape was clearly over, it was best to become philosophical, despite knowing that by the time Von Bracken had gotten through with him, he would weigh 150 pounds. Along with this, he would be peeing down the side of his leg and whimpering about diverse fictional swill like that sap Winslow.

In a way, the ants might be a better choice.

Another visitor appeared.

Around the end of the hedge a wren hopped, and its tail coverts flapped upwards, suddenly, in alarm at seeing Wagner lying there, tortoise-like, turned over on his carapace, legs skyward. And like a tortoise, Wagner could not regain his legs. He felt an excuse was in order.

"You see, Wren," commented Wagner, "there are certain things not done in an RV. And taking a crap is one of them, especially when you don't fit in the fucking toilet."

The wee bird nodded, took a delicate two hops, and flew off. Wagner imagined it would flit to the other side of the church—to dig around in the detritus in peace, without being hindered by a talking leviathan.

Wagner had chosen the worst time in the entire history of his life—and possibly several other lives if he were ever granted them—to discover that, upon falling, he could not rise.

While tussling with the steering wheel, he'd been forced by natureto cram his mass out the RV door and waddle madly for the wealth of bushes, shrubs, and general undergrowth that had essentially turned the churchyard into a jungle.

It was all that goddamned peanut oil and breading in Dixie Charlie's fried chicken. There were massive subsurface rumblings in progress that had to be respected.

His diminutive hospital gown held up with one hand while clinging to a tree with another, well, Wagner's efforts were certainly not a charming sight nor a fitting homage to the church's overall function. But, the deed got done.

The fateful moment occurred upon his return-waddle to the RV. Wagner had espied the side entrance to the rectory's overgrown garage, so, what the hell, he checked it out. Wagner's escape had been fueled by so much thievery, it was best not to allow any potential opportunity go neglected. There might be alternate transport in that garage, less conspicuous than the RV.

And Wagner wasn't far wrong. The garage—though crammed with contents ancient—had only recently been home to an automobile of great size. A tarp, clean and neatly rolled up, was stacked on a bench; on the dirt floor was the outline of its recently departed occupant, including metal platforms to keep its tires free of the dirt.

"Aw, shit, it was probably a Rolls or goddamned Jag."

Wagner cast off this cursory oath concerning his near good-fortune.

Looking about, he observed no more opportunities or support, and he exited. Wagner took a turn towards the RV, and he remembered being in a hurry—knowing Taffer would sooner as opposed to later bring all Hell's Fire down upon him. He needed to get gone.

It was at this precise moment-of-thought when the fateful stroke fell in the form of a cursed root. It snagged his instep with fiendish surety. But still he was initially confident he'd avoid the fall. For good reason: Being of diverse great sizes for many years (e.g., Extra Large, Huge, Extra Huge, Hormongus, then his zenith—Stupendously Mammoth), Wagner had become an expert non-faller and un-faller.

Ninety-nine percent of all humans not stupendously obese or aged and frail did not have to view falling like Wagner. Even at St. Finny's they'd asked, "Mr. Wagner, can you get up if you fall?" for they equipped most "clients" (they avoided the term *patient* at St. Finny's) with emergency necklaces. Upon falling you'd press a button and people would come running to where you lay.

Wagner, of course, had told them to go fuck themselves, and when they'd foisted it on him anyway, he dropped the necklace in Dr. Von Bracken's fish tank. Though he had not fallen in a few years, when he last did he had been able to rise. It was a helluva effort, but he could.

So, as his body fell forward—the root snagging one foot, his mind sensing disaster quick as a cat eats sardines, Wagner swept the other forward. But it too—defying the odds—snagged on a root, and Down Went Wagner. He plowed into the viney earth with such force that a brilliant shaft of silver rammed upwards through his brain.

When he opened his eyes—for he had come close to being knocked out—he was on the ground, a dozen feet from the closest object—nose in the dirt. Despite rolling onto his back, then returning to his belly, then onto his right and left sides, he could not even begin to rise.

His vast bulk needed a minimum of one handhold above him—the ground would not do. And, like an upside-down giant Galapagos Tortoise, he lay sprawled on the ground, helpless. This was a fuck of a way to end an escape.

He was close to weeping when the ants showed up, enabling Wagner to take his mind off his own problems. He considered the joy his carcass meant for his newfound invertebrate neighbors.

Yet his primate pursuers would probably show up first—whomever Taffer had contacted—and ferret him out at once. Thank goodness, the Salmon Queen, he knew, would link with typical firmness his well-being with the $75-thousand reward. Wagner well understood that, in his inimitable style, he'd made some enemies in North Carolina.

Milepost 57.1
Beware of Falling Rocks, Next .2 miles

Mo Taft had earlier kicked his son Ezra's ass for not keeping him apprised of current events—like rewards for escaped lunatics—and certainly for going to the law. That was stupid. When his brother-in-law the Sheriff showed up with Taffer, he might have kicked Taffer's ass but they were in a hurry. Still, his wife had to break up a shoving match between Sheriff Lawty and Mo arguing over the reward.

Relative peace re-established, they took off for town. Mo and his boys followed the Sheriff's multi-antennae'd SUV in that week's latest stolen transport. It gave opportunity for the elder Taft to lecture on matters educational and punitive.

"When ya' encounter sumpin' requirin' some sense, you look up your Pap, you dumb shee'yits. Now the ree-ward is gonna' get sliced up like sweet potato pie. When th'yis day's done, I'm a-gonna keek yo' asses proper-like."

Mo Taft was fifty-seven years old and from Tennessee and still could kick a considerable amount of North Carolina pine-humper's ass on any given day. Plus he kept in practice by raising boys. Only by kicking ass could a father adjust them to a society inherently hostile and menacing.

Mo's boys—especially Taffer—were tough customers, yet in this county, despite their considerable reputations, they dwelled in the formidable shadow of their father.

Mo Taft was a seriously bad som' bitch . . . and then some.

13

The ant in charge of FOOD RECOVERY AND ENGINEERING showed up with two or three hundred of his Finest and Most Obedient not too long after Wagner awakened from what might have been a nap. A swoon?

When in the midst of disaster, how could one tell?

When the engineer ant saw what lay before him, a strange event happened: He began to run wildly in circles, waving his tiny antennae about in the air, clearly overwrought by the visual confirmation of his scout's report. At that point, seeing this collapse of leadership, his dragoons attacked, tearing him apart. They took off in diverse directions with bits of their supervisor's body, perhaps for an illicit snack under the oleander.

To Wagner, this savage manifestation confirmed for the thousandth time that life was a son-of-a-bitch, and how success was no guarantor of happiness.

These musings on natural history stopped when he heard vehicles pull up nearby. Wagner began to prepare an opening statement for the constabulary, when the full significance of the ant tableaux struck him: In an instant, he resolved to be baptized in yak crap before yielding to the forces of dismemberment. What he'd seen was a metaphor sent by the gods!

A quick look informed that all wasn't lost. Though unable to rise—he could roll. Next to him was an enormous hedge long-ago grown into a forbidding wall of vegetation. Though most rolling into this formidable barrier might bounce off, Wagner's bulk was another matter. Brute momentum might cause the barrier to cave in, engulfing either part or all of him; he would at least be out of view.

Goddamn! It was worth a try.

He heard the arrivees wending their way towards the battered RV—then Wagner rolled once, twice, three times—propelling him into the hedge with admirable force.

And by Jesus, Mary Baker Eddy, and Joe Smith, if it didn't work!

Though his naked skin was prodded and jabbed with thousands of fiendish branches and sticks, the shrubbery closed part way behind him. At least this would compel searchers to dedicate minimum energy into a search. Now, Wagner could only wait.

The searchers scrambled about the RV. Door open. Door shut. Then voices, but he recognized none of them. Ah! Then he caught wind of Taffer's low drawl, that reptilian motherfucker! But, sadly, details were not audible.

Voices rose and fell in a cadence of disagreement. Wagner took heart: like rapacious brutes worldwide, disagreement set in amongst the pack. These quarreling voices drew nearer as they headed for the garage. He lay quite still.

He saw only feet sweeping by. A Bubba Oath demanded silence. There was silence. Then a concluding obscenity and pro-fane rhyming couplet, and Wagner smiled at this larval bud of American poetry.

Next, the squeaky hinges of the garage side door; a pause. (Oh, this was audio-drama par excellence.) Then another bubba voice—deeper and more scornful, declared, "See they'yah. Fat som' bitch boosted Parson Bandyleg's goddamned DeSoto. So, there goes your seventy-five-thousand goddamned dollars!"

"Mo Taft, is it possible fo' you to shut the fuck up fo' a second. I'll dial thee'yis DeSoto thing in; ha'in't no seventy-five grand leavin' this old boy's fuckin' county."

Taffer's voice was now audible—oh, how it elevated Wagner's ire just to hear it. Why Oh Why had Wagner been so compul-sively decent and humane?! He should have knee-capped the miserable prick.

They now stood virtually right above him.

"Ah'm shore glad he left ma' pistol, Pa. He was a goddamned menace with tha'yat ol' som' bitch."

The voice identified as Mo Taft had an edge to it—a tonal quali-ty of cunning and ruthlessness lacking in Taffer's. Wagner logically associated the name Mo Taft as that of the patriarch, heavy with menace and contempt.

"If ya hadn't allowed hee'yim to catch ya with yo' face out, ya would'nah had to worry, would ya, Boy? Plus, ya'd have yo' godda'yammed teeth."

There was a morose grunt from Taffer, as a way to resist back talk. Mo Taft allowed an ironic chortle, then under-voiced, "Damned straight. You watch tha'yat tongue, boy. Ah'd keek yo' ass raht he'yah."

Wagner then heard the cell phone click shut as Commander Bubba finished his call. To his relief, he recognized the frail voice of the ancient black man approach. In it was annoyance.

"Jus' what you all doin' hea'yah, Sheriff?"

"Somebody made off with your DeSoto, Parson. You see the guy in that RV parked over yonder?"

"Sho' did. Nice fellow. Donated some whitening fo' ma' coffee few hours back."

They moved from earshot, and Wagner allowed himself slow, silent breathing. Jesus! Despite the countless prods and pokes from the shrubbery—as if he was sharing a sleeping bag with a porcupine—he felt his optimism grow. A miracle just might be in the making, of which Wagner was the principal benefice.

Because of Divine Intervention mixed with Hasty Thinking, his escape still had life in it. Not a lot, but some.

Milepost 57.2
Tunnel Ahead: Please Remove Sunglasses

In a classic touch, Lulu ran off while Moynahan was exercising her during the flight change at St. Paul/Minneapolis. Matters were complicated. Moynahan knew at least one of Younghusband's ferrets was tailing his ass. Changing planes, though, always fucked ferrets over royally, and by the time he changed in Buffalo, the bastards wouldn't know whether he was in Kalamazoo or Kivalina. But now Lulu.

"What in hell kind of cat is it anyway?"

The shift commander at Airport Security was confused, and when Moynahan repeated it was a Mottled Macedonian, things became no better, especially when he described Lulu.

"Holy shit! Is it muzzled?"

So, Moynahan passed up his Cincinnati connection, instead renting a car and supplementing Airport Security's search for Lulu. With a $5,000 reward ("Alive, please") interest in Lulu's return ranged from keen to frenetic.

This delay threatened Moynahan's layover in Gainesville, Florida, where he and Crazy Sue would screw each other's brains out. It would devastate Wagner if he knew Moynahan—a virtual brother—harbored a sexual obsession for the same woman he did, slaking his forbidden thirst more than once. Moynahan had violated all rules of good fellowship, and knew he was a shitheap of a human being.

Months before, when Wagner insisted on rescuing Crazy Sue from her latest and meanest pathological relationship in North Carolina, Moynahan had pleaded, "Don't go near her, Wagner. Trust me, old friend, I know what I'm talking about. There's something rank in this. She's without scruples. She has more personalities than a troupe of actors, and all of them are fucked up."

But Moynahan knew that Crazy Sue did things—drew lust from men in such powerful spasms— that, once tasted, her waters left a thirst never again satisfied by other women.

Milepost 57.25
An Escape of Style

Von Bracken did not desire an indefinite professional furlough in an American jail, so getting out of the country fast was imperative. This was the wrong moment for Greta to be dallying at malls, but she'd hardly know he was gone until they canceled her credit cards.

He'd send for her in good time.

And before this day ended, that Asiatic harridan Mrs. Wagner would have far more than Von Bracken's credit cards canceled.

Still, it wouldn't do to rush away shabbily dressed, plainly luggaged, or boringly transported.

So first: he packed his matching alligator-skin suitcases—themselves worth nearly $20,000 American. Second, he would don his Gambollini driving gloves, cruising blazer with matching trousers, shoes and shirt, and take the lift down to the parking garage.

And there—third, was parked his life's joy, his alloy-silver '78 Alfa-Romeo.

So, with this wonderful troika of class consumer goods, Von Bracken would play goodbye United States on the asphalt keyboard of Interstate-95 all the way north to Dulles International.

Von Bracken allowed himself a smug guffaw, for once on I-95, pursuers would need a pair of Cobra gunships to catch him—and sundown was minutes away. Arranging the suitcases just so in the boot, he went back upstairs for a few finishing touches. 'But, not to tarry, Von Bracken!' he hummed to himself—reminding of the necessity to get his ass on the road.

Yes, getting gone was the absolute priority.

Once in Zurich, he would be out of harm's way. In Switzerland, they awarded scientists prizes for innovation that in the States were prosecutable offenses. The American scientific community was frozen within clinical paradigms steeped in endless convolutions of testing and re-testing.

And in Switzerland, he would retain potent bargaining power over Herr Wagner. Oh, yes!

She'd learn that tampering with Von Bracken was a different matter than dealing with entrepreneurial swine. Back in his Zurich offices, he'd deal with the Wagners without fear of Colonel Younghusband's thugs. If necessary, he'd hire a half dozen Tamil Tiger security people—in great abundance in any Zurich restaurant.

In the world of obesity control, Von Bracken knew that with Sodium Anhydroxaline he had uncovered the Fountain of Slim. (In fact, might that not be a snappy trade name? He'd have to remember that.)

Oh, God! Think of the money.

How many people were worried about their weight, worldwide?

Perhaps it was ten or fifteen million in Europe, and Gottenhimmel! It was double that in the States! Americans—especially American women—were, every Jill and Jane of them—obsessive/compulsive when it came to their butts and hips.

When class reunion season began, American women nationwide bailed off bridges and office buildings rather than face peers who'd squeezed into dresses two or three sizes smaller than theirs.

Sodium Anhydroxaline was a veritable El Dorado of wealth when such brainless flocks abounded. Every obese female in creation, and especially those with money, would come crawling—if necessary, on bloody stumps!

Yes! Sodium Anhydroxaline ran fat off mammalian bodies faster than, well, faster than it did off Oolong the Orangutan at the children's zoo in Zurich. It was there he and Fritz Mueller discovered it. ('Jesus, God, Joseph and Mary! He and Fritzy had sweat that fat tub Oolong down 118 kilograms in almost as many days.')

After Fen Fen and Redux took the big one-way trip down the poop chute of infamy and lawsuits, the market was wide open for something, and Sodium Anhydroxaline could be it. And by God, Von Bracken intended it would be, despite some ongoing physiological quirks.

And what better clinical population to perfect it on—to work out these quirks—than those societal endzone dwellers—the morbidly obese, the MegaFatties, those Lords of Lard. So what if Sodium Anhydroxaline had a few untested clinical zones. If one were looking Mr. Death straight in the puss, what did the small stuff matter?

In fact, right now, it was those untested zones that was going to pull Von Bracken's gluteus maximus and minimus out of the soup.

Going back into his townhouse, he removed the $50,000 in cash from his emergency stash, loaded up his money belt and strapped it on. Peace was close at hand.

Once in Zurich, he would call Mrs. Almighty Wagner and let the old bag see his trump card! Without a series of follow-up medications, her foul-mouthed, abusive pig- of-a-son would be a pile of skin, with eyestalks atop it within three weeks! Perhaps a few bones protruding.

And therein was Von Bracken's bargaining power.

He allowed himself something of a satisfied laugh as he took the lift down. God! It would be good, returning to Switzerland. It would give him time with Chatzi their Ukrainian maid. ('Oh, God, there was sport enough in that little roly-poly for any three men!')

"Absolutely uninhibited!"

Von Bracken said this out loud to the elevator door as it slid open. But the primitive, male warmth rising through loins took a swan dive when Von Bracken's view of the garage was occluded by that stupefying mass of humanity that always attended Mrs. Wagner.

Then Colonel Younghusband stepped into view.

The Behemoth's massive arm extended, blocking the automatic door from closing. Younghusband's voice was steady, even pleasant.

"I say, Doctor, Mrs. Wagner thought Stromboli and I might pop over. I hope we haven't interrupted."

Von Bracken felt his bowels liquefy. There must be something he could say, but at the moment Von Bracken could think of nothing. Absolutely nothing.

The Salmon Queen Meets the King

The diminutive shooter refused all deals in lieu of prosecution for attempted murder. No, she would not return to Anchorage with a considerable cash payment and no baby Wagner. All deals had to include Baby Wagner. Her son. Junior's son.

"But you'll go to jail for years," her public defender decried. But she resolved to fight it out in court. Before a jury. Before the entire Seattle newspaper(s)-reading public. And radio. And the youthful Seattle television stations.

As he did with all such claims, Junior denied everything. But to the Salmon King, the presence of an actual child required absolute truth-finding.

So, for the only time in Junior's twenty-five years, the Salmon King rolled up his sleeves and, calling upon his rugged youth as dock foreman and beach-gang straw boss, booted Junior's carcass around the Wagner mansion. Yet despite sniveling and cries of pain, Junior held out.

He had never, never touched the girl. He'd had nothing to do whatever with her!

The now guilt-ridden but righteous father demanded a late-night meeting with this 'lying tart.' With a sure royal touch, he'd get the goddamned woman to accept a deal—or else!

The Salmon King met the future Salmon Queen at 2:00 a.m., September 24, 1948, in the King County Holding Facility for female inmates.

The Salmon King was about to lay out his harsh ultimatum when from under her jail dress she removed a jumbo black-and-white Rexall print of Junior. He was dressed up as King Neptune, and next to him were embraced fondly his two cannery mermaids—most prominent being a frowning, soon-to-be-fourteen-year-old, future Salmon Queen.

She looked steadily at The Salmon King and explained, "It was the cannery July 4th beach party. I have two of those." And that concluded that.

14

After Wagner had slain the sixteenth or seventeenth division of ants, he supposed the Ant Commander had reflected on his casualty rate and decided, "Ah, screw it. Sooner or later whoever that vicious bastard is will die. Then, we have him."

Wagner was almost lonely for ants, despite their rather dark intentions. Now, he was wedged in the midst of the church shrubbery—unfound, unable to move, rise, or do anything. He could pee himself; he'd managed that many times through the late morning and afternoon. Now, the thirst had him on the rack; Jesus, God and Mother McCree, The Fix still had him wrapped tight around the metabolic axle!

It was sometime during late afternoon that Wagner realized he was left with a short and somber list: (1) Either he was going to cry out for help, thereby rewarding his rescuer with $75,000, then be provided with an express ticket back to St. Finny's, and Von Bracken (that miserable fuck!), Winslow, and the entire disastrous North Carolina backlash, complete with diverse criminal and civil ramifications resulting from his escape.

Or (2) he would continue to lie here, losing consciousness via dehydration, and eventually becoming mummified and/or devoured by various members of the animal kingdom. Oh, yes— someone might run across his skeletal remains. And perhaps identification would be possible if a coyote, a stray dog, or a family of raccoon hadn't trotted off with his skull for an intimate little gnaw-down under a porch.

Of all the lists he'd constructed, this was Wagner's most dismal. And not unlike other times in his life, Wagner fell into a straight-down funk. In such a frame of mind, he was unable to face either choice. And now, there was nothing to assuage it: not Kokanee Joe's chicken. Not even any franchise take-out food, national or regional, each one a sonnet to Wagner's pallet: Domino's Pizza, Lin Quan's Chinese, Colonel Sanders' (grease-infused pre-digested) Chicken,

Sailor John's Deep-Fried Fish (and potato byproduct), Russian Joe's Piroskis (with sour cream-garlic spuds). Nothing. Fucking nothing. Zilch. Zip. Zero.

What a way to end a life dedicated to social justice. Unheralded by a hostile society, Wagner had lavished his unasked-for, unearned capitalist millions on projects that turned the table on corporate blood parasites fattened by a lifetime of non-stop, unregulated feeding.

And through this, he'd not even made friends. He knew, that save for Moynahan and Leggy Peggy, everybody hated him. And certainly the Salmon King would feel likewise about his infamous grandson, if he'd known how far his darling grandson's politics would take him. Even before he'd died, the Salmon King had been crushed by Wagner's radical bent. The Salmon King had felt betrayed.

O the anger and frustration of it all.

And betrayal! And by Wagner's own mother? There had to be an explanation for it. Oh, surely the sexually inverted Oswald had urged her to this. She was pushing seventy—could finally the Salmon Queen be losing her grip, allowing puny crustaceans like his Uncle/Brother Oswald to manipulate her?!

God, it pissed Wagner off to think of that punk Oswald fucking over his mother—manipulating her. He groaned, tried to roll over, but was painfully impaled by yet more hedge branches and sticks.

He began to reflect that his situation—all due to betrayal—was not unlike that of Fatty Arbuckle, who in 1922 had been framed big time in San Francisco with a lousy wannabe actress-hooker—like he himself had been by Crazy Sue, that double-dealing cunt! (Oh, what a miserable-ass bozo she'd made out of Wagner.)

But unlike Wagner, Roscoe Arbuckle was one of the Most Famous Fat People of the 20th Century. And despite his mother, Oswald, or Crazy Sue, Wagner had to learn by example of the Great Arbuckle.

Wagner let out a whooping "YES" into this prisoned greenery. For Fat People were almost invariably dragged down into the mire of humiliation by the Norman Normals. Much like the Immortal

Arbuckle. Paraded out before a mockery of a slimline society and dragged into the muck by moral midgets.

Yes, Arbuckle had been utterly and absolutely ruined for all times by that goddamned trial, by betrayal—of friends, agents. All envious—interested in bringing Arbuckle down. Oh, people, people!

Wagner's lousy goddamned enemies would have endless choruses of "I-Told-You-So's" and countless sadistic giggles out of his apparent end—here in the shrubbery of North-fucking-Carolina!

Wagner grabbed a wad of vegetation and tried to sit up straighter. When one of the larger variety of sticks jabbed his scrotum, he roared, feeling both present and past pain.

Of Arbuckle's pain! Of Arbuckle's humiliation! And Wagner delivered a King Learian bellow into this cursed southern air: "OH MOTHERFUCKER AND SCRAMBLED EGGS!!"

Arbuckle's career as the world's funnyman ended just as Wagner's campaign to give the little guy a chance was now ending, the valiant struggle against the onslaught of greedy shitheads that functioned as corporate doyens in the business warrens of Order Rodentia, all winding up as a buffet line for an ant colony.

Oh, SWEET JESUS! This universal social evil caused Wagner's rage to surge.

He took a fresh power-hold on the woody base of the closest hedge and pulled. He'd be dipped in guacamole and pig feathers before allowing himself to be hornswoggled by a lousy fucking bunch of shrubbery!

Arbuckle had gone pussy, and had given up—by drinking himself to death. But by fucking Moses, Jedadiah, and the Holy Ghost, Wagner was not Arbuckle—perhaps he didn't have the Great Man's talent, but he was meaner. If anyone doubted that, just go ask those fucking ants!

"You hear that!? GO ASK THOSE FUCKING ANTS!"

A flock of starlings flushed at the sudden and impressive volume of this shouted question. While pulling upwards, the force of Wagner's efforts flopped his 435-Pound bulk onto his side—and despite sticks puncturing port and starboard, Wagner kept it up.

"BY GOD AND ARBUCKLE! TRAP ME, WILL YOU!!"

If Wagner's vegetative prison had been viewed from outside, an imaginative witness might conclude that within this quaking dark undergrowth, two rhinos were struggling over a nearby willing female.

Wagner threw every molecule of bulk and force against this vile, cruelly ensnaring vine. His banshee voice flushed birds from the peaceful thickets of the overgrown churchyard. And then, in one cataclysmic whoop of rage and fury, Wagner leaned back, and howled to the heavens—cursing every foul demon of fate, not just for him, but for the pathetically martyred Arbuckle.

"I'll tear the fucking core of the earth up by these roots. I'll kill all you rotten, no-good motherfuckers! YEEEEE-YIIIII O'WHO-HOOOOO!!!"

Milepost 57.3
Deer Crossing, Next .4 Miles
Peggy II

Fifteen minutes from Minneapolis/St. Paul International, Peggy took a Valium to ease the terror of landing. There was also anxiety over the worsening situation with poor Mr. Wagner. When Lulu ran off from Mr. Moynahan, he made an urgent call for Peggy to fly south and take over the search for her. "Time is absolutely precious, Peggy," he explained, "I've got to get right on this shit."

So, while Moynahan raced east to facilitate Mr. Wagner's escape from North Carolina, Peggy knew she must attend matters regards Lulu. Loyalty, above all.

She threaded long knobby fingers through salt-and-pepper hair and knew it was a mess, but what could she do now? Once at the gate, she was thanking Fate for continuing in one piece when two men loomed up before her. "Are you Miss Peggy Rothstein."

Oh God, Police!

Peggy shrank against the exit door of the plane, looking with old terror at leather belts holding guns, pepper mace, and implements of hostility. During her forty-five years, and as many protest rallies, Peggy survived beatings, hosings, attempted and successful rapes, gasings and kickings— so was positively anxious about police.

She recovered, though, when they announced their purpose was to drive her to where drug-dogs cornered Lulu beneath ground service equipment. Thankfully, selfsame pooches gave up their wildlife tracking careers when they came face-to-fang with a Mottled Macedonian. Above and beyond all, Lulu hated dogs.

In her carry-on, Peggy had "Lulu manna": rabbit haunches; but sadly, they were peppered with downers.

Lulu, Peggy knew, would come to her——and would be famished. Peggy hated betraying the animal's trust. If there was a single thing Peggy valued most, it was trust. And after that, reliability.

"But, weren't they the same," Peggy once asked Wagner—rather Mr. Wagner—and after a brief preamble of F-words, he'd growled, "There is

such a thing as reliable villainy. So, no. Though, in your case, yes they are."

Peggy knew, of course, what 99.9 percent of most people refused to recognize about Mr. Wagner. At heart, he was kindly, despite the fact he openly cursed human society, treated almost all individuals shabbily, and held mankind's institutions in open contempt. "You see," she'd tell unconvinced friends, "I suspect he's had a most unusual life."

15

Wagner struggled to remember how in Great Swarms of Warthogs he'd come to be standing up.

"Jesus Fucking Christ!"

His voice was a raspy *bassofundo*; his throat, a fiery pipe. Wagner reeled and leaned desperately against the garage attaining as much stability as possible.

However. Whatever. Forever?

Oh, the hell with it! Questions didn't matter now. What mattered was that Wagner once again was afoot. He swore to never fall again until he weighed two hundred pounds and could spring up like Man Mountain McGillacuddy and Crusher Yakamura—Wagner's favorite pro-tag team.

In fact, before him, the shrubbery had all the appearance of surviving a visit by that infamous duo: The largest of the bushes had been uprooted, and, along with roots and wads of dirt, sprayed in every direction.

His hospital gown—never a garment to cover much of his imposing exterior anyway—was now less suited to its task. It was shredded and smeared with dirt and body fluids diverse, including blood. Blood?!

"Jesus!" He took immediate inventory of Body Physical: Wagner's hands were bruised and cut; his shoulders and back felt as if he'd competed in a tug-of-war with a brace of elephants. Knees ached; arms tingled. He remembered the cursed branches and sticks prodding and sticking in parts tender.

Yes, the blood made sense.

Wagner now understood the basics: He'd risen during a rage, another resulting from his meditations on the injustices incurred by Roscoe Arbuckle. For a moment, he was confused. Best to put this conundrum on hold.

For the present, he realized that being earthbound most of the day in the goddamned shrubbery had dehydrated him, and potentiated The Fix—making it more effective.

He needed water, for The Fix was clearly not flushed from his body—in fact, it was a helluva long ways from being flushed from his body.

Plus, of course, he had to get the hell out of here.

There could be no more missteps. Oh no, not again.

Wagner was bloodied, yes, but he was UP and kicking. He was now, more than ever, a self-actuated, hyper-intensified bad-ass motherfucker. He'd incurred setbacks during this escape, but the fact was he had emerged a long goddamned ways from being ant bait.

Shoving off from the garage, he remembered the Sheriff's search party, including that slimeball Taffer. He suppressed a chuckle recalling the half-wits erroneously concluding he'd run off with the preacher's goddamned car.

A DeSoto, of all things.

What a prime assortment of dunderheads they were!

"Praise the Lord, but you look a mess."

Wagner found himself confronting the elderly preacher and his dog. Within the moment, an itemized list popped into his head—possibly one of the quickest lists he'd ever generated. And a damned accurate one it was!

(1) With a simple phone call, this Ancient could bag seventy-five G's—far better pickings than skimming off the top of the Sunday collection plate; (2) Since the old fool didn't know his own car was gone, he might be around-the-bend in the brains division; (3) Wagner loathed bible thumpers more than any other job category, this one included.

He eyed the old man up and down, and decided to play him along. Though Wagner knew himself to be, essentially, a fine humanitarian, he resolved to be unscrupled in maintaining this renewed liberty. His escape had experienced a rebirth, and Wagner wouldn't allow it to slip away. This old gatekeeper was all that stood between him and freedom.

Milepost 57.35
Reptilicus Has Re-Escaped

The Director for the 2nd Unit working on the remake of THEM for Turner Broadcasting had just re-blocked spacing for the giant ants when the helicopter landed—ka'plop—right in the middle of his set.

Flying into a rage, he charged it, but was tackled by his lighting director—a veteran of the (first) Gulf War—before getting himself decapitated. By the time they let him up, a toothy Englishman named Mushusland, Mulhulland, or whoever-the-hell stood in the midst of the mess he'd made. He asked breezily if indeed his property "chaps" had rented an antique DeSoto from so-and-so.

Struggling past those restraining him, the apoplectic Director sputtered venom and would have throttled the son-of-a-bitch if those restraining him had allowed. He did manage to howl, "You've completely fucked my set up! Car! I'll show you a fucking car!"

The young woman with the North Carolina Film Commission interceded. She then noticed the Commandant's Eagle on the shoulder of the State Trooper standing next to their toothy drop-in. Spotting her ID tag, this official stepped over and added sotte voce—though never allowing his smile to languish, "Young Lady, I'd have this silly shit answer the English Gentleman's question A-Sap, befo' I shut yo' water down."

Managing to bring Mister Director back to planet earth, he looked to the Commandant of the State Troopers, then while glaring hatefully at his greater enemy, who of course was Colonel Younghusband, admitted after checking with his property director. "Yes, we did rent a DeSoto. Now may we get back to what's left of our set?"

And nodding their thanks, they left.

The set manager estimated it would take more than an hour to put various equipment back in place, and repeg the blocking strings for the giant ants. Furthermore, clouds were moving in from the east. The lighting director was not optimistic.

The Director ranted; the Director raved. He called a half dozen persons on his cell phone. In truth, he acted like the asshole he truly was.

The young woman with the Film Commission was thoroughly disheartened. Her appointment to the North Carolina Film Commission was supposed to have been reward for being student director of the Governor's campaign. It was not a plum deal. Lemon, was more like it.

Unleashed from Hollywood—or from wherever they kept them—and allowed to wander the hinterlands, cinema and television types acted like hybrids between 19th-century Russian Boyars and rapacious Ostrogoths.

Well, she'd had enough.

She not only had sworn off politics, but she was on the cusp of deciding to never vote again.

HISTORICAL LANDMARK #15
The Salmon Queen Prevails

By the third day of negotiations, the future Salmon Queen, despite both her and her attorney's inexperience, had the long end of the stick. The Salmon King's weary attorneys bargained the situation down to a list he could live with: (1) She would marry Junior, but by proxy, for she never wanted to see him again; (2) Monarch Foods would pay for her upkeep and education through her twenty-first birthday, and (3) for the infant's support until he was age twenty-one; and (4) the most difficult point of negotiation: she would have sole custody of the child.

"It was the photograph, Mr. Wagner," the lead attorney had observed. "It meant Federal rape charges. Even if Junior had been acquitted, it would be ruinous to the label. Her age."

But the Salmon King raised a weary arm, and growled that he "damned well knew about her fucking age," and the lawyer left him sitting in his darkened eighth-story office in downtown Seattle.

O it was a goddamned dismal situation.

He took stock: For cautionary legal purposes, he'd dispatched Junior's fornicating, lying posterior to Monarch's new anchovetta plants in Tierra del Fuego weeks before.

Everybody from Aaron Aardvark to Zeke Zymgosk told me he was useless, and goddamnit, he is.

Confronting reality was ugly business: He was a widowed forty-seven-year-old with a Weenie-Head for a son and a grandson he could not see. And, for Christ's sake, he'd been outmaneuvered by a fourteen-year-old native girl; and here he was, absolutely and completely fucked up.

It was a situation that would piss anyone off.

For the Salmon King's money, Junior could stay in that godawful southern blowhole until it sprouted palm trees sixty feet tall. Fact was, his late wife Uma had cautioned, "Always watch Junior, Husband." And he had not. Yes, his was a goddamned sorry-ass situation.

Milepost 57.4
Washouts Ahead!—Emergency Road Advisement!

When the Johnson Birthday Party opened the door to Uncle Haslett's Soul Food Express, they saw not only a white delivery driver, but one dressed in a minister's gown. Plus, he had all the appearances of being Uncle Haslett's best customer. The delivery itself was difficult: The Too Good Chicken was flat missing; Uncle Haslett's Cornbread Stuffed Chicken was there, but only half what they'd ordered; the Slap Yo Momma Meatloaf and Momma Haslett's Fried Catfish were all there, as was Momma Haslett's Calves Liver and Chitterling Loaf. And the cornbread. Thank God, it was there.

When Mrs. Johnson called Haslett's, she pointed out that the delivery driver had waddled off without collecting any money. "Furthermore," she added, "when I asked him about the Too Good Chicken, he answered very rudely. Biggest, strangest ol' white man I ever saw."

16

Except for the tips of Taffer's liberated clodhoppers protruding from the hems of the minister's gown, Wagner felt his clothing situation bordered on perfect. It reeked of mothballs, but what the hell, better than a bloody, soiled hospital gown.

Parson Bandy Smith petted his dog absently and free-formed about the gown's former occupant.

"He was a big old man, with a God-given talent for preaching. When they lynched him, his head liked to snap off."

The lynching business returned Wagner's mind to basics, though the Ancient Preacher's motives still remained a nagging issue.

"Lynching? What lynching?"

"Why, Reverend Byers. They lynched him for taking the Jefferson boy's side." He looked Wagner up and down, nodding. "My, it does fit you nicely." He smiled with satisfaction. "I reckoned you and Reverend Byers were about the same size. Praise the Lord."

Wagner decided to take the grisly matter of the late great Reverend and the Jefferson boy no further. The tiny radio on the parson's countertop continued with gospel music, and a glance at an old mantle clock gave clear warning: In ten minutes it was coming up on the hour.

Shit! News time. All the latest and greatest. Wagner must make an immediate exit.

The Ancient certainly could not know Wagner's market value. But why question the man's ignorance? Better to get the hell out of there before he wised up.

Still, his mind seemed aware enough. Since leading him into the parsonage and ministering to Wagner's basic needs, Parson Smith demonstrated senses not dulled by age.

And here was the radio?

Maybe his poor cranium was stuffed with so much Christian horsefeathers there wasn't room for matters practical. Wagner long ago had recognized that such milky doctrine clouded and addled those afflicted.

Parson Smith took out a tiny biscuit and held it before his dog who stared at it, uninterested. The old man shrugged, then looked Wagner up and down, nodding.

"You shorely are welcome to stay, but seems the whole country is looking for you, Praise the Lord. An's the machine come and towed 'way your little trailer house." He sighed sadly, and concluded, "Ah'm 'fraid the po'leece' will soon know the movie folk rented my car again. Oh, they'll come lookin', praise the Lord."

The Parson's information level dropped upon Wagner like a gladiatorial net. A chill took hold, and he felt the distant talons of St. Finny's tightening.

What about this old, old man?

Wagner frowned, weighing each word. Nothing made any goddamned sense about this old fossil. *What the fuck, Wagner, just be straight out with matters.*

"With seventy-five G's, you could sponsor an entire tent revival. When they get here, they'll probably lynch you for bullshitting them about the car."

In a surprise move, the old man popped the dog biscuit in his mouth, and talked around it.

"Well, Suh, they didn't ask me about the car, Praise the Lord. You must be a Pilgrim—a stranger in these parts." He nodded, then chuckled—though there was no humor in it. "Around he'yah, a black man don't fetch the age of one-hunnert-'n-one and mess in white folks' affairs. This su'tunly is not Raleigh, or some such big city. This is ol' time Nawth' Carolina out here, suh. And, I might add, the Good Book teaches that bee-trayal for Mammon is to incur the eternal fires of perdition. Praise the Lord."

Wagner and the Parson Smith meditated on scripture for a while, the parson slowly chewing the biscuit. Then Wagner's roving eye caught sight of the phone book. Long ago, he'd learned a valuable tactic about phone books, and reaching over he nabbed it.

"Know of any good home-delivery chicken joints, Parson? Dinner's on me."

Wagner was anxious to play some of his own traveling music, and he loved irony—more than anything. And wouldn't it be wonderful irony if food—which had gotten him into this mess—would be his ticket to ride?

Oh, Wagner! You Old Devil. You're an unprincipled genius!

Milepost 57.45
Warning! Soft Shoulder, Next Mile
Oswald II

Oswald spent the day closing the Carolina Packing Acquisition for considerably less than market value. Alone or no, he decided to celebrate. Oh, it was all fine for everyone to be worried about his swine of a brother—or uncle, depending on one's view.

Actually, Oswald thought of himself as avuncular—made him feel superior to Wagner. A person could have a swine of a nephew just as they might a swine of a brother. What was different was having both in the same hideous package.

Well, I shouldn't ruminate on that.

This was his night. Not that anyone would compliment him, including his mother. You know, faithful old Oswald just went around making a $35 million profit in a single day—making everyone unbelievably wealthy.

But I shouldn't ruminate on that either.

He should concentrate on having a good time, but the spirit of victory was spoiled. Absent. Fizzled out.

And it was Wagner's fault. A blight of a human being would be putting it weakly. Nobody would blame Oswald for his idea—in fact, it was a fine idea.

So: I shouldn't feel guilty about what I did.

He tried that out loud—looking at himself in the mirror.

"I don't feel guilty about what I did?"

Yes, repeating it out loud helped. Often, his psychiatrist had suggested this technique—sort of transactional reality grounding.

Fifty thousand dollars in Canadian Gold Maple Leafs, hand delivered, to any peace officer apprehending Wagner—on top of Monarch Industry's more conventional $75,000—would cork that Great Fatty up like a cricket in a jar. "With that," the Commandant had confided to Oswald, "a damned old black snake dipped in Vaseline couldn't squeeze over the state line."

And the commandant would keep Oswald's added incentive confidential, of course. Especially from his mother. Police were good at keeping things to themselves. And the Black-Snake-in-Lubricant analogy—Oswald especially liked that, though he kept it to himself.

So, no! Oswald did not feel guilty about this gold mapleleaf business. It was in everybody's interest to keep Wagner in North Carolina. Even Wagner's.

17

Wagner's escape had experienced dynamic renewal. Astride the old Harley three-wheeled motorcycle, he felt the night air ripple around and through his gown, over his oh-so-recently tortured epidermis.

The experience was like being blow-dried by the Gods. Behind him, the now-empty box of the delivery vehicle sported a plastic statue of that Immortal of Soul, James Brown, in an eternal freeze-frame of two-and-a-half-foot-high plastic and glitter. This late 20th-century promotional masterpiece included the master's plastic cape. Its entirety was illuminated from within by a pulsing red light.

Mr. Brown's front and backsides sported letters proclaiming "Hazlett's Soul Food Express" to the passing world—or that portion of the world Wagner was passing.

Wagner decided his conveyance, though not the most discreet vehicle, was devilishly indiscreet by its glaring indiscretion. *O Increasing Irony!* Wagner loved that. Was irony itself becoming a *leitmotif* of his escape?

By Wagner's acquiring the motorcycle, everybody was happy within this burgeoning matrix of irony. Cheered by it all, Wagner constructed, extempore, a helluva list, one of his keenest: (1) The Hazletts' youngest son's business acuity made his parents' tiny business richer with $12,000 of Winslow's money; (2) Wagner had wheels, plus [2a] the Hazlett Express cell phone, [2b] a county/state map and flashlight, and [2c] the tri-wheeled conveyance came complete with a half tank of gas. (3) The Hazletts would be sensibly discreet about their transaction, thereby allowing his pursuers to update their membership in Wagner's favorite club, i.e. [3a] the Inky Darkness Club, those kept in eternal darkness about anything connected with his escape; and last but not least, (4) when Wagner used the parsonage's john, he'd stuffed five hundred dollars in the centarian's false teeth holder.

With all that Christian nonsense in his head, Wagner knew the Ancient could use counseling, or at least a better class of tea biscuit.

Wagner was semi-inconvenienced by the young Hazlett's sense of integrity: Despite any amount of money, Wagner had to swear both to the young man and Pastor Bandy Smith that he would deliver a goddamned shitload of soul food to a birthday party.

Carefully, the young man had drawn a simple map, for the destination was only a few blocks from the church. While thus occupied, Pastor Smith offered a farewell blessing, "We thank you, Oh Lawd, for on this night, you brought Brother Hazlett together with this pilgrim-in-distress. So bless both. Praise the Lord."

Once free and away, astride his spiffy set of wheels, Wagner of course dismissed the idea of delivering a bunch of food.

Fuck 'um. In this world, it's Devil-Take-the-Hindmost.

Pulling off at a nearby secluded glen, he popped open the rear compartment's door and beheld a vast treasure of culinary Valhalla. It was pregnant with food—and such food! It emitted powerful aromas; Wagner knew the Gods themselves would have fallen over backward and passed fucking out if they had a sniff of this stuff! Plus, in a separate compartment were chilled half gallons of pop. God Almighty! How could anyone pass something like this up?

Milepost 62.6
Caution! Slow to 15 mph., Hairpin Turns Ahead
Next .3 miles

#1 Motel Twist: The Desk Receptionist at the Ponce De LeonAirport Inn faced the indignant man, repeating, "Ms. Sue Charles checked out. Both she and Mr. Moynahan."

"Hardly, goddamnit. I'm Mr. Moynahan, you threadhead. The one paying the fucking charges here, which I'm guessing are considerable—you know, on the card number given to you over the Internet."

"Listen, Sir, it isn't necessary to call people names, here."

"Oh?! Well, if I'm Mr. Moynahan, and she left with Mr. Moynahan, who in hell did she leave with? So, if you aren't a threadhead, why do you run charges on a credit card from an unidentified man?"

"I'm ringing our resident manager, sir. I don't get paid for listening to abuse."

The clerk watched the alleged Mr. Moynahan storm out to his limo, say something to the driver, then put his hands to his hips, staring into the night.

The clerk thanked God he was doing the night receptionist a favor and his regular shift was days now. Nights were when the Gearlooses and Moonhowlers checked in.

This Moynahan fellow wasn't the first who claimed they'd checked out when trying to check in. Why did normal, good things change, but the weird, kinky stuff never did?

#2 Mobile Phone: Mo Taft snatched the high falutin' cell phone from son Ezra after he'd yakked a half-hour non-stop with Maze Carlisle, his homelier-than-fatback girlfriend.

"Give me that som' bitch, fo' ya wear out the batt'rees. We hain't got no charger 'cause some careless sort stole eet without one."

Mo Taft aimed a remonstrative stare at Taffer, who now drove through the North Carolina evening on a quick return to the Reverend Bandileg Smith's church. Mo ruminated on matters tactical.

"While tha'yat dumb-ass brother-in-law of mine ees out huntin' wild geese, us'uns is gonna' be kickin' some preacher ass and gettin' back on the trail of tha'yat seventy-five thousand smackers."

"Reverend Bandilegs didn't bull'shee'yat anyone, Pa. He just stood there."

Mo didn't answer Taffer. Both were good boys, Taffer brighter than Ezra. But like Mo had explained to their Ma, there was more North Carolina in them than Tennessee. "Back home in Tennessee," he explained, "havin' the name Taft meant bein' cagey. An' ah' means to be a decent Pap to them boys. Damned straight."

18

Wagner had problems. He couldn't urge this aged motorcycle over thirty-five miles per hour, plus consumption of a six-pack-and-a-half of pop required him to pee every ten minutes.

And navigation remained problematical: There was a well-used map amply lubricated with Hazlett's Too Good Chicken drippings in the courier case, yet the batteries in the Hazlett flashlight were weak, making roadside reference difficult. Plus, his maps ended at the North Carolina/South Carolina state line. So, Wagner experienced a tad of anxiety not having full information about which crossing went where. More guessing was necessary!

During the last two pee stops, Wagner tried unsuccessfully to extinguish the light within the King of Soul's plastic thorax, with no luck. Mr. Brown's brilliance raised hell with Wagner's privacy situation. Having one's gown hiked up while peeing—with no undergarments therein—made a less than favorable tableaux in the murky shadows cast by passing headlights.

Well, no escape was perfect, especially this one.

Best to remember that, privacy or no, his lot had improved exponentially over what it was hours back.

Wagner felt in an unselfish mood.

Despite evil, self-serving motives, ingrained instincts of fellowship compelled him to deliver the soul food—at great risk to himself. He had to admit—essentially, he wasn't the rat-bastard people thought he was.

Simple expediency dictated he ignore his promise to the naive Hazlett boy. Yet there remained feelings of gratitude. So, following the lad's instructions he'd graciously completed the delivery.

True, Wagner had been somewhat cross with the old bag who'd whined about the missing Too-Good Chicken. But Hazlett's chicken challenged even the culinary prowess of Kokanne Joe's, so Wagner had overindulged a bit.

But the hell with all that.

Now Wagner was South Carolina bound. Hopefully, Spartanburg, population forty-three thousand, with the famous Spartanburg Memorial Airport. With his formidable research skills and his laptop, he'd researched his appropriate port-of-departure while inside the confines of St. Finny's.

And Spartanburg was launch pad, so to speak, of Wagner's Plan Blue.

In Spartanburg, Wagner would charter the sleekest, fastest corporate jet possible from Kittihawk Charters. Oh, that would be a momentous event: Winging his recently incarcerated carcass back to Alaska, and the comfort of his suite of offices—the world editorial headquarters of the *Northern Socialist Review* and The Northern Institute for Social Reprisal.

From there he would launch a withering assault on both private and public institutions in North Carolina. He'd slam the Doomsday Book on the conniving motherfuckers who'd rained agony and humiliation on him; they'd be reduced to heaps of bankruptcy slips—litigated into a pool of legal sewage.

Here he was—Wagner (he visualized this in very large lights), social essayist and innovator, worth dozens of millions in his own right—riding a fucking beater motorcycle adorned with a ghastly artifact of American idolatry.

While cruising through this deep, Tarheel night—not really knowing where in hell he was going—every rural and semi-rural scum from Aaron Aardvark to Zeke Zymgosk was out to bag him. Jesus Christ, just the thought of the inequity of this pissed Wagner off to the tenth power!

But cool down, Wagner. Think straight. Think right.

This time, if he pissed away his freedom, Fate would not be so kind. With seventy-five G's hanging on his head, the hounds were keener, meaner, and less easily thrown from the scent.

So, if circumstances required Wagner to sit astride this mobile monstrosity proceeding at thirty-five miles per hour over the phantom backroads of North Carolina, then that's the goddamned way it must be. He took a fresh, bold grip on the handlebars—keeping that old throttle cranked full out. He allowed a smug chuckle, and Wagner felt at once more cheerful.

Watch out, you Spartanburg sheep shaggers!

Oh yes, as soon as Wagner could find out exactly where in hell it was, he was hell-bent for Spartanburg.

Milepost 70.5
Chances in Hell

The Salmon Queen fingered the spreadsheets with Carolina Packing acquisition data while looking onto the gardened hotel terrace. Within minutes of their regular morning work session, she and son Oswald had had words and he'd sulked off to his suite.

It wasn't Monarch Food business that led to their disagreement, but the usual: Brother Wagner.

She loved Oswald, but Oswald was different from Wagner, and he—Oswald—was forever putting the most self-pitying spin on that.

She allowed a regal sigh, and moved her diminutive frame to one side, sliding feet beneath her and massaging a chronically rheumatic left foot—a remnant of an ancient scuffle over garbage in wartime Otaru.

Oh, perhaps I should not have had a second child.

The Salmon Queen's wealth of conflicting memories surged back. There were problems from the beginning: The eleven-year-old Wagner, of course, didn't understand how he could no longer be the center of her attention, and his grandfather's—but mostly he was confused as to why she would even want another baby. Also, the infant Oswald was the son of the Salmon King.

"But Mother, doesn't a son take precedence over a grandson?"

But she struggled away from these reflections. More to the point was: How could Oswald have assumed she would not find out about his added reward of gold-on-delivery? And of course she was angry—he hadn't even stipulated his brother be unharmed.

"You want him harmed. Even dead!"

And Oswald's normally detached, even cool, demeanor developed a sudden fissure from which oozed old bile. He pitched his croissant over the edge of the terrace and barked, "And why shouldn't I! The arrogant, cruel swine! And Younghusband is supposed to be doing Monarch business, not spying on me."

And so terminated that business conference!

She was at least thankful for some good news: Her medical consultants, after debriefing that awful Dr. Von Bracken, had reassured that this drug used on Wagner might just work itself out, even if they didn't get to him within the next few days.

"But," they'd added, "much preferable is beginning a course of treatment at once."

North Carolina authorities, eager for upscale Monarch Foods to invest in the stubbornly gray-collar pork market, were eager to please. In fact, the Attorney General himself guaranteed the Salmon Queen that Von Bracken would be seriously involved in odd jobs around the state park system for the next 180 days. After that, they'd toss him to the Feds. She patted the AG on his cuff, and said, "Good. I'll hold you to that, thank you."

It wasn't that the Salmon Queen could never be bullshitted by men—oh, she could. The point was that over the years, she'd dealt out severe retribution to such fools. Consistency of consequences was the answer.

She'd learned this, among the other less civilized facets of business, from the Salmon King. "Little Lady," he'd invariably advised, "those who play, must pay. Nail their double-dealing hides to the wall for all to see. That's where the old ounce of prevention comes in."

HISTORICAL LANDMARK #18
The Salmon Queen's Widowhood

There were four halcyon years for the Salmon Queen. Wagner grew, a hale and robust baby, and the Salmon King paid once weekly visits to his grandson. She began her education at Seattle University after completing elementary and secondary school in one year. Business courses were her common sense selection. She excelled.

She scraped by on the meager allowance agreed to in the settlement, living in a small apartment on Queen Anne Hill. It was a few days after the end of the Korean War when the Salmon King appeared midweek—never his usual time—with housekeeper Katrina at his elbow. The Salmon Queen knew the moment she opened the door that Junior was no more.

Katrina took Wagner out for ice cream while the Salmon King stiffly explained, "He drank himself to death in Chile. It was my fault. We never spoke again, you know."

And he left, muttering something about their agreement remaining the same. "Unchanged," was how he'd put it.

When Katrina returned with an ice-cream-smeared Wagner, she expanded with details: After the end of the anchovetti season, the now 380-pound Junior had challenged four Dutchmen to a drinking contest during one of his week-long debauches at the Santiago Grand and had collapsed, never reviving. He was thirty-two.

He'd literally drunk himself to death.

"And Himself" (as Katrina always referred to the Salmon King) "is not well. He sits in his office. Doesn't even conduct business." She looked guiltily at the Salmon Queen, and got to the point. "Fact is, why don't you and the boy come up and spend the next weekend at the mansion. It would help his grandfather."

Junior could have turned to stone, for what she felt; also, the Salmon Queen harbored considerable ill will against the Salmon King. Even at eighteen years of age, her penchant for remembering friends and never forgiving enemies was well developed.

Katrina could see her turning matters over, so added,

"He's a forty-nine-year-old widower who's lost his only son. The babe is all he has now."

And she agreed, because he was Wagner's grandfather, albeit a hesitant one. And in the Salmon Queen's bones was an undying respect for blood ties. That was enough.

19

Thankfully, it was Sunday. And the clerk at the Crossroads All Hours Minimart had mistaken Wagner for a preacher. He eyed the wall clock that read 1:30 a.m. and commented, "On your way to church kinda' early, aint'cha, Parson?"

"Souls aren't saved during convenient hours, brother. Praise the Lord."

The clerk re-plugged his dubious mental powers into a television fervent with drama courtesy of *The Dallas All-Wheel Monster Truck Competition*. He chewed a thin lower lip as the tension of the final event rose.

While Wagner maneuvered his cloaked frame through the store's narrow chip and snack department, he kept a weather-eye on the clerk while loading up. But the wretched creature remained devoted to the quasi-primates bashing each other goofy in their four-wheel-drive genitalia.

Wagner returned to the pumps, replaced the gascap, and stared suspiciously at the All Hours glittery façade. Might that little piss ant of a clerk be as lunk-headed as he looked? Would he really not associate the non-stop media burpings about rewards for a fat lunatic with his customer—an overlarge white preacher, live and unrehearsed, right before his proboscis?

Perhaps, but the South Carolina state line couldn't come soon enough for Wagner. And surely, he was on his way!

Since coming by his novel means of transport, Wagner's sense of optimism had grown steadily. After Wagner drove down the road a half mile and pulled behind a defunct produce stand to sample his booty, he decided that once again Dame Anonymity was blessing his path. The store clerk, poor sot, had missed the financial opportunity of a lifetime.

So, in the eternal light of Mr. James Brown and the anemic illumination offered by Brother Hazlett's flashlight, Wagner snacked on pork rinds and cheese sticks while perusing a state map of

North Carolina. He tried to make sense of blue, red, and interstate roadways while downing a quart of apple juice for regularity and general overall health.

The Hazlett Soul Food cellphone, miles back, had been put to skillful use: Since Moynahan was busy with Wagner's Plan Blue, he was absent from home. Yet Wagner's friend and attorney's answering machine offered more technological wigglings than some heart-lung machines, and using diverse codes, Wagner gained electronic admission to it—and left an update.

Then, he repeated same with Leggy Peggy, though somewhat surprised that his faithful and woeful Business Manager/Editor was not at home.

"Oh, not another spate of drag-ass boyfriends," lamented Wagner out loud, a wave of pity almost overtaking him momentarily, until his own plight erased Leggy Peggy's problems.

After all, he remembered, the poor woman wasn't comfortable unless she was barricaded in her bathroom calling 911 about a madman outside with an ax, or some such outrage.

With a curse to petty bourgeois, hypocritical, Green Party jerkoffs, Wagner tossed aside pork rind and cheese stick wrappers, then started in on the half dozen sandwiches and opened a container of orange juice. He had to keep up the peeing; otherwise he knew The Fix would turn his liver to basalt.

Between satisfying bites, Wagner's long apprenticeship with charts and maps under the Salmon King's tutelage paid dividends: He ascertained that he'd driven in the opposite direction of South Carolina for the last one and three quarter hours.

In point of fact, he was now closer to Virginia than South Carolina. By quite a few miles.

"Shit—oh rotten eggs!"

They would ('they' meaning everyone in the world, from the Abyssinian Volunteer Fire Brigade to the Zydeco Swing Kings) would of course expect him to be heading north into Virginia. Diverse sorts—both official and private—would be lurking behind every rain barrel and rusted tractor, waiting for their shot at wealth and accompanying fame on the afternoon sloptalk circuit.

Wagner used all his mental discipline to calm himself—to remember the Good about this escape, rather than the Ugly. Wagner reminded himself that—theoretically speaking—during an escape, there was no 'wrong direction,' if indeed one's flight rendered one increasingly distant from one's pursuer.

And this thought offered him balm.

For he was all of that—more distant from St. Finny's, The Fix, and everyone else intent on clapping him back in that phenomenally overpriced Lard Lodge.

Milepost 76.0
Road Advisory: Wildlife Viewing Area: Game Unit 2C
Vehicles Stopped on Road, Next .1 mile

"No one said you were a disloyal Israeli, Abraham, just stupid."

Major Beinhorn's attractive Semitic features slowly darkened into a sardonic grimace as she steered the car through the North Carolina hinterlands, "Your late femme fatale, this Oriental Mata Hari has caused my section not a few problems, Abraham."

This late business saddened Abe. Yes, Jai Ling had ruined his career, jeopardized his country's security, and effectively established Abe as a grand schlemiel before God, Country, and Family. Still, she had defied every stereotype about Chinese women, and had been a wild, unparalleled, loin-pounding ride.

"His problem, Major, I think, is most American; he thinks with his dick."

Technical Sergeant Yeleni guffawed, as did the Major and even the massive, stolid, newly assigned Massad agent sitting next to him.Actually, Abe wished the hell he were American—or, at least All- American. He might bail out at first opportunity, and tear into the undergrowth. But no, he was a loyal Jew in the wrong line of work.

But not for long: If they did not recover the cell phone, he would be court-martialed and sentenced to ten years of hard labor.

If they did recover his cell phone, he would also be court-martialed; but instead sentenced to two years on a mine-removal squad. Abe would supervise Palestinian prisoners, hopefully ones without desires for martyrdom.

Ten years imprisonment, Abe mused, might be better than two years on mine-removal squad. After all, he was only thirty-one, and being forty-one and in possession of all one's body parts was far preferable to being thirty-four and stumping about Haifa on a converted skateboard.

20

Wagner became philosophical about his escape. Crossing into South Carolina, then the fourteen miles into Spartanburg, was now simply a matter of several hours along a clever backroad route compliments of his own intellect, and of course the North Carolina map. A spirit of forgiveness began to develop.

Now, with a pre-dawn wind at his back, at times the old three-wheeled Harley rattled along at speeds of almost forty-two mph.

These last forty-eight hours had been a taxing ordeal. Since buggering off from St. Finny's (so adroitly, so beautifully) there had been an array of challenges. Yet Wagner had been their equal, despite a few noteworthy but essentially minor setbacks.

Still, in the midst of this more reflective mood, a shadow of bitterness crept over Wagner, and he swore out loud into the night air, "The motherfuckers will pay for what they've done."

And he meant it. Oh, how Wagner meant it.

But now, he struggled to retain the Tao of his escape: Wagner was mindful of the night air lacing over and around him, causing his gown to set down a peaceful continuum of muted popping sounds.

For a beater of a motorcycle, Hazlett's ancient beast was well muffled, and if anything, added counterpoint to the ambiance of Wagner's spiritual rejuvenation.

The road was wonderful: Singular, peaceful and without complications such as houses, traffic lights, or even signs. It was merely a road with a broken line bisecting its ebony surface. And this overall simplicity contributed to a steady improvement in Wagner's mental state.

After all, for the last eighty days, he'd been in a helluva pickle, with medical gremlins crawling all over him. Plus, the rotten sons-of-bitches had starved the holy living shit out of him.

Oh, those specks of offal. I'll kill 'um.

Once again, he found himself angrily chewing the night air, and reminded himself that the Tao of this Road could not be found in clinging to the Red Dust of his recent confinement. He had to release this, despite the down-and-dirty conglomeration of fuckheads he'd been forced to consort with to get this far.

Fortunately, there was additional balm.

Having almost thirty dollars of junkfood in him, plus three or four quarts of pop, helped Wagner's system stay centered— unplagued by a persistent hunger, with him since birth.

True, Wagner's experience in the churchyard had demonstrated a dark dynamic to his obesity he had never confronted. Positive, intelligent measures had to be taken to reduce. He accepted that.

As soon as he returned home, and slipped back into his routine— savored his freedom—he would lean-out big-time, as he had so often in the past. Cut back on the junkfood, even Kokanee Joe's fried chicken, save for perhaps a night or two per month.

When it came to weight reduction, Wagner knew his way around. Oh, did he!

Any doctor or nutritionist—and Wagner had gone through a train-load of those assholes—would pronounce time and again, how a slow, gradual weight loss was far better than this quick stuff: the gimmicks, the shots-in-the-butt, the gut-cuts, skin plasters, balloons-in-the-stomach, and diverse sorts of emetics, pills, pyramid-shaped sleeping tents, Middle East hypnotists, and cockeyed coal-walkers and liver-extract imbibers.

No, these were all Horsefeather Promises and Sawdust Dreams. Wagner had a more than passing familiarity with good, reasonable diets. Every one of them was just a matter of discipline and intent.

Of course, that greatest of all Foodheads and Obesity Doyens, the Great Arbuckle, had quite tragically gone on a diet-of-misery resulting from alcoholism, a chronic abscess on his butt, and utter depression at being framed by all his arse-sniffing Hollywood cronies.

Betrayed—like me. Yes! Like me, Arbuckle. I know where your pain was at, my friend.

If Wagner had any hair on his ass, he'd turn this fucking piece of shit around, and head for St. Finny's, and fight it out right there.

Withdrawal wasn't his cup of tea, and no truer fucking words were ever said! Where in hell would Charles the 12th of Sweden have been if he'd retreated in the face of apparent overwhelming might?!

Fucking A-Rights Johnny!"

Yes. Yes. Now Arbuckle, though lacking Charles the 12th's resources, did try and fight the system, but ended up 160 pounds, dead-ass drunk without work, and with everybody writing him off as a sexual ogre.

"Oh, those lousy cocksuckers. What do they know! What do they know of the fucking pain!"

Wagner shouted his defiance ala Ahab into the dank, petty-bourgeois North Carolina night. God! He was retreating—giving way to the forces of evil, tail tucked under his gown—going belly up!

A Wagner does NOT GO BELLYUP!

Wagner took a firm, fierce grip on the handlebars, and decided to turn back—turn west, and confront Von Bracken, that dirty sodomite and all these petty demons. Yes! Go chin to chin with Von Bracken—eyer of medium-sized goats and llamas.

Wagner laughed, and even managed a jubilant bounce, causing his aged vehicle to sag then rebound momentarily. He allowed himself a whoop—*Yes, even deer weren't safe around that pervert Von Bracken.* Wagner chuckled—yes, even extra-large specimens, like that framed in his headlight managing a perfect, glass-eyed dumbfounded dumb-beast stare for that infinitesimal breath of time prior to the motorcycle's imminent impact.

Milepost 81.6 — Road Advisory
Wildlife Viewing Area: Game Unit 2B
Vehicles Stopped on Road, next .1 mile

Stopping the car before the church, Mo Taft wasted no time with detailed planning.

"Now, we'll sound bottom of this he'yah Reverend Bandilegs situation."

While they got out, Mo quickly used the cell phone to tell his Old Lady they'd be late to breakfast. But, when he got out, he saw he had family problems.

Taffer looked at his feet, then over at the dilapidated overgrown church, and managed, "Pa, me and Ezra have a raht hard time bracin' an ol' neegra man, a preacher, thay'yats over a hunnert year old. Hee'yit hain't raht."

Mo moved to one side, and regretted not kicking both their asses more frequently.

Since he had time, Mo Taft figured he'd do so right here—or at least Taffer's, usually the ringleader of the two. Before Mo could execute his trademark sidewise sneak-kick to the balls, a Lincoln Towncar cruised up and stopped; three men and a woman got out.

Immediately family differences were put aside, and the three Tafts thought and acted as smoothly as a Roman Legion: They spread out, Taffer to the rear of their car, Ezra to the other side, so the strangers could not see him reaching inside his overcoat.

The woman stopped a half dozen paces away. She didn't smile.

"You have a cell phone that belongs to us. Please hand it over, no questions, and we'll be on our way."

Mo stalled with a bit of diplomacy.

"You the Hay'yed Pussy 'round c'here, Honey?"

She stood a bit straighter—and Mo noted the size of the third man ranged between a landfill black bear and a septic tank.

"The cell phone, please."

"Don' know what ya's talkin' about."

She moved to one side, and Mo saw a poisonous little metallic snout protruding from the smallest man's leather coat. At him.

Now she smiled.

"You were kind enough to make liberal use of it. So, I'm not guessing, as to whereabouts. Our cell phone. Now."

At the same moment, Taffer moved a bit—and when the two other men's, plus the woman's, eyes snapped in that direction, they were looking at Ezra's sawed-off shotgun. In full view.

Yet their gunman's attention remained tightly focused on Mo's midsection. Mo noted these were no beginners. Just the sight of Ezra's weapon usually gave pause even to veteran officers.

"You-all is a lookin' at an ol' Spanish ten-gauge loaded up with buckshot and rat poison. Not as fancy as your'un's, but down hee'yah, ya' gotta' pardon our'n country ways. "

Experience enabled Mo to identify the root issue: a)This matter revolved around a cellphone they'd come by without cost. So b) anything gained by it, would be net profit.

Yes, root issues: A man's ability to make sense of these was what Mo's Pa claimed separated a businessman from your run-of-the-mill cordwood and smokehouse thief.

Milepost 81.9
The Rude and The Worthless

Colonel Younghusband looked across at Mrs. Wagner and thought that no matter how much fish oil his Missus took, she still didn't suffer the years as easily as Monarch Food's Chief Executive Officer. Years back, Herself had advised Mrs. Younghusband that fish oil is what made the skin retain youthfulness.

"Ma'rm, you look positively youthful this morning."

And she thanked him, even serving him tea and allowing that strange, decidedly Asiatic halfsmile to flicker across her dark features.

Then Younghusband commenced his seventy-two-hour situation report:

"There is really no sign of him since the Church business, though we know he acquired some means of transport. Possibly," here Younghusband shrugged while sipping tea, ". . . possibly as innocuous as a taxi. After all, there's Dr. Winslow's money. But let me assure, Ma'rm, he's still within the bounds of North Carolina."

She continued to listen, without asking questions—without visible response—until he got to Wagner's assistant, seemingly marooned in a Minnesota motel with the vicious creature which passed for Wagner's pet. Herself "tsk-tsked," and mused, "Peggy Rothstein. The poor woman. Did you know she looks after Wagner? The only one who cares." Then, while Younghusband paused with not a little interest in this rare aside, Herself pinched off a bit of croissant and looked off-terrace before nibbling.

"Do make sure she stays safe, Colonel. Mr. Moynahan isn't dependable."

"Yes, Marm. Now: Speaking of which the good counselor is continuing south from Gainesville on something of an erratic course. Seems to have disconnected from events or plans in North Carolina, Ma'rm, in interests of pursuing that tart."

"And she's with one of your men," she offered a sardonic (could it be?) still disapproving sniff, followed by a pursing of lips?

"Yes, Ma'rm. Albans, a solid sort. Believe me, it was best to sidetrack our good counselor, even though we've monitored the messages and such. Never can tell, with those two."

But as he approached the end of his report, Younghusband was surprised when Herself took a note from beside the tea service, and sliding it across the glass tabletop with a delicate fingertip, nodded for him to read it.

"SQ: I'm well. And I forgive you. Love W."

Even Younghusband experienced confusion until Herself explained.

"My confidential answering service in Seattle received that about two hours ago. You see, Colonel, since his earliest years, when he began going off on his tangents, I made him promise he would always let me know, at the very least, if he was all right."

And when Younghusband left her suite, he paused in the entryway to gaze steady-eyed upon Stromboli who, apron on, was hog-wrestling several unfortunate bouquets of flowers while studying a book on Japanese flower arranging.

"Stromboli, whatever are you doing?!"

The mammoth man, somewhat embarrassed, admitted in halting English that his longtime fiancé in his Sicilian village had complained of his lack of gentility. Herself had recommended this new hobby as a way to render him more sensitive. Artistic. As Younghusband returned to his suite, he admitted there was much to write the Missus this day. Whenever he was away, even years ago when he was held hostage by the bloody Israelis, he wrote her twice weekly.

As much as circumstances permitted, he allowed her a glimpse into his world, for it was one that intrigued her. They were always something of a team. Now this week, there were topics rich with characters: Stromboli strangling carnations, baby's breath, and roses; a fatally obsessed barrister; a wandering wildcat; stunningly criminal hillbillies with a stolen cell phone; and the continuing mystery of "SQ," the incessant sobriquet, or whatever, by which Herself's oldest invariably referred to Monarch's CEO.

"Why don't you just ask her what SQ means, Dear?" the Missus had asked more than once. To which, Younghusband pointed out—as always—that questions of this sort weren't asked. In the world of personal security, information (either its presence or absence) was taken, traded and/or uncovered/discovered—but never offered. Absolutely out of the question.

The Salmon Queen's Vision

The Salmon Queen did not move back to her apartment in Queen Anne Hill, but instead she and son Wagner took up residence at the Chinook House, the Salmon King's thirty-eight-room mansion on Seattle's Capital Hill.

On one of his visiting days with Grandson Wagner, she ended her long silence with the Salmon King. He gently removed her leather-bound graduate business project from Grandson's clutches—he'd been using it to take swings at the cat. He thumbed through it.

"What's this?"

Katrina, always present for the visits, looked from one to the other.

Would she answer or not? Finally, the tiny woman—for the Salmon Queen was now all of that—held out her hand, watching him turn the pages.

"That is my senior project. I graduated from Seattle University last May."

"I know that. I'm not a fucking idiot. I live here."

"You must not use such language around my son. He's starting school soon."

"He is my grandson and this is my house."

"And I know that. I too am not an idiot."

Katrina, standing with the boy in hand—she'd been dressing him in preparation for the zoo—glanced from grandfather to mother, dumbfounded. No one, ever, spoke to the Salmon King in that fashion.

The Salmon King stopped paging through her senior thesis. They were eye to eye. Two feral cats leery of each other's power: his phenomenal economic authority that spread across six states and three countries; her legal and moral authority of Wagner—for though Grandfather and Grandson had grown close, Mother and Son were as one.

The Salmon King placed her prospectus on an end table and said, "For twenty-six years, I've found that people like good, safe food at low prices. Only a fool would pay five times the market price for a can of sardines."

The Salmon Queen was surprised that with just a few turns of pages, he could discuss her project. She gestured at the report.

"Similar logic could be used regards a Ford versus a Bentley."

Her point was a hard rhetorical grounder between first and second—and the Salmon King watched it burn into center field, untouched.

Katrina's expression reflected surprise at this strange direction in topic. The Salmon King reached out, picked up the thesis, asked if he might read it over at his leisure. At that point—and only at this point—can it be rightly claimed that these two members of salmon royalty formally met.

Had it been a win for the Salmon Queen? A stand-off between the two? Later when Katrina confessed to the budding businesswoman that she'd feared for her well-being, the Salmon Queen smiled wearily, shook her head, and replied, "The father, thank goodness, is nothing like the son."

21

Wagner, and what remained of Hazlett's delivery motorcycle, came to rest upright 180 degrees in reference to his original direction-of-travel. It had been a singularly eventful ride: Always blessed with extraordinarily fast reactions, Wagner avoided the deer, instead colliding with a formidable row of rural mailboxes.

The bulky motorcycle, plus its not inconsiderable pilot, had mowed down the boxes with a grand flourish of sounds: crashes, gratings, metallic screeches—mixed liberally with Wagner's horrified, pain-driven howls and whoops.

The first rural box Wagner assassinated was fashioned from welded log chain as its vertical riser, the box itself a massive mockup of a barrel stove: Wagner only remembered this initial box looming up in the motorcycle's single headlight. He'd slammed into it directly, sending the windshield of the metermaid's vehicle folding violently over Wagner's cranial vault.

At that instant, the circuitry of his central nervous system sprayed a wonderment of heavenly bodies through the yet conscious sphere of his brain.

Struggling to remain alert, Wagner found his vision obscured by the *plasticus obscura* of the windshield, smashed flat against face and head.

After the initial smote of vehicle against mailbox, the rest was a cavalcade of cacophony and horror-show violence. Mailbox after mailbow was slain in a noise-filled domino-effect, though each mailbox's demise came at a slower rate as Wagner's transport slowed.

When fully stopped, Wagner was treated to a strange, new perspective: The headlight remained on, but now bent upwards; it projected a clear, white beam into a dense pine canopy. Through this column of light, mail not picked up the day previous fluttered earthward—a shopper here, several envelopes there—and even torn remnants of a yard sale sign—all came earthward before

Wagner's eyes when the windshield fell free from his skull, allowing unfettered vision.

To his left, the bobbing posterior of the deer disappeared into the forest. *The wretched bastard stayed around long enough to see the show,* lamented Wagner—yet grateful he could still think anything.

A trickle of blood seeped from his forehead causing near panic: Had he fractured—even split—his skull!? Feeling with his hand, he diagnosed a modest gouge at the hairline, and held the flat of his palm against it.

He felt the chill of shock settle across him until realizing with dismay—in fact a helluva lot of dismay—that it was not the chill of shock (as yet) but the sadistic absence of Reverend Smith's loaned gown. His trajectory through the boxes had torn it free from Wagner's body. Wagner was naked under the canopy of heaven. Well, almost naked, for Taffer's largish field boots remained. Finally, Wagner found voice.

"You fool, Wagner. The deer would have been a softer target than these goddamned mailboxes!"

Wagner's sense of mercy and compassion for animals and other creatures innocent had tossed him into the stew pot.

When he looked down, Wagner saw that though yet astride the vehicle, the posterior portion of it had been severed neatly from the anterior. On the road, the box of the motorcycle, complete with wheels, had come to rest. Somewhat behind this, lying upon the centerline, was Mr. James Brown's statue, its light finally off. Using badly mangled handlebars to push upward, Wagner attained a standing position.

The first vehicle along would be treated to a unique tableau: They would see Wagner standing there, shod in great clodhoppers, naked before all amongst the scattered ruins of rural Americana and the twisted chassis of this nation's last motorized conveyor of Slap Yo Momma Meatloaf.

Milepost 82.0
Caution! Construction Ahead
Frequent Breaks in Pavement: Next 1.2 miles

Mo Taft was not the sort to overlook an opportunity to make some spare change.

"Seein's tha'yat cell phone's so impaw'tant, you give us a grand, an' eet's all yers, and they'll be no need for shootin'."

"Bullshit. The phone. Now."

She extended her hand, gesturing for him to hurry. This, he knew, was a hard woman. Mo long maintained that a hard woman was worse than four of the orneriest men.

Mo—only too often—had the sins of his offspring visited upon himself. This was another instance. He took a weary breath.

"Well, seems we got a Mes'kin standoff. Tell ya what. I'll fight any them three dumb shee'yits—-'cludin' that big ol' side of pork belly standin' they'yah. Ah wins, we gets two grand; you win, you geet the phone."

The four interlopers looked at each other, and something like an approving rumble escaped from the maw of the behemoth. Mo reckoned this hulk might take a tad extra doing, but for two thousand, no problem.

Finally, the woman nodded—and sweeping off her coat, revealed a lot of femininity in very appropriate places. Mo whistled, was about to compliment, but she cut him short.

"I accept. With one change. You fight me. No holds barred."

Seeing boundless humor in her offer, Taffer and Ezra began to laugh and heehaw—respectively. Mo groaned.

"Shut yo' traps, ya' wuth'less piles of crowbait!"

Silence.

Unlike himself, Mo's sons weren't men-of-the-world. His record of fighting females was mixed: Twice with his wife (one and one), once with his daughter-in-law (a clear win), and with two different Korean prostitutes overseas (another one and one). Easily, the second fight with the hooker was the most instructive.

Mo scrambled for an exit strategy. This cell phone situation was migrating from Sorry-Ass to Fucked-Up. Pure and simple.

22

Wagner was sure no one would drive past the accident site without stopping. This would be the only positive effect of a 430-pound man, naked save for boots—standing dazed on a secondary highway.

The rest were negatives.

In the diffused illumination of the vehicle's skyward headlight, now growing dimmer—Wagner waddled about searching for remnants of his gown. The pathetic state of his recently departed vehicle confirmed that its fate was a most definitive sort of demise; parking tickets, soul food, and fleeing madmen were now firmly in its past.

How Wagner escaped with only a head gouged and minus his minister's gown was something, as yet, he wasn't prepared to accept. Frankly, of late, his luck had turned to the profoundly shitty.

Then he found the gown. It was actually quite intact save for a rent from the neck to bottom hem. Thus ventilated, it peeled away from his body like corn husks from a tamale.

He slipped into it like he might an ultra-whopper-sized hospital gown with gold fringes. Holding it closed at the side, Wagner modestly assessed his torso and lower body for major/minor wounds, abrasions, plus road or mailbox parts embedded in his epidermis.

Thankfully, save for the head wound, it was definite—Wagner was relatively unscathed!

There was no shortage of pressing considerations for Wagner. In fact, right now lamentations and numerous obscenities might—at a minimum—soothe and assuage Wagner's demolished plans. But an older, more primordial urge took hold.

Wagner recalled that in the now-dismembered rear box of the motorcycle were the remainders of his generous repast purchased from the American primitive back at the crossroads market.

It wasn't until he'd opened the jumbo bag of fried pork rinds and a quart of orange juice (the pure stuff had cost far more, but regards vitamin C, Wagner was a zealot) and was well into each, when the Hazlett cell phone rang.

Since he was in semi-darkness, the cell phone's dial pad betrayed its location by its glow—inside the carcass of a recently fallen mailbox. It chirped its plight dutifully to Wagner.

While taking a lusty swig of juice—needed to facilitate the passage of pork rinds down his gullet—Wagner bent over cautiously. In an interesting bit of navigation, the gadget had retreated rodent-like into its current metal hiding place. He eyed it suspiciously.

It kept ringing.

Wagner fielded it, wiped off pork rind grease, and pondered things: It, of course, would *not* be Moynahan—they, as always (and Jesus Christ, especially now) would only communicate via the cunning lawyer's labyrinth-like answering machine.

The Salmon Queen's answering service could not have gotten the number—but Wagner wondered. Could they? Even the most banal of capitalist lackeys was acquiring increasingly spiffy tracing gadgetries. And, of course, by now, Wagner's new means of transport might be public knowledge.

So, that left a short list: (1) It might be one of three or four hundred thousand people interested in him answering—thereby broadcasting his precise location; (2) Wherever Leggy Peggy was, she'd violated his clear instructions, and instead of going through Moynahan, had dialed him directly. Earlier he'd left the cell phone number with her, but in Wagner's usual code—a mixture of her telephone number, his social security number and the street address of Kokanee Joe's. Even the FBI's most evil number freaks had not cracked it.

The ringing stopped.

Wagner grunted an appreciation of this return to silence. The orange juice was already working: He shuffled to the side of the road to void his system of (hopefully) the last remnants of the vile Fix. And not too soon. Vaguely, he recalled a drift of purpose and resolve just seconds prior to his "crash and rip" collision.

He was thus involved when in the far distance—from the direction he'd come—he noticed headlights. Since leaving the market, he'd seen only one vehicle. This was his second.

Wagner palmed the cell phone and touched his money poke for reassurance, then—in the manner of a Victorian dowager—tucked his gown to attain maximum decency.

He headed towards a pathway leading down into the pine woods, yet he saw it was rife with snags. Aware of his inability to rise in the event of a fall, Wagner picked his way along cautiously. To help, he picked up a stout branch, and proceeded into cover like Oedipus bound for Colonus.

Best to lay low and wait this one out.

Milepost 82.1
Construction Area:
All Traffic Fines Tripled

When Taffer stepped forward, Mo Taft's quest for an exit strategy arrived by—was it divine intervention?

"Ah'll fight her, Pa. Get maw'self some feels of them big titties."

Sans the suit jacket, her sweater, especially the neckline, demonstrated a revealing design regards nature's endowment. In fact, both Ezra and Taffer eyed that part of her anatomy eagerly.

"Your pistol."

She pointed at Taffer's jacket, beneath which was parked his horse pistol. Her astuteness was not lost on Mo—for Taffer was not half-bad at concealment. When Taffer handed the pistol to Mo, his affection as father combined with his teaching skills caused him concern: "Well Boy, ya' watch her han's an' not them jugs, and 'member what your Pa taught ya'."

At precisely that point, she raised first her left and then right foot, and removed her shoes in a dainty but graceful maneuver—tossing the pair to one of her comrades.

Later, Mo decided it was this bit of feminine craft that covered her palming the knife—distracting Taffer for that critical split second during which she executed a wide and powerful leg sweep. And though Mo had a brief surge of optimism when Taffer successfully jumped over her leg sweep, this was short lived. She sprang up behind Taffer, cutting off his left ear and then pressed her terrible blade to his throat. Mo had to admire the speed and precision of her moves.

Taffer's howl—simultaneous to his ear landing at Brother Ezra's feet—caused his sibling to look down, at which point the Behemoth (with uncommon swiftness) yanked Ezra's shotgun away, breaking it over its owner's head, poleaxing him to earth in the classic tradition. Her hand reached out, and a lethal purr in her voice conveyed sincerity.

"The cell phone—and down with your weapon. Now!"

Mo, sensitive to his own survival, concentrated on the nasty muzzle protruding from the smallest man's coat: his steady, inky-black eyes remained fixed on Mo.

Always the realist, Mo dropped Taffer's pistol. Then, reaching very, very slowly into his pocket, he took out the cell phone and handed it over, though allowing a disapproving grunt.

"Well, hell. Ya' needn't'a gotten so all-fired shitty 'bout thangs."

As he took out his handkerchief and fielded Taffer's ear, Mo reminded himself that the struggle to pass on all he'd learned to his boys was never ending. Certainly there was still a ways to go.

23

The oncoming vehicle turned into one, two—then an apparent convoy. Wagner hunkered down into cover, wondering *Now, just what-the-fuck is going on?* In the Oncoming Vehicles Department, they were anything but in a rush. A caravan of garden snails would have made faster progress.

Disgusted and nervous with the wait, Wagner picked his way from hiding. After checking the progress of this strange caravan, he went to the defunct rear section of his motorcycle and raided his still well-stocked junk-food larder. Despite conspicuously lousy luck in the geography department, Wagner's digestive system was coming back to center: The copious but diverse genres of snack food he'd purchased were soothing the rough spots in his enamel-lined alimentary canal. Soon it would return to its pre-St.Finny's processing ability.

Munching corn chips, he slogged back into hiding, experiencing a hybrid of emotions: from worrying about how in hell he was going to continue his escape to what sort of random weirdness he was, once again, about to encounter.

Pondering these sore issues, he experienced insidious self pity set in, a long-time favorite in the pantheon of Wagner's patron deities.

Since escaping, he felt that the very gods opposed him. A list of woes worked its way into his thinking processes again. He composed while chewing the last of the corn chips, washed down with a dramatic swig of an orange juice chaser. Lists, the certainty of lists, put him on friendlier ground:

Certainly NUMBER ONE on this list, would be that goddamned Winslow buggering off with him from St. Finny's—uninvited, and certainly fucking unwanted. Wagner became annoyed just thinking about the unparalleled cheek of the hapless son-of-a-bitch. Winslow had nearly cost him the entire escape, plus he'd turned Wagner into a felon subsequent to events at brother Pine Jack's beer wallow.

So, yes—Winslow, doped down to amphibian intellect via The Fix. He was Item One on Wagner's list-of "fucked-up-events - that-can-make [and have made]-a-mess-out-of-my-escape."

Suddenly:

Onward Labor's Children,
Marching for to seize
All worker's rights
From Country Porker's Meats. . .

The semi-harmonic wisps of "Onward Christian Soldiers" drifted into Wagner's atheistic lair. Quelling an immediate instinct to moan, he noted the modified lyrics, containing familiar key words.

Shrinking back into the shadows, he was able to recognize that vehicle headlights began to illuminate the physical remnants of his recent efforts at wildlife management.

Wagner heard car and truck engines amongst the singing.

. . .Not to cut or wrap
pork ribs, steaks or squeals... .

The singing slowly faded—a voice at a time, then ceased. All vehicles stopped, mutely confronting the roadside tableau of Wagner's accident. A low, clearly African-American voice rang out, "It's a motorcycle. Looks like that crazy motha' fukka' Pedro really fucked it up."

Wagner's curiosity—despite events—was aroused by this procession: In the lead was a long flatbed trailer towed by a battered diesel truck. On it was, from all appearances, a portable music hall review. In the midst of the flatbed was a raised platform; in deference to movement, its occupants—a mariachi band, complete with costumes ala yard-wide sombreros and braided, multi-colored suits—sat on barrels.

Wagner had to grant this: A barrel sitting, truck-borne mariachi band passing by in the middle of the night on a backroad in North Carolina seemed an unlikely sight.

Around the musicians, singers and other audience members sat on bales of hay. Behind the flatbed and truck was an assortment of jalopies. By contrast, these vehicular relics made the procession's rear-guard even more of a stand-out: a long, ivory-white stretch limo in full waxed and gleaming regalia, including privacy windows, cruised regally at the rear. Brushing Cheeto crumbs from his gown, Wagner scrunched away from the reflected headlights, muttering, "Now, what in the fuck do we have here?"

Since escaping, Wagner's world had flopped around—the unlikely switching with the likely. Hopefully, this design was temporary.

But as he struggled to visually assimilate all of this procession, the less it seemed it was temporary. And a closer look did not render the visuals more coherent.

Against the cab of the flatbed was a cage occupied by two pigs with a human occupant squeezed between. The pigs slept sound-ly, though the swine's cage-mate was a long ways north of bed-die-bye time. With the truck stopped before the remnants of mailboxes and motorcycle, the caged man sprang forward, and clutching the bars, bellowed, "Good! He's fuckin' dead. And soon you taco benders and nigger cocksuckers will join him. Yeah, that's right! You'll fry!! Kidnapping is a capital offense. You'll all fuckin' fry. You hear!?"

The man's ferocious vituperation startled one of the pigs, who awakened with a snort—shifting its porcine bulk against his human neighbor, squeezing him voiceless in mid-cackle.

Responding to his bile, voices of outrage flared from a hostile audience—followed by an aerial volley of beer cans, their con-tents marking trajectories by broadcasting pinwheels of foam into the night.

"Shut yo' motha'fuckin' racist mouth, you sorry-ass piece of shit."

Several of the frothy missiles struck the outside of the cage, splattering both species within—the pigs grunted with outrage, compressing their human neighbor even more in their panic.

In the reflected lights, Wagner saw that atop the limousine

was affixed a plywood cutout of a giant pig with a red "X" across it. Under it a sign read,

Country Porkers Inc.: Unfair to Workers!

Others joined a large black man who had begun to search for the aforementioned Pedro; a few began preliminary lamentations over the alleged motorist. The black man, though, seemed more annoyed than alarmed. "Pedro, where in fuck . . . Pedro, you som' bitch!! You hea'yah us? Pedro. You greaser som'bitch, GODDAMNIT, YOU ALIVE?"

Concern for Pedro ceased at the instant the pejorative epithet "greaser" was given voice. Wagner watched as nearly a half dozen Mexicans closed in on a quartet of black men. The gestures and postures were at once, menacing.

Hey, usted ennegrece a diablos, no está llamando a nuestro amigo un engrasador, o usted puede ensamblar quizá ese cerdo blanco en la jaula.

Wagner's understanding of Spanish and signing in International Heinous Gesture informed that peace and fellowship weren't in the offing.

The four blacks confronted the six brown men: Hackles rose, hormones pumped, ethnic and racial stupidity flowed. This was all wonderful stuff to the caged man. Popping out from between the two pigs, he laughed gleefully.

"Fucking Great! Rip each other's throats out. Ha Ha Ha!"

The group was torn between whether to visit violence on their uncaged or caged antagonists.

It was a tough call.

On the flatbed, a half dozen women—some black, some Hispanic—made their decision: Catcalls, obscenities, and a volley of tossed beer cans, including a single clear plastic water bottle, were all launched at the cage. With this new volley, both pigs snorted in alarm, and this time, they nearly pancaked their human neighbor.

This noise-filled episode resulted in the limo's door bursting open, and Wagner was instantly impressed. Admitted into the night was a personage whose *physicalus entiretus* could be spun as nothing but unparalelledly *vast*.

He was at minimum six-and-a-half feet tall, weighed in somewhere around three hundred, and wore a garish three-piece suit. In a swagger, he deftly brandished a brass-headed cane, pointed at the potential combatants and bellowed—Stentorian tones swept about the night air with unfettered authority:

"Vat in ze fokking goddamn hell you dumb shits think maybe you doink stopping here?"

Locked and held in the authority of that voice, all turned. Yet several of the women aboard the truck recovered at once—and laughed, offering a sarcastic volley of oo'ing and awing. This semi-immortal looked over at them, changing his cane's aim from the men at the side of the road to the women on the truck. When he waggled it theatrically, the women increased their taunts.

His response was to tender a few pelvic thrusts while casting rakish looks at them.

"Hey, you fokking wom'ins, Woody's so much lover guy that he suck your guts out, an that's no shit, sweet babies."

That did it. North, south, east, and west—all broke into laughter, save for the cage's occupants. The pigs settled back into snoozing, and their human neighbor—lacking any other place—sat atop one of the oinkers who emitted a *pro forma* grunt of complaint.

"Woody become bigtime fokking union guy in Gdansk before you fokkers been born. Woody know by fighting right in the middle of ourselves, you making to fok up. Sonofabitching solidarity, babies, is the big thing. Got to be."

But there was the matter of the wreckage.

"Woody man, lookit. Pedro's stacked up his ride."

Mr. Woody knotted up his pale features and sighed with saintly patience. He offered a toss to his mane of black hair, then, stepping forward, he tapped Hazlett's motorcycle with the dragon-shaped head of his cane.

"To begin with, babies, Woody is saying you are not only dumb shits but blind. That's not Pedro's muzzer'fokking bike." He looked to the blacks then the Hispanics with unconcealed scorn, then tossed off a contemptuous laugh.

"Now let's get our asses to damned meat plant, babies, before TV truck guys haul ass, go home, and all Woody's work is for bullshit."

Wagner was relieved that their urgency exceeded whatever instincts they had for Good Samaritanism. Now, when all was quiet upon the highway and the procession's participants were headed back to the vehicles, Wagner's cell phone rang from within his clenched right paw. This time, its cheerful ring was not muffled by the acoustic confines of a mailbox. Its dutiful voice was clear and faithful.

Several dozen startled gazes fixed on the precise spot in the woods where he had heretofore been hidden.

Milepost 98.5
Caution: Water on Highway, Next .2 mi

Moynahan and the limo driver parted ways in Sarasota when he found the irresponsible bastard nursing a quart of VO stashed beneath his seat. This explained his refusal for higher speeds—clearly the sonofabitch had a phobia against balloon blowing and line walking.

He, of course, had to go.

"I'll act as my own fucking driver," he'd told the limo operator back in Gainesville, ringing off in mid-objection.

All subsequent speeding citations, and there weren't really that many, Moynahan stuffed in the Caddie next to the cell phone. From Sarasota, he made better time south to Fort Myers. At that juncture, he had closed within four hours of Crazy Sue and that lascivious backdoor humper masquerading as him—rutting his brains out with the faithless harlot on his credit card.

Moynahan was plagued by rising fires of sexual obsession as he sped towards Miami. But there would be a payoff!

This sado-sexual coquettishness was what Crazy Sue used to intensify their initial sexual contact—whenever and however it happened. Oh yes, thought Moynahan with delicious anticipation. Our first few orgasms will probably register on regional seismographs.

She knew—above and beyond all things—that even if the sotted Floridians built a bridge to the Dry Tortugas, Moynahan would follow her. Crazy Sue's current sidemeat bagatelle's use of his credit card (as both she and Moynahan knew) was the asshole's downfall. Moynahan's longtime gumfoot operative in Anchorage tracked them almost to the minute via that card, providing a square-meter perfect locator beacon. Last, as a minor side benefit, with this heavy card use, Moynahan was building up bodacious frequent flyer miles.

He'd just reached the outskirts of Miami and was closing fast on the last Crazy Sue coordinates when the phone rang. It was surely his detective with final coordinates! Moynahan answered with a victorious whoop—he had cornered the bitch now! Yet his loins went slack when—instead of his gumfoot's voice—he heard a desperate Peggy, even more desperate than *usual, and few could get as desperate.*

"Mr. Moynahan! You answered! I have had Lulu for some time. Where are you? Where do I go from here? I hear really weird things from North Carolina."

Moynahan pulled over beside the road and struggled to switch major emotional topics.

Jesus, he thought, I seemed to have forgotten all about that goddamned North Carolina mess.

Milepost 98.6
Grease and Antipathy

Despite his sulk, Oswald indulged himself a chortle when he heard his brother/nephew was riding across the North Carolina countryside on a motor scooter—or whatever.

"A convenience store clerk saw him."

Younghusband had concluded his brief update just prior to Oswald's and his mother's morning work session. Since the previous day's business and been cut short, their agenda was unusually long. There would be no talk between mother and son about the day's previous troubles.

She and Oswald shared the common trait of not chewing over disputes. Nonetheless, Oswald enjoyed the idea of Wagner reduced to skulking about on a motorcycle.

"Mother, has Wagner ever driven a motor scooter?"

That came up, out of the blue, as it were. She slowly took off her reading glasses and looked steadily at him.

"Motorcycle," Younghusband corrected as he excused himself from their presence.

The Salmon Queen reflected, and shrugged. "I don't remember if he has."

They both paused a moment—considering that: The image of Wagner riding across North Carolina on such a strange, small conveyance. Wagner was renowned for his admiration of large vehicles—whether equipped with wings, wheels, or keels, he liked them large.

The Salmon Queen's attentions returned to business—safer grounds—and aired what was bothering her since looking over the current Carolina Packing prospectus.

Oswald fish-eyed the slavish Younghusband making his exit and only begrudgingly relented his hold on his mental snapshot of Brother Wagner astride his motorcycle.

"Why did Carolina Packing not resist a takeover?? They could have done better."

"I thought they did. They actually struggled quite noticeably."

He nodded proudly as Younghusband was replaced by two CPA's, escorted in by Katrina. They made their usual groveling kowtows to their masters while laying out briefcases and notebook computers—getting ready for MEI's final push into the European upscale pork market.

The Salmon Queen's instincts in business were almost as keen in the Dark Zones of Screwings and Hornswogglings as her late husband—the notoriously wily Salmon King. She had learned from him as he had from her more subtle, technical side.

Years ago, when acquiring a tuna label down on its luck, her spouse—right in the midst of a most civilized business setting—shocked the young businesswoman by looking across at the heretofore silent CEO of the firm—who had been letting his accountants and lawyers do the dealing—and told him, "I knew, Harold, you were going to screw me over this deal, but I didn't think you were going to try and fuck me."

The negotiations had collapsed at once, only to eventually be consummated later that year with fairer arrangements. But, at the moment, the Salmon Queen had been shocked. Yet, though she could never approve his choice of words, the lesson had been made—voiced by the Salmon King during the ride to the airport that morning.

"When they're weak and cornered, watch out! Trouble brewing."

The Salmon Queen Meets the Metropolitan of New York

By the time the boy Wagner was seven, Katrina and all the household staff at the Chinook House assumed Wagner's tiny mother and the Salmon King were involved in a growing and successful business relationship.

So, during a soon-to-be memorable visit to the Seattle Aquarium, Katrina's mouth dropped when informed otherwise. Since she too was of the Orthodox faith, the future Salmon Queen confided that "since Himself and I are, well, related, there is a problem with the church regards marriage."

The thirty-one years age difference plus their former (albeit by marriage) relationship was something discussed by all but mentioned by none in either party's presence.

Days later, this bit of generational weirdness touched down on the desk of His Most Reverend Bishop Ortosky, Metropolitan of New York, spiritual leader of North America's Orthodox faithful. This request for Holy Dispensation created problems historical and theological. His administrative assistant had worked up a fact file.

"Theodosic the Second of Bulgaria was given such a dispensation for marrying his daughter-in-law."

His Most Reverend Bishop replied tersely, "That was in 1180, Mikhail."

"Actually, 1188. It was suspected, though, he'd at least condoned the murder of his son. And he held those clerics not in agreement hostage in the event the dispensation was denied."

The Metropolitan opined this was poor precedent.

"There must be other dispensations—or even petitions for dispensations—for fathers-in-laws to marry their daughters-in-law."

"There was Algarth the Fourth, Duke of Tula-Saxony, to marry his son's wife. He'd died in the invasion of Russia—1699. The son, that is."

"Hmm. But was there a child, please remind?"

"Yes, your Holiness. Two. But the daughter-in-law was Catholic, and she converted. Still, it remains a precedent. Actually, your Holiness, the only precedent."

Both drank tea and looked out the windows of the Orthodox Administrative offices onto the East River, losing themselves in thought.

"Yes. But In our case, Mikhail, the father-in-law is converting to Orthodoxy And from what faith, please remind?"

"Judaism, your Holiness."

"Oh. I had forgotten.

"Actually, I don't think you knew"

"Well, that brings up thorny theological issues, in addition to the dispensation matter."

"Yes, Holiness. Surely."

The two clerics sat in mute contemplation. The call, Father Mikhail knew, was his Holiness's—a conservative man in matters of church doctrine. Perhaps this silence was Father Mikhail's opportunity for a finesse.

"There is the matter of the old church, and the fifty patented acres at Bear River, in Alaska."

"Please remind, Mikhail."

"Mr. Wagner—the father-in-law—intends to donate lands and structures to our Alaska diocese. In fact, he has. Virtually. His company owns the defunct cannery there."

Father Mikhail saw theological matters shift to friendlier climes as his Holiness pondered: Typically, when he was leaning towards issuing any dispensation, His Holiness slowly raised his hand, inserted a finger into his vast, impressive gray beard, and wound up a thick ribbon of it, then unwound.

There would be a little humming, too.

While His Holiness was thus occupied, Father Mikhail took up a writing pad and began to compose the rough draft of the letter of dispensation. In matters canonical, His Holiness was a man of sage and prudent behavior.

24

Wagner sat in one of the limo's posh leather seats and listened to Haywood Cherkoski lecture on his first-hand experiences during Poland's Solidarity labor movement. A young man—suspicious of itself to Wagner—he bore names from parents schooled in North America radicalism.

"My father love this Big Bill Haywood guy. So, Woody is named like this Big Bill Haywood. My mother listens to records of singer and American party guy Paul Robeson. So crazy papa and momma again names Woody Robeson, too." He opened another single-serving bottle of champagne, passed it over to Wagner, then opened a second for himself.

His lecture wove haphazardly between autobiographical, the historic, and present-day situations. *Let 'em rant*, thought Wagner. Beyond and above all else, he wondered if this crazy dose of compressed gas and horse manure knew of his passenger's net worth regards ratting him out to North Carolina goons.

Once again sitting tight and keeping a keen eye out for opportunity was Wagner's only shot. At least, he still had the Hazlett cell phone. Woody sneered and gestured downroad with the hand holding the champagne.

"And now, Woody is awesome labor dude here in states. Tonight big labor protest at MOTHER PORKER's Packers #1, and tomorrow night at MOTHER PORKER's Packers #3 over in Medicine Springs."

Several times, Herr Woody took and received calls, mixing in languages as diverse as Afro-American dialect, Spanish, Polish (or Russian, Wagner couldn't decide which), and Woody's own sub-jargon of jaw-bending accented English. He'd alternately shacken the limo by slamming the seat with hand or cane—laughing, or admonishing.

Dead ahead, off the limo's hood-ornamented bow, was the procession, moving steadily at ten miles an hour. Three vehicles ahead, the truck with the mariachi band slowed even more, as the musicians struck up a lively tune—all of this in mime for Wagner due to the limo's superb sound proofing.

Wagner nursed his champagne with little interest—he preferred chocolate bars and cashews to booze, having thankfully not inherited his father's fatal penchant for Sir Barleycorn. Though a long-time labor scholar and, of course, sympathizer, Wagner desired muchly to avoid public appearances at this present time.

Zipping his cell phone closed with a smug chuckle, Woody emptied the small bottle of champagne as though it were a Dr. Pepper or Fresca, burped and switched his dubious attentions to Wagner.

Wagner went on full alert—this giant, verbose bird could be anything from a baseline troglodyte to a Rhodes scholar. *Be cautious, Wagner. Be cautious.*

Woody raised a massive index finger, smiled mischievously and, waggling it at Wagner, wondered out loud why such a freak of nature like Wagner would be out in the middle of the night mucking out motorcycles into mail boxes. He concluded by shaking the finger even harder, "And don' shit the Woody guy, be straight."

Wagner thought there was no percentage in concealing the truth. "I'm a messenger from God."

Milepost 110.5
Peggy in South Carolina

When Peggy arrived in Spartanburg, South Carolina, she was plagued with questions, worries, guilts—and just about anything and everything that could plague a middle-aged woman carrying a stoned Mottled Macedonian cat in a medium-sized dog carrier.

Why had Mr. Moynahan called from Miami, Florida, when she thought he was in North Carolina, or even Washington, DC, with the escape car?

Why had he ordered her to South Carolina?

Why didn't Mr. Moynahan know anything? In fact, it was Peggy who had updated Moynahan, who'd updated herself on the Internet from her motel room.

Where was Mr. Wagner headed? Was he headed anywhere? And why did that awful man follow her from Minneapolis/St. Paul to Atlanta, where she was forced to change planes three times before shaking him, schlepping Lulu every inch of the way?

Or had she shaken him?

Who did he represent? It couldn't be the FBI, or could it? The Foundation had made powerful enemies on the right; hence, it adorned most Justice Department subversive lists. But old-style socialists had become yesteryear's news, so due to budget priorities agencies had moved on to terrorist groups. But, then again—was there renewed Justice Department interest? The Foundation hadn't inadvertently funded a terrorist group, had they? Such a blunder would be her—Peggy's—doing, as she screened all applicants.

Or was it those awful business people who worked for Wagner's mother? That Colonel Somebody?

Something akin to terror shadowed her heart when she thought of Gully, her last boyfriend. He'd sworn to kill himself or her if she did not quit the Foundation and move with him to Australia. When she'd told Mr. Wagner, he'd called Gully into his office, and, lulling him off guard by talking dingo hunting, stepped on his foot, breaking it in six places.

Might Gully be walking well enough to stalk her again? After they'd operated, doctors said he would be on crutches for a long, long time.

Then there was Peggy's disobedience.

Few knew about Wagner's heart problems. Yet it was this drastic situation that had caused Peggy to take the most disloyal, awful step six months back. After his attack, she'd called his mother and told her. She had not known.

She, Peggy, was a mother, but had not anticipated such a drastic maternal move as institutionalization. Ultimately, had Peggy betrayed Wagner—or saved his life? Oh, this had become such an awful mess and she, Peggy Rothstein, was responsible.

25

When informed he occupied the same space as a messenger from God, Haywood Robeson Cherkoski, aka "Woody"—the truly big-time labor guy from Gdansk—rocked with laughter. Wagner continued it straight, *Best to keep this fucking primitive laughing.*

Outside, there was a sudden urgent rapping on the privacy window; Woody's laugh melted into an angry sneer.

Their procession had stopped.

"Cogsuggers, wha' in fok hoppening?!"

Exploding out the limo door, Woody delivered a not-so-accidental shot to his caller's kisser, knocking him sprawling in company to a painful whoop.

In the short second it took Woody to charge from the door, Wagner saw the man fly tail-feathers over beak. Had he recognized the afflicted but none-too-silent prisoner from the cage? The door was slammed, and Woody's torrent of mangled oaths was almost entirely muted. But the percussive soundtrack increased.

The entire limo began to rock as Woody slammed somebody or something against the sturdy vehicle once, twice, and even thrice.

"Hey, you crazy bastards, watch my rig, goddammit to hell."

The limo driver—up to now a silent figure—jumped out his door, leaving it open. Now, the entire soundtrack became clear, and Wagner tried to make an iota of sense from what was a degenerating degree of civility.

There was mayhem and hullaballo outside, joined by the protests of the driver. The main percussive track was seasoned liberally with thumps and bumps, counterpointed with feminine screams; all of this accompanied with masculine-grunted continuo. But dominating all was Woody's basso-profundo roars of outrage, "You greedy cogsuggers! Chicken liver fuckheads!"

The driver, clearly for his own safety, dived back into the limo, closing the door quickly. He looked back the fifteen feet to Wagner, and objected, "Those crazy bunch of faggot bastards! And Woody is worse than any of them. Listen to them! Just listen!"

And then took out a nasal inhaler, cursed when he found it spent, tossed it aside, and ripped open a fresh one. He inhaled deeply, cooing, "Oh, yeah. Fuck-all! This is good shit."

Then settled back, happier with the world.

Wagner had no time to reflect on this bit of pharmaceutical trivia, for the massive rear door swung back open and readmitted a ruffled and somewhat damaged Woody.

His dress shirt, which had sported two mamba-king style ruffles, was missing one, plus his green sport coat, complete with pocket heraldry, lacked a sleeve.

"Woody kick heavy ass," he boasted; then he looked at his damaged attire, and growled, "Fokking goddamn actors! Turn pussy on Woody."

He slid out a massive wardrobe drawer from beneath Wagner's seat, clicked on a courtesy light and decided which of the half dozen complete suits to select. Then remembering the driver's disloyalty, turned back, adding, "And you too, you fokker! You shut fok up or Woody kick your ass, too."

Wagner thought over what seemed, to him, the key word of the scene: *Actors?*

Without pause Woody narrowed down his quest to a pair of garish sports coats and dress shirts; deciding which to don, he began changing. For the first time, his attentions turned to Wagner, and the man's massive brows which shielded great eyes became cautious—he clearly weighed what to and what not to say. He came to a decision and motioned outside with a brusque toss of his head.

"Woody have trouble. Members scared shitless of MOTHER PORKER cops and goons. To pull off this big protest thing, I scored on some actors. You an actor?"

"You mean on the truck. Actors? The guy in the cage?"

"You got right! All 100% New York deli hams."

The driver, somewhat jollier now, had volunteered this. Woody darkened—and pointed at him.

"You shut fok up and drive, you smar-ass mosserfokker."

Woody shrugged into his coat and undervoiced a few more odiums. He then checked a small drawer, which contained an assortment of ties—all sporting hideous iridescent artwork. While sorting he talked business.

"Guy in cage tell Woody, 'I played Hamlet.' Hah! Big-time actor?! Naw! Big-time bullshitter and mosserfokker to Woody, who pays this som'bitch two grand. Then go chickenheads."

"Actually, it's chicken-hearted."

"Chicken-shit, is what Woody says. Now, you actor? Want to earn from Woody five hundred dollars, no bullshit. Right now! Fifteen minutes gig, nuzzing to it."

"Me?!"

"Oh no, not you. Woody meaning maybe Donald Fokking Duck! Of course, you! Five hundred dollars, right now. Nobody want this big part now."

"Part?"

"Yah, yah! As Inspired Speaker. Like kickass Tony Bickkerson or Jimmy Shaggart on info'mmertials—you know. Goes everywhere, those guys. Pussy up the ass! Those mosserfokkers. So, Woody does intro but needs good speaker. Labor speaker. Woody's English fokked up, no shit."

The implausible offer appealed to Wagner on its most primitive level, while at the same time singing a Siren's song to his frustrations. Long an academe, funder and ideologue of labor and socialist causes, Wagner had secretly nursed dangerous fantasies of Wagner, the brilliant rhetorician—a romantic mix of Mother Jones, Eugene Debs, and the original Woody—Big Bill Haywood. Instinct and vanity combined into a single bolt of inspiration.

"OK. But you paid one fuckhead two grand, now want to give me five hundred. It's clearly dangerous work. I've got another price."

Woody appraised Wagner with something like respect, for, if nothing else, showing a keen sense of opportunity. Wagner leaned over, remembering, for modesty's sake, to hold his gown together, and pointed outside. "What I want is your word that after my speech—no matter what happens—I'll be provided at once with direct, high-speed transport into South Carolina via this richly out-fitted vehicle of yours."

Woody and Wagner confronted one another, proboscis to pro-boscis: Woody tapped his cane thoughtfully against the palm of his left hand, while Wagner leaned back, waiting.

Wagner pointed south.

"By my reckoning, it's eighty-seven miles that way."

Woody's brows again washboarded up for a moment—and when he was about to open his mouth, he thought better of it, then point-ed coyly at Wagner.

"OK. But, no qu'vestions."

"None at all. Either way."

Woody's paw came out, and Wagner took it. This was America, American, and Americana in one vast utterly insincere and dis-sembling shake of the hand. Wagner was There, Woody was Here—and they needed each other for the time being.

Jesus Christ and Mary Baker Eddy, how more American could you get?

Milepost 131.1
Caution: Low-Flying Aircraft

Moynahan braced himself during the takeoff of the Piper Aztec, but even the sensation of his innards staying earthbound couldn't detract from the horrible guilt that plagued him.

Next to him, a braggart of a pilot named Rodrigo "Big Lindy" Hernandez—pilot and charter member of "Truth over Cuba"—bloviated about his leaflet runs over Havana. But this swagger went unnoticed. Moynahan's guilt dominated.

How could he—Moynahan—have allowed his best friend to be hung out to dry by the wretched Bubbas and Bubbettes of North Carolina? And all for—all!!—for just the even-up statistical chance of a phantasmagorical synaptic-scrambling sex binge with Crazy Sue?

That medieval fat farm doctor probably had Wagner (O, the poor sot!) tethered to a leather and oak slat chair in the charlatan's equally medieval clinic. Hadn't Wagner bailed him out—how many times had Wagner come through when it was Moynahan who had gotten crosswise with fate?

It wasn't enough to be pronging the very woman Wagner obsessed over, for whom the poor slob had incurred indefinite incarceration. O what a treacherous fool Moynahan had been.

Moynahan looked below at the Florida beaches sliding by as they climbed, winging his way to Spartanburg, South Carolina. He would now get On The Job, and pull Wagner's bacon from the fire—like the Lion of the Law he truly was. Moynahan could promise this much: When he got on someone's litagatory shit, he stayed on it.

On the beaches below he watched as the sun glistened off a shoreline littered with multi-storied hotels waiting for just the right hurricane. While they executed a gentle low altitude turn, and on a relatively vacant beach—Moynahan saw a familiar feminine form running gracefully towards the water. Behind sat a man on a beach blanket watching greedily.

Long tresses of red hair trailed behind her almost down to her ample buttocks (barely concealed by a lower part of her meager swimming costume). Even Big Lindy forgot about his exploits over Cuba long enough to admire the woman's entry into the water. In fact, he even reduced climb-rate.

Moynahan knew those strawberry tresses anywhere, and especially those buttocks. Oh, Blessed Jesus and Sweet Baked Potatoes!

"Land, goddamnit! Right there. Now. Land!"

"What? You loco, man! I can't here."

And the pilot's jaw dropped when Moynhan reached over, punched in the throttle and turned off the switch.

"You can now, mi amigo!"

And down, down, down you go.

As the ground reached up, Moynahan eyed Crazy Sue in the gentle surf, looking up at the plane as it sideslipped in for its power-off rendezvous with terra firma. She slowly strode from the water, giving a dainty hike upwards on that portion of her costume that covered her most fiercely delectable part.

She gave a toss of her head, as she followed the beachward glide of Big Lindy's aircraft—and smiled.

For Moynahan knew she knew. Already, his maleness was beginning to cook!

Oh yes.

26

Woody's Traveling Thespians, with Wagner as its star attraction, arrived at Mother Porker's #1 ten minutes prior to change of shift. Buildings, towering brick smokestacks, exterior walls and fences were festooned with Mother Porker's logo—a matronly, chubby pig, knitting old-time long underwear, wearing glasses with words underneath proclaiming, "Old Time Goodness Since 1894."

The Old Time Goodness concept clashed when Wagner saw the plant looming out of the North Carolina night. It was a gigantic affair, covering a good hundred acres, complete with employees' parking lot, a half dozen security gates, and service outbuildings all dominated by a great mountain of the main plant. Lastly, a lock-and-load chain-link fence surrounded the entirety.

Was it a prison or a workplace?

"We work out at Gate Number Three."

Woody primped a bit while Wagner read the "script," written by none other than Woody Himself. Since he wrote English far worse than he spoke it, Wagner gave up. Woody assured him that winging it should be routine for an actor with such obvious talent as Wagner.

Their procession approached the battle works of Gate Three deliberately.

There Wagner was somewhat—well, actually very much—impressed with the presence of Sheriff's deputies and Mother Porker Rent-a-Goons. They paced and/or bided time in multi-antennaed SUVs behind the fence: Stolid, Caucasoid grimaces looked out from behind the galvanized grid works.

On a makeshift stage a smallish Chicano with a bullhorn presided. His flock numbered at most no more than two dozen. He spoke ebulliently—first in English, then Spanish.

"OK, brothers and sisters, here's the kick-ass surprise I promised."

On cue, the 'prisoner' in the cage roared out obscenities and racial epithets at his fellow artists, and the audience—mostly Hispanic, with a few blacks mixed in—was treated to their first kick-ass scene when diverse missiles were hurled at him and his porcine cage companions.

Woody strode out of the limo onto this scene like Caesar before siege works in Cisapline Gaul: Freshly and gaudily attired, carrying his walking stick, he grunted only half approval.

While the attentions of those on both sides of the fence were diverted with this raucous vaudeville, Woody called over one of the female "workers" who—functioning as wardrobe person—began hasty emergency repairs on Wagner's gown. Woody beckoned by name to his colleague—a man named Pedro—who eagerly jumped down from the stage.

"Woody guy! Where you hombres been? I'm dying here," he looked Wagner up and down. ". . . and who in hell is this guy?"

Woody ignored the question, instead taking a half dozen strides over to the truck. Clearly his mariachis had misgivings about the cultural attitudes of those on the opposite side of the security fence.

"Hey!! Play zat' fokking music, you goddamned sonsbitches! We got half of Mexico coming out this place in five minutes! Play, you mozzerfokkers!"

They commenced on something less than a single beat, but nonetheless, they began. The small man shook his head and scratched his jaw with the bullhorn.

"Man, this is not good." Then, looking again at Wagner, he asked, "where do you fit in, amigo"

"I fit in, hombre, as your inspirational fucking speaker."

Milepost 138.1
Severe Sidewinds
Campers and Vans, proceed with caution

"They'll never get the bastard, and I've got five crisp ten spots in the till says they won't."

Kokanee Joe's challenge had gone untaken. During that first day Wagner's escape immediately entered popular folklore at the misanthropic philanthropist's favorite Eagle River eatery.

It had been late morning at the legendary chicken house when the news of Wagner's breakout, via Peggy, had landed on Kokanee Joe's doorstep. A quartet of Joe's aficionadoes, bent over coffee, pondered Wagner's chances, but remained several miles less confident than Joe.

"Bullshit, Joe, you can't fight the system."

"No, 'specially what passes for a system down south."

"Down there, you don't fight the system."

"You can say that again, McGee."

But as Day One developed into Day Two and Wagner remained free, Kokanee Joe's wisdom moved into the mainstream.

"Well, Joe, you old bastard. Maybe you're right. They might not catch the commie bastard."

"Goddamned rights I'm right, and he's not a communist, you ignorant fuck; he's a socialist. How many times did he explain that shit. A scholar like Mr. Wagner talks, you should listen. You might learn something."

Every morning, as they did this morning, his regulars showed, expecting an update.

They watched as Joe supervised his two middle sons in the Changing-of-the-Oil ceremony. Kokanee Joe squinted into the overhead lighting and pondered matters of quality control.

"Half the outfits in the entire Anchorage area renew their deep fryers twice, maybe three fuckin' times a week. And that's it. Me?! Pure, one hundred percent peanut oil from West Africa, change it every day. Costs me bigtime. But, here: quality counts."

"Joe we've heard that before. Hell with that; make your phone call. Find out the latest."

"I did. Peg left for South Carolina. Spartanburg, she said. In fact, I got her in-flight. These days, they got phones every goddamned place."

"Why South Carolina? Big Mouth is in North Carolina."

"I know that, for Christ's sakes."

"Then why would she go to South Carolina?"

"Because . . . Christ. I don't know why. She says, he's still in North Carolina, but nobody knows where."

Point was—the meat of the matter—Wagner was free, and would remain free. Joe nodded his head wisely, adding, "I'm amazed they bagged the som'bitch in the first place."

The two clients now dug into their breakfast hashbrowns and a.m. scrambled nuggets with vigor. Between wolfs, one—a long time denizen—shook his head sadly and lamented, "It was the woman, Joe. Egghead or no, he thought with his little head instead of the big one."

Joe walked down the row of deep fryers and adjusted each, testing the still-cool oil with a stainless steel dipper for clarity and body. He took a breath and turned his thoughts back to Wagner and looked sadly at his morning faithfuls.

"Did you ever see that woman?"

They thought, but admitted ignorance. Joe took fresh towels, and distributed them to each cooking station while looking out onto the Richardson Highway and the flocks of commuters spilling towards Anchorage. Then, beyond this to the expanse of flatlands at the head of Cook Inlet. He grunted his point.

"To see is to know, as they say. He came in here with her a couple of times."

Joe took a breath, tossed the last towel onto his left shoulder and despite long admiration for Wagner, could not steel himself to deny a natural force as sure as the movement of geese north and south with the seasons.

"Yeah, it was the woman."

Milepost 138.2
Deus Ex Machismo

Colonel Younghusband was sure that Oswald, always his nemesis, would see that he would be blamed over this Carolina Packing mess.

For the second time in as many days, Younghusband avowed that retirement could not come too soon, even if it meant knocking about across an American desert in a smallish caravan with the Missus.

It was just all damned frustrating.

What was the main focus of his job?! Was it keeping track of that behemoth eldest son? Or the needful hush-hush bedroom baubles of Herself's youngest? Or, blast it, the security issues of Monarch Enterprises International (MEI), the job he'd been hired for originally?

And Now?

Well, now the North Carolina Packing sitrep was anything but good. And as Younghusband entered Herself's suite, there IT was: Mrs. Wagner, with the briefest of glance, communicated every molecule of her disapproval. She might as well have announced on a loud-hailer, "And you don't know where Wagner is, do you? And you've nearly allowed Oswald and MEI to become euchred by those reptiles from Carolina Packing. You should have known of this subterfuge, Colonel—you, of all people. I depended on you."

Yet her silence said this and far more. But years in the military provided him with needed survival tactics; hence, Younghusband knew precisely how to proceed: He would boldly take full responsibility for security lapses, despite critical failures on his staff.

Stromboli closed the door behind him and a trio of MEI lawyers. They too—perhaps even more than Younghusband—were rigged for silent running; in fact, until located in a sailing vessel in Puget Sound, the senior of the trio had been expertly incognito. Younghusband opened with an apology for something he had no control over whatsoever. A safe flourish.

"Terrible weather, Marm, or I would have been here sooner."

And he waited: (Hold on YH, Old Boy).

The lawyers began: "Certainly," they droned, "if they had KNOWN of the labor problems that compromised one of Carolina Packing's labels, negotiations would never have been halted. But . . ." (ah, here there was a cool, calculated glance at Younghusband) "since this had not come to light, well, how could they have known?"

"It did not come to light because our security people were asleep at the wheel. I certainly did not know."

Oswald looked pointedly at Younghusband—one thing, the little puff never hid his feelings towards him. If there was one thing Herself valued, it was absolute fairness to all employees. She avoided labor unrest as cats aviod water balloons.

"Can we renege? MEI has a spotless record with its employees, plus a long policy on social justice. We were in front of BEN AND JERRY and even POLAROID in this. So?"

The lawyers—sitting haunch to haunch—became the Simian Triplets, sans hands to mouth, ears, and eyes. Finally, the master yachtsman of the three shook his head,

"Not without extensive litigation, which would certainly move up to the federal level, Mrs. Wagner. And get in the business sections of—well, the media."

Herself stood when Katrina entered and served tea and cakes at the suite's teakwood buffet. Katrina—always Herself's best friend as well as attendant—cast a sour look around the room before wheeling the service caddie out.

"So, we were euchred," and she allowed a sigh while urging all to move towards the buffet. "So Colonel. What is the situation at ... What label is it?"

"Mother Porkers, I believe, Marm. They have three plants. All three are affected."

She repeated the name with irony, then despite the situation, smiled. And when it grew into a diminutive laugh, all joined in—save Oswald, of course. Which was understandable, for as Younghusband knew, purchasing Carolina Packing was Oswald's project in the first place.

So Younghusband joined in on the mild laughter while pouring himself tea. Mother Porkers indeed!

HISTORICAL LANDMARK #26
The Monarch and the Salmon Queen

The Metropolitan who provided the dispensation for their marriage, it is said, went on permanent spiritual retreat when, a few years later, he learned there was a child by that union.

His successor took the matter of this infant's baptism and chaotic consanguinity into canonical advisement, but was never heard from on the matter. When, each month, their petition was pressed, it is rumored His Holiness wept.

The Salmon King and his young spouse gave it all up, and Oswald Innokenty Wagner was baptised without issue into the Lutheran Church. "We're a two-church household," the Salmon King would tell anyone who asked. ". . . and two churches are a helluva lot better than one. Cost effective, too."

As a gift to his bride, The Salmon King deeded outright the Monarch label and its principals to his newly invested Salmon Queen. For years, it had been in disuse, tradewise, "And if you can make something out of old Monarch, you're welcome to it."

By the time of Oswald's birth, it was discovered that customers indeed would pay five to six times the price for a can of fish if suitably labeled and marketed with a bit of snobbish pizzazz.

"Damned if I wasn't wrong," The Salmon King declared gleefully to all business associates. He was proud of his new wife's business acumen.

But the Salmon Queen knew Himself's heart; hence, she guessed the truth of his gift. The Monarch label had been his first, and its decline had always hurt, despite the current success of a half dozen others. "It is fucking amazing, my Dear, what pretentious lithography and glossy puff-ads in arse-sniffer magazines will do."

"Please. The boys."

"Of course, my Dear, of course."

Any and all of Seattle's Social Register Rats initially assayed dark scenarios and motives for this odd marriage:

"It's revenge."

"Simple financial convenience, of course."

"Just a semi-ordinary gold-digger."

"She's a comely oriental wench. Pure male vanity."

And these were just the headliners on a long, long column of motives vast, varied, and chuckleheaded.

The two motives omitted were the most ordinary, but these made poor copy and poorer conversation. Yet the staff in the Chinook House—especially Katrina—knew without fear of guessing. And the ugliness of the couple's earlier dealings was now past. Also, the Salmon Queen's business slowly—her concept of upscale food items caught on re: other products—and as the ancients said, "Ultimately, the Gods shine upon those who most deserve it (plus can handicap skillfully in races one through nine)."

27

When Wagner was helped up to the plywood platform, crowds of shift workers were already spilling out of Gate Three. Pedro—Woody's smallish business agent—rattled off salutory Spanish; the mariachis played; the workers, for the most part, formed a semi-circle around the trailer. Behind, the caged man screamed at them—conveniently switching to Spanish invectives. The crowd took part in booing and jeering. Holding up his hands—Nixon in China style—Pedro called for a pause in the music, then began an introduction—in Spanish, naturally—to the Woody on Wheels Show.

"Speak English, motherfucker!" Several dozen blacks screamed out in semi-unison. Clearly, the proletariat angst Wagner saw acted out earlier was present in reality also. Despite grumbles of Hispanic discontent, Pedro switched to English, cajoling his audience towards international brotherhood.

While this continued, Wagner saw a television truck ramble up, spilling technicians and production people onto the lot. Intense, they set up without pause. Woody greeted them, arms open, his English sentences rear-ending each other like demolition derby beaters.

He even slapped one of the female production people on the butt, and was playfully slapped on his posterior in return. Wagner felt he might have been witnessing baboons socializing.

"And, we have a special speaker for all you brothers and sisters, man!"

Wagner's attentions were drawn back to Pedro as he began his introduction. *Your time is at hand, Wagner,* and he began to think through a few catchy openers—for with crowd management and public speaking, the mob's spirit had to be seized in seconds.

While thinking thus, Wagner noticed an enigmatic vignette that diverted his attention from his imminent debut in public speaking. It was, in truth, quite bothersome.

Since all attention was on the stage, Woody took opportunity to approach the fence. Though a rack of lights had obscured the view, when they were suddenly moved, Wagner's view became unimpeded. Woody stepped up close to the fence. A Deputy sidled close to Woody, then confided something. He checked his watch and nodded, and Woody looked at his watch and also nodded.

Then they nodded together.

They were definitely a pair of nodding sons-of-bitches of the Old School. At the once, Wagner sniffed a *Rattus Norwegicus*—and a wharf-sized specimen at that.

"Hey, Gordo, what in fuck is your name? I gotta fuckin' introduce you, man!?"

The musicians blasted into a brassy version of "Fanfare for the Common Man," mariachi style. Wagner's anger deflected his curiosity from Woody.

"Well it isn't Gordo, you sawed-off little shithead. It's Volpone. My name is Volpone!"

Overlooking this edge of friction, Pedro raised his hands, silenced the band and announced, "And now, a great labor speaker from New York City! My old friend and great spokesman for labor, Mr. Volpone. Let's hear it!"

He repeated it in Spanish while beckoning for Wagner to come forward to the skeptical applause that began.

With no more time for thought, Wagner stepped into the breach.

Pedro thrust a bullhorn in his face, and warned, *sotte voce*, "They're ready. Make it good, Gordo."

Milepost 138.3 — Point of Interest
Nasty Summit: Elevation 1,091 feet

Undersheriff Goodwin J. Slenderberry, along with deputies Lofton Chiles and Vasily Rodinov, cruised the line between North and South Carolina. The Undersheriff, referred to as "GS," pondered matters fiscal.

"Fifty thousand in gold coin, topped with $75K in official reward, would put me aboard a Bahama cruiser bigger than Susy's tits."

Deputy Chiles glanced in the rear of the SUV at Deputy Rodinov and nodded—confirming an earlier assertion he'd confided to his equal. He drew himself up a notch, preparing to be righteous.

"Maybe out in California, GS, they don't know 'bout equal sharin', but in Nawth Carolina, that's how we work it."

GS smiled—in the dashlights, his white teeth shone an unnatural green against his ebony black skin. Turning onto a main highway he visited a laugh on the concept of sharing.

"This is my territory, my idea, so son, shut the fuck up. It's like this, you gotta deal with the concept that my black ass gets the boss-end, and your cracker butt gets what I says it'll get—along with the old Commissar in the back seat here."

Deputy Chiles sipped at a coffee and groaned.

He was probably the only born-and-bred North Carolinian peace officer with a California-born black man for a boss, and a Russian émigré for a partner.

"Your kin might have North Carolina in their blood GS, but you hain't got nothin' but L.A. dollar signs in yours."

They turned down a smallish road that led to a bridge overlooking a stream—the geographic demarcation point between the two states. Deputy Rodinov yawned and confronted the pre-dawn countryside with a less than optimistic gaze.

"This Wagner guy. We never seen him anyway. So nobody shares shit."

GS fiddled with the scanner, then gave a glance to Rodinov via the mirror and, taking out his cell phone, hesitated before dialing.

"One thing I like about you two, you're both as smart as it takes to pee downhill. Neither of you moho's could catch a goddamned train unless

they loaded you on."

"An' ah' suppose you're Einstein, right?"

But Chiles put no energy in his rejoinder, and Rodinov didn't even try—or care enough to try. It was late, and a twenty percent share for a fleeing fat man was probably a myth anyway. And twenty percent of nothing made nothing.

Nothing rather said it all.

28

Wagner felt the crowd's energy; he enjoyed it. My God and Mary Baker Eddy, he flat-out was getting into this shit. Where had public oratory been all his life?!

No failed attempts at inspiring the populace for Wagner! These were Workers. His lifelong cause. Victims of Capitalism. And now it was Wagner's turn to depart the theoretical fiddlefaddle and get with the heavy lifting of social activism. Furthermore, Woody and this maggot Pedro had a surprise coming their way.

During his formative period Wagner spent four arduous seasons in Chile with the Salmon King as his *aide de camp*—whipping the anchovetti operation together. Spanish!? Hell, Wagner spoke it like a goddamned native.

With an eye towards crowd demographics, Wagner noted that those who lingered were mostly men, while the women walked directly to the parking area.

Good! This would be a speech for men! Hispanic men!

When he began in Spanish, he saw the drama it effected on the crowd. To speak in the language of Lorca, Neruda, and countless other poet/social activists made this an almost holy moment.

Naturally Big-Voiced, unlike the puny insect Pedro, Wagner lateralled the infernal bullhorn to his smaller companion on the dais. Simultaneous with his opening words, he waved an angry fist into the air.

"Friends, Fellow Workers! Welcome! Now is the time to come to your senses and realize what fools you've been made to look by these Yankee Capitalists!"

Wagner knew it was a dynamite opener. The crowd hushed. Woody's mouth dropped open and he glanced helplessly to Pedro who was so flabbergasted, he ignored Woody's frantic request for simultaneous translation. Behind the fence, the Bubba constabulary was confused.

"Now is the moment to halt your ceaseless cutting and trimming of pork shoulders and ribs—while watching the white scum get fatter with all the easy jobs. And you, friends? The bosses work our brothers and sisters like the pigs they lead to slaughter!"

A spontaneous roar swelled, as a vast breaker might upon a perilous rocky coast. Wagner knew he had the crowd, held it squarely. Now everyone—all the workers—pressed forward, thirsty for each word. A surge of power and infinite truth seized him, and then—something else, too. A singular inner voice cried out, *Go for it, Wagner. Go for it! The next shot must be your finest!*

"While you live like animals, the rich Yankee capitalists give fat white babies to your daughters and women back in the resorts and hotels in Mexico. You are treated like women because you behave like women! You rot here, working for little money and allowing your manhood to drain onto the monied floor of your enemies, mixing with the blood of pigs. Look to your manhood and pride. Revolt! Tear this place down until there is nothing left but a burned hole in the earth, and then shit in that hole. Destroy Capitalism! Don't stand around like dumb animals. Annihilate forever those who make pimps out of honest men and whores out of your innocent daughters and wives."

Pedro's presence of mind resulted in an impressively rapid assessment of looming calamity. He cast panicky right and left looks—appraising the crowd that now pressed forward—then tossed the bullhorn and bolted.

Though his Spanish was poor, the Big-Time-Labor-Guy-from-Gdansk obviously concurred, and as Pedro executed a Cisco Kid vault onto his motorcycle, Woody decided to accompany him as passenger. Clearly the speed of departure took precedence over the size of conveyance.

Yet, in a deft two-stroke move, Pedro kick-started his mount and parried the massive Woody with a second deflective kick to his chest—and sped off in the manner of an animal fleeing a burning hay barn. Woody was left sitting flat on his butt, flapping his arms and bellowing in outrage, abandoned to fate. His stentorian curses were lost in the angry clamor of the crowd.

Swift action now dominated: The television truck was first to catch the wrath of that portion of the crowd opting for immediate action. Mirrors, doorhandles, and external electronic gizmos were torn off like hunks of damp bread. Then began the traditional side-to-side rocking of the entire craft.

The truck's media aces spilled out—fleeing hands over posteriors—clambering up the twelve-foot high fence. They ignored the bobbed wire atop it—slithering between and over the strands, leaving bits of clothes and skin attached.

Woody yelled at Wagner, but Wagner could not hear. No, no! He could no longer hear.

His rage against Mother Porker's Chasm of Capitalism had turned the corner, and Wagner no longer cared about himself, or anyone.

But the hired thespians and musicians on the tractor-trailer combo *did* care. Using the wily Pedro as an example, one jumped into the truck cab and started it. Even the former Prince Hamlet, while exiting his cage, shouted to his colleagues, "Jesus Christ, let's GO!"

But quick thinking Mother Porker employees had other plans for the big rig! Pushing Woody's actors out and aside, yanking the driver from behind the wheel, they commandeered the great vehicle, and turning it about (only narrowly avoiding smishing dozens of their fellow protestors), aimed it at the security gate.

Their strategy didn't require a Lee or Grant to appreciate: The cops and goons scattered like jackals, save for one stout lad who ran to his Bubbamobile and took out a shotgun. But aside from those taking action, hundreds of workers stayed and LISTENED, and Wagner was driven to continue.

During his initial words, Wagner saw the knots of confused black people falling back. He knew language should not stand in the way of what he must say. Deciding *Fuck all to multi-ethnicity,* he switched to English.

In his heart he felt an unstoppable wrath and primordial urge that moved beyond mundane labor issues at Mother Porker's

Number One. No, this was a larger, global conspiracy: These socially pulverized workers were up against the same merciless capitalist machine that the Great Arbuckle had so bravely opposed—yet so piteously failed against. Wagner knew that his voice was the spiritual reprisal of all the world's Arbuckles.

"All of you poor-ass Motherfuckers—black, brown, purple—are flat fucked—just like the Great Arbuckle, who never had a goddamned chance against Hollywood Capitalists. KILL THE SONO-FABITCHING CAPITALIST BLOODSUCKERS, BEAT THEM TO DEATH LIKE YOU WOULD BEAT COMMON VIPERS IN THE CRADLES OF YOUR BABIES!"

Wagner looked out upon the destruction and chaos, and knew he'd turned the hour to the advantage of the working classes. His public speaking premier had been an unparalelledly four-star operation.

Milepost 138.35
The Dawn Patrol

The meeting between Mrs. Wagner, Oswald, and MRI's harried lawyers was abruptly shattered with a scream from the suite's kitchen. Stromboli—with uncommon speed and grace for his massive size—had almost reached the Dutch-style door when Katrina reeled through it, her hands held to her wrinkled face.

What she exclaimed was in a language no one understood, save Mrs. Wagner. They used it between each other rarely. The Salmon Queen gestured urgently to the television remote.

"Turn it on."

In seconds, there was the mid-morning Action Central News running hot tape of the now notorious labor riot at Mother Porker's Number One. That alone was bad enough corporate news for MRI—but oh, that wasn't what shocked Katrina. No, not at all, and of course—neither the Salmon Queen.

Though the lawyers did not recognize Wagner, his family did—including Younghusband. Despite the poor lighting and long gown, the Salmon Queen and Katrina—even if there had been no sound—knew in an instant. To Wagner's devoted child-mother, along with his loving nanny, his oratory, clearly gone ape-shit, was a vision into the glowing coals of Hades.

At the moment before cameraman #1 was pulled down from the truck and plowed under by the mob (caught faithfully by camerman #2), Wagner riled away. The Salmon Queen, stunned, lamented, "What on earth?! It has to be that foul medicine given him?"

Katrina embraced the Salmon Queen and wept. The CEO of Monarch Enterprises International looked grimly at Colonel Younghusband.

"Do something, Colonel. You've seen enough," and, gently pushing Katrina away, she took the remote, clicked off, and repeated, "You've all seen enough. So: All of you! Do Something!"

And the Salmon Queen did the most extraordinary thing, something no one had ever seen: Angry, and intense, she threw the remote onto the floor, glared at all present, then led a weeping Katrina into the suite's pri-

vate quarters—consoling her in that strange, unintelligible language.

When Stromboli was herding the lawyers out, Younghusband took a minute to make phone calls on the suite landline. While calling, he glanced back into the suite and the strange sight said it all, regards Wagner Family Politics:

Oswald had picked up the remote, turned the set back on, and (itself an unusual flourish) sat Indian style before it. He took off each of his shoes, then each sock, and allowing his toes free wriggle, watched with unconcealed interest and glee. All his attentions remained on the set, and in his increasing joy Oswald even began a sort of Tantric right/left weaving.

Younghusband was not the only one to notice this: Moving through the corridor towards the elevator, one of the lawyers managed to delay any reaction to this tableau until the door closed and they were descending to the lobby. Exchanging looks, the senior partner shook his head and drawled, "That, gentlemen, is one strange family."

Milepost 138.4
Steep Downgrade Ahead
Check Air Brakes

Moynahan escaped from Dade County Sheriff's deputies by stepping out the back window of the men's room at the Esso Super Stop. In a clever reverse, he stepped immediately back into the lady's room, which was fortunately unoccupied. While waiting, he combed his hair and straightened up a bit.

Thinking he'd buggered clean out the back, the two deputies shouldered their way through the door, vaulted a rickety wood fence, and pursued a non-existent Moynahan into a trailer court.

Seeing that his double-reverse worked, the cool-thinking attorney strode confidently back through the store. At the pumps, he held up a trio of C-notes, asking an elderly black patron, "Could you run me to the airport? I'm a little late."

Safely away from the Esso Super Stop, Moynahan's driver asked, "What all them bulls want you for?"

Moynahan narrated his recent unscheduled landing on the beach; him jumping from the plane, tackling and assaulting the dirty son-of-a-bitch who'd been running up HIS credit card in HIS name while on a Tour-de-fucking-Florida with Crazy Sue.

The man nodded, appreciating the moment.

"Now I reckon that was one surprised motherfucker."

Remembering the recent donnybrook, Moynahan inspected a badly bitten left hand, cursed a bit, then fished out his second pair of glasses and dabbed at a gouge on his forehead. The black man whistled, "Man, I hope ya give as good as ya got. Yo' all tore up."

Reaching into the only untorn coat pocket for something to wipe a smudge from the glasses, Moynahan took out what felt like a marble, but in fact was a glass eye.

Moynahan and his unexpected combat souvenir exchanged blank stares. His ride gave something of an approving grunt, and complimented, "Well, you musta' done OK. You got his eye."

29

When events made the transition from chaos to mayhem, Wagner's megalomaniacal mist cleared sufficiently to realize he was going to be torn flesh from bone by the mob. Perhaps his reawakening was facilitated by the gunfire.

It was either a Mother Porker's Rent-A-Goon or a deputy who'd fired the shotgun—but it did little good, and far more harm. At that point, the captured thespian tractor/trailer combo bashed through Gate Number Three, sending the armed deputy sprawling after his initial warning shot into the air.

Then, with suspicious timeliness, the Sheriff's helicopter showed up, letting loose Beirut-sized canisters of tear gas. Its rotors broadcasted this vile mist everywhere, making certain all participants, regardless of affiliation and intent, had their fair share of the eye-smarting, snout-stifling stuff.

As a bonus to this impressive pandemonium, bales of hay used as seats and abutments on the flatbed trailer burst from the impact with the gate. Now, hundreds of pounds of straw swirled with gas and dirt, creating an maelstrom unsurpassed.

Wagner might spend years in future contemplation, but they would never provide the answer to how he (and others) ended up seeing well enough to dive into (in Wagner's case) the posterior-most seat of the limo.

Arriving at the limo more or less at the same moment were (1) the driver, then (2) Woody and (3) an unidentified but terrified Rent-A-Goon, who at once entered into a hand-to-hand brawl with Woody between the rear and middle seats.

But the most influential and vocal arrivee, surely, was (4) one of the pigs, so recently freed from its theatrical confines upon the truck. Semi-blinded and in utter porcine panic, it pitched into the front seat at same moment the driver started the vehicle intending a getaway in a zestful Dillinger/Baby-Faced Nelson tradition.

But the pig—squealing piteously at top volume—and surely not knowing where it was—sought the lowest, deepest "hole" (true to its kind) for shelter. And in a limo, that was the peddle-well on the driver's side.

Wedged against the accelerator, piggy enabled the vehicle to start off with a grand snort of speed. The driver (already in a rage over the clear and present danger to his vast vehicle) screamed oaths of fear and anger, and while he steered, fought with his unwitting assistant engineer.

But the accelerator wasn't the only peddle in the animal's makeshift shelter.

Twice, all the limo's occupants were pitched forward with headlong abandon when the pig covered the brake peddle while cringing from the driver. This catapulted Wagner into and upon the brawling duo of the Goon versus Woody. And menacingly, it also allowed a dozen or so rioters to throw themselves over the limo's exterior. Joining the fray, as it were.

One of these wielded a bludgeon, and immediately began smashing in the security windows on the port side. As safety glass sprayed over the limo's multi-specied occupants, the driver howled, "OH, SWEET FUCKING JESUS!"

But either on purpose or via random event, the accelerator again dominated, and as the limo attained awe-inspiring speed while hurtling from the parking lot, it sprayed external riders port and starboard.

And with that, the long cream-white vehicle sped with abandon into the early North Carolina morning.

Milepost 149.1
Switchbacks Ahead: Proceed with Suspicion
Switchback #1 – Adopt a Switchback
The Benevolent Society of Police Officers

What did Trooper Aldrove see passing by in the half light of dawn? Its force and speed was such it left swirling dust devils of dirt and leaves in its wake. To his right, in front of still-closed Magnolia's Grocerteria, a sleeping dog jolted awake. But the hound saw nothing but dying wisps of dust devils. Deciding it was yet another doggy-dream, it shifted to another position.

Had Trooper Aldrove been dozing?

Just a cadet months before, Aldrove's late-night patrol area was his first assignment. Rich with diverse racial sorts, this area seemed to be just what he'd hoped for. Being among the new generation Southern police officers, Trooper Aldrove enjoyed the challenge. And he never dozed.

Traffic infractions were his principal assignment, and looking at his speed gun—left on by accident—he read 116 mph. This was reality. But how could it be?

Gotta be fouled up.

But then, he remembered the dust swirls, the blurred slash passing north to south. The truth was, hours of training had not yet led to instinct: A veteran officer would have been in pursuit within ten seconds. It took Aldrove a full half minute.

"Jesus, at 116 miles per hour, he's got almost a full mile on me."

30

In the overall category of limousine rides, Wagner conceded this one was the worst on record. In the altercation between the rear and middle seat, which now involved him along with Woody and the Goon, a savage bite was delivered to Wagner's lower leg—a wild attempt to free them of his four hundred plus pound bulk and avoid major internal injuries.

In another context this scene (the squealing pig in the peddle well, the brawl amidships) had potential as a salute to a Mack Sennett comedy. But chances of this vanished when a horse-sized pistol emerged from the blur of the melee.

With hammer back, all comedic potential vaporized.

Wagner, after emitting an agonized yowl, knew at once that it sure as hell wasn't his gun, so that meant it belonged to either Woody or the Goon.

At that instant, the gun fired.

And unlike a comedy, it wasn't fired harmlessly through the roof, but directly towards, and at—as accurately as Wagner could tell— the driver, who immediately bellowed out.

Wagner acted!

He seized the hand that held the gun that pulled the trigger that probably killed the driver that would result in the six-ton limousine smoking into the North Carolina woods at well over one hundred miles per hour.

But, the vehicle sped on—still semi-controlled.

Somehow, the round had not annihilated the driver. Taking his chance, Wagner closed his massive grip on the wrist until the weapon dropped. At the same moment the pig, bleeding and screaming in unbelievable volumes as a result of a gunshot wound, fled its hole. The unfortunate beast hurled itself up and over the frantically laboring driver—into the back seat—becoming a fourth participant in the melee. In doing thus, it profusely illustrated the old saw, "Bleeding like a stuck pig."

Wagner, though intending to parry it away, caught the small porker, and in doing so, came eye to eye with it. In the hapless creature's largish piggy ear was a perfectly round bullethole.

"OH, JESUS, BUDDHA, AND MARY BAKER EDDY!"

Wagner was absolutely surprised to discover that those words were his and that he'd invoked the names of the prophets while holding a pig to his heart.

Was this the appropriate moment for a spiritual revelation?

Milepost 161.5
Switchback #2–Adopt a Switchback
South Carolina Chapter, National Alliance for the Morally Burdened

Undersheriff "GS" Goodwin J. Slenderberry didn't know wealth was headed his way when the rookie Aldrove lost control of his cruiser at Beyer's Bend, sending him rocketing into the puckerbrush. The neophyte was broadcasting a Code 65 when he'd lost it. In the parked Sheriff's vehicle, the three questing lawmen listened to his last calamitous moments on the overhead speaker. GS and his deputies had little use for State Patrolmen in general, and the inexperienced Aldrove in particular. Deputy Chiles rolled his eyes, then drolled, "Dum' som'bitch. Now I s'pose we gotta fetch up the pieces."

The trio lurked at the historic junction of N.C. State Routes 13 and 29. GS drew a resigned "do the right thing" breath, and, just as he started their cruiser, his cell phone rang.

When he rang off, deputies Chiles and Rodinov knew something was up.

"News! That was the wife. Goddamned if the Fat Man isn't headed our way. Charleen saw it on Action 10 News just now. Some sort of riot."

"Riot?"

"That's what she said. On this highway. This way."

Deputy Rodinov knew his priorities.

"Well fok that state guy, big time. Let's head for the bridge, get that big fat bastard."

All three knew that on this highway, there was but one portal from North Carolina into South—that was Steenman's Bridge, a narrow wood affair. With siren and lights on, GS needed no further prompting. Steenman's Bridge was two minutes off via a kidney-addling shortcut. All grimaced painfully as they were tossed against seat restraints while GS drove headlong—whooping for glee over their oncoming triumph to riches. If any of the three thought of Patrolman Aldrove, they might have surmised he was dead anyway. So, wherever the officer was, he'd wait.

31

Wagner considered whether the tragic still-life beside State Route 29 was Sophoclean, Days-of-Our-Lives-ian, or an overwrought hybrid between both, which to Wagner, would make it O'Neillian. In any dramatic spin, though, to recreate these present scene-ettes might challenge the most adroit set designer:

Against the State Route 29 sign, the limo driver reclined, weeping deeply, lamenting the disfigurement of his life's investment.

"Jesus Christ, me and the old lady dealt blackjack to tight old bitches for seven years to buy this rig. We had an investment."

Then, through tears, he glared with undiluted odium at Woody who, a few feet down from the driver, sat squarely upon Mr. Rent-A-Goon's torso, a character he'd recently beaten senseless.

The driver thrust a dagger of an index finger at Woody, slashing the air into ribboned swirls.

"You four-flusher. I should shoot your fucking ass."

At the word "shoot," Woody looked to Wagner, though quickly returning a weather eye to his vanquished opponent lest the miserable bastard attempt to squirm free.

Thankfully, Woody needn't fear the driver shooting him because Wagner had the pistol. Sitting half in, half out of the limo, the now infamous demagogue tended his bite-wound using the limo's first aide kit.

The fourth participant and mourner was the North Carolina State Patrolman. He sat cross-legged down-highway from the driver, mouthing a semi-intelligible sing-song, for sadly the poor devil had been knocked fruitcaky, perhaps permanently.

The hapless officer had tottered onto the asphalt from the cruiser-wide swath in the woods. Departing Route 29 at 110 mph, he and his capsule (for at that speed, shouldn't a vehicle assume a more appropriate term?) leveled six or seven acres of dwarf low-bog cedar before stopping.

His tunic was shredded, a small rent exposing a hairy nipple being the only clue that once thereon had rested a badge proclaiming him *uno ladataum officialus*, late of the North Carolina State Patrol. Tatters of air-bags hung from his anatomy, and a bulbous contusion—still swelling—rendered his forehead Frankensteinesque. It wasn't a pretty sight.

The missing fifth survivor of the escape from violent death was the pig.

Wagner had watched it flee, squealing into the underbrush, assumedly in search of its ancestors, to live out its life as removed from *Homo sapiens* as possible. A hole in the ear was a small price to pay for such a unique education.

"Raindrops, listen to the tanktops. Ragbottom, flaggertiles, sla'bom, sla'bom."

Woody grew impatient with the patrolman's ongoing syntactical succotash.

"Vy don' you make to shut fok up, you som'bitch fokking cop. Lucky we stopped, help this guy. Huh?"

He looked at Wagner, including him into the fellowship of his rhetorical question and inviting him into his world of *agent provocateur*, double-crosser, and betrayer of labor ideals. Wagner lowered his robe over the treated wound, and observed, "Don't even speak to me, Woody, you miserable two-timing pile of carrion. You see, it's like this, I'm going to shoot you. My only question is where? The guts? balls? Or, perhaps I'll be a humanitarian, and smoke one through that degenerate brainpan of yours."

"My vote is for the balls."

Woody raised his hand when Mr. Rent-a-Goon made his suggestion—causing the trapped reptile to cringe against the ground.

Oh, my Brothers and Sisters, this had not begun, nor had it developed into, a friendly rest-stop.

When the limo rocketed off from the Mother Porker's Den-of-Mayhem, the driver—already half crazed between controlling the vehicle and struggling with the pig—wailed in frenzied outrage, "Shit oh Dear! Now we've got a cop on our butt." But the pursuit had been brief, for within minutes the pursuer's vehicle went cat-tiwompus.

If it weren't for Wagner's armed insistence, of course, they would not have stopped at all.

"The poor fucker could be dying, you inconsiderate fucks!"

The others didn't share his concern, but, following long tradition, respected his weapon.

When the occupants of the limo had spilled out onto Route 29, and during savage but revealing vocalizations accompanying Woody's subduing of his enemy, Wagner gleaned much truth.

It confirmed what Wagner had suspected: Woody—the Big-Time-Labor-Guy-from-Gdansk—had been paid off by Mother Porker's as agent provocateur. On the trumped-up charge that Woody's labor melodrama was "incitive conduct," choppers, company goons, and sheriff's deputies, including some in choppers, had been standing by—scripted to render dramatic resolve to the show. In more than one way.

Wagner's speech had, ironically, rendered the fictional, real—plus added a dash or so of vituperation and deadly menace. Mother Porker's union-busting strategy had worked too well.

Wagner gestured down the highway with the weapon.

"Fuck it. Neither of you is worth a bullet. Start walking, both of you worthless specks of phelgm. Now, goddamnit! While you each have two goddamned feet."

Wagner supposed it would be emotionally satisfying to shoot off one or both of their feet at the ankle, yet more civilized instincts prevailed.

Better to have both brutes bipedal to keep each other company, taking in the blush of first light during a dawn promenade. The shyest and most subtle of sunrises shone gracefully through the eastern, pine-rich skyline.

But, despite his compassion, there were still complaints.

"But, da'yam, that's mah .44 mag," the Goon whimpered.

A shot fired into the morning air ended his sniveling, and Woody and his companion skulked off in the manner directed. The trooper, unaffected by the hip-howitzer's report, giggled a bit, then began to pore over the toes of his left foot. His recent deforestation efforts had peeled off his footwear, rendering his occupation easier.

Wagner decided the pistol's heft was not half-bad, and seeing that the combative duo wasn't moving fast enough, decided, "Oh, what the hell," and fired again. This time, he sent a round ricocheting off the asphalt a few yards to their starboard. This projectile spat heinous fragments and sparks, creating an angry but splendid-sounding whine as it spirited into the morning air.

"Oh! Holy Fokking Chris', mon!"

Woody and his comrade's pace at least tripled; in fact their strides approached Olympian proportions.

Oh, that was better.

The limo driver was not interested in side issues. Instead he still lamented the dents, rents, and smashed-in portside windows on his limo. Wagner looked up and down the road.

Fast thinking and action were absolutely required.

"Listen asshole, shut the fuck up. See here," Wagner removed a wad of C-notes from his poke—his one powerful tool of Americana remaining. "These, I'm sure, will repair your fucked-up limo, and see this, here's another thousand if, but *only* if, you get me into South Carolina and to Spartanburg. So you're still in business."

The driver looked to Wagner, then the wad. The moolah facilitated an immediate return of his composure. Wagner gestured towards South Carolina.

"Well, shouldn't we be going? Like fucking *Now*?"

The driver followed Wagner's gaze downroad, into North Carolina. On the horizon—moving their way fast—a fine array of red, purple, blue, and green emergency lights was visible in the morning light.

And to the west was the menacing pop of helicopter rotors. Clearly, help was on the way.

The driver hustled toward the front of the limo, but motioned to the front seat when he saw Wagner move towards the rear,

"Not back there, man. No airbags. Now, let's get this mother-fucker rolling!"

Oh Yes! Wagner liked this change in attitude!

As he plopped in next to the driver, Wagner knew that with a mechanized lynch mob hurtling towards them, it was absolutely necessary to rely on one of the Salmon King's trusty axioms: "Grandson, this is a situation where the Devil will kick-ass on the hindmost."

Milepost 169.4 Miles
Exit Ahead: No Services Available:

A Federal Air Marshall aboard Flight 185 from Miami to Atlanta was in semi-hot pursuit of a skyjacking suspect known only as "Moynahan." He'd been diverted aboard from other duty and knew nothing except that this Moynahan had attempted hijacking a single engine aircraft to Cuba earlier that day. Yet when the Marshall rushed to deplane in Atlanta, he was arrested by Airport Security who concluded he was Moynahan bolting from the plane to make an escape.

"Goddamnit, I'm not Moynahan! I don't even know what he looks like."

"Well, hell, sorry. But we don't either."

By the time all the players were in the right places, Flight 185's passengers had gotten off and it was damage control time.

Airport Security, the U.S. Marshal Service, and the Georgia State Police cordoned off Concourse B, simultaneously setting up a perimeter around the Boeing 757—a continuing flight, hence half full of passengers bound for Raleigh-Durham.

Striding up and down the aisles, lawmen fish-eyed passengers until one slunk suspiciously into the toilet. Assuming he was Moynahan, they extricated him at once, only to discover he was "Scanner" George Hodgeson, wanted on a federal warrant for counterfeiting and interstate flight.

They were right, but wrong.

After securing Scanner George, they continued to look for this Moynahan fellow. The delay was now approaching an hour. An overwrought businessman en-route to Raleigh commenced reviling the U.S. Marshall, even threatening to punch him in the nose. So, the businessman was arrested for Obstruction of Justice and ended up sharing the courtesy cart with Scanner George.

Meanwhile, Airport Security decided that the skyjacker—as Moynahan was temporarily known—was perhaps not on the plane. But how in hell had he gotten off in mid-flight?

But then there was a break: A stewardess from Flight 185, with keen presence-of-mind, provided the searchers with the complimentary 1st-Class handkerchief that Moynahan (sitting in 4-A) had discarded in the seatback pouch. They brought in dogs.

One or two whiffs of this and the hounds' noses were smack on his trail. They clambered into a men's room in the main terminal and alternately bayed and scratched at the door of a handicapped stall—with one dog slipping under it. The pursuers indeed found the handkerchief's owner—involved in a welcome home backside bong-bong with his male lover. Neither participant was the notorious Cuban Hijacker (as Moynahan was now known).

To save face, police arrested the pair for Public Licentiousness and Sodomy.

Embarrassment became total when the Airport Administrator tendered a critical comment during a live interview, saying that physical descriptions, back in his day, were a necessary part of nabbing a suspect. "No wonder this bird got away." He had a good but embarrassing point: The Air Marshal, Scanner George, and the Handkerchief Owner were as similar as Before, After, and In-Between.

And Moynahan—the Cuban Skyjacker? He was still at large and a menace to air travelers everywhere.

32

The limo driver whooped in victory when he left both helicopters behind. He opened up the double-paneled sunroof so he and Wagner could see overhead. Their annoying followers would be back as soon as the limo emerged from the deep trees.

"Tipping a tail rotor into those trees at one hundred-plus miles per hour would drop those choppers like dirty shirts," the driver chortled. "Fuckin' pilots are all pussies."

To celebrate their newfound privacy, the driver took out his inhalant and rewarded himself with a hefty sniff. He handled the speeding limo like an elderly lady might wield a Lincoln Towncar in a church parking lot.

Wagner noticed that the pig's hooves had wiped out the limo's instrument panel—or, more to the point, the speedometer.

"How in fuck fast are we going, and what is that shit you're hitting off of? I assume it isn't for asthma."

The driver—as Wagner was relieved to see—put his other hand back on the wheel, but he kept the inhaler, cigarette style, between index and middle fingers.

"Oh, probably 110, 115. This som'bitch weighs 5.8 tons. Has a fuckin' mill in it—I bored it out to 585 cc., and added a goddamned military supercharger I scavenged from an old P-38 Thunderbolt that crashed behind my parent's farmhouse in Jersey." He nodded proudly, then glanced at Wagner (just a brief glance, thank god) to see if these facts impressed. He completed his litany after taking a mini hit from the inhaler—a pleasurable shiver caused his eyes to roll back, but only momentarily.

"The tires are the same custom eighteen plies all the Mafiosos' limos mount around New York and Atlantic City. I could drive at this speed across glass, nails, rails, spikes—even fuckin' four-inch abutments—and they wouldn't mean a goddamned thing, man."

He smacked the flat of his hand onto the dash and whooped, "Isn't a fuckin' thing without fixed wings that can keep up with us on the straightaway."

He flicked his head sideways, took a hit from the inhalant, and with a nod towards his pleasure, affirmed, "Oh, Jesus, this is good shit," and handed it to Wagner. "Try this shit, man."

Wagner declined at the same moment he spotted a familiar white bag in a compartment between him and the driver. Though smished a bit, it was a familiar container; its presence in his life had been absent for over three months. At first, he doubted his senses, but then his throat closed up tighter than a dying man's at the sight of distant oasis, and he knew: This fucker was for real.

He touched it. (Oh yes! It was real all righty.) This multi-blessed find was a stunningly magnificent white bag pregnant with bakery goods.

Despite his situation—all other instincts (e.g., fear of death, maiming, imprisonment, ruined health, institutionalization, etc.) retreated behind the most dominant of all: The orgasmic feel of sugar, dough, and oil (and skillfully selected flavorings) blended into that vast culinary opera known as custom-baked pastries.

And, partially due from all the activity and stress, Wagner was hungry. Goddamned, he was hungry! Thirsty, yes—but hungry more.

When he picked up the bag, he saw it was full of plump, fresh-baked Cinnamon Turbans glistening with sugar and raisins. Oh, sweet galloping motherfuckers from Elyssium—Wagner's favorite!

"Hey, don't eat them all. They're for my kid's birthday."

"Fuck you. I'm paying the bills. Anyway, I'll buy your goddamned progeny two hundred pounds of them in Spartanburg. So drive."

Wagner discovered he could not reach into the bag while holding the pistol, so he put it down. Now, with a free hand, he dived in. The driver took another vaporous hit—a healthy sniff up each nostril—enjoying the delightful spasms that passed, wave-like, along his narrowish shoulders.

Looking sideways at Wagner—now ingesting with clear pleasure the first Turban—he smiled wondrously, asking, "There's two dozen of those fuckers. You can't eat them all," and turning his attentions to the road for the brief split-second it took to pass a school bus, looked back—adding, "Can you?"

Wagner swallowed the first, started on the second, talking around it.

"Of course I can. I wouldn't have started if I couldn't. Watch out for the goddamned truck."

But, as he did the cars, the driver slipped around a milk-tanker so effortlessly and skillfully, it made even Wagner pause in his chewing.

"You're good."

The driver nodded, and with a flip of a button, the sunroof began closing.

"Goddamned rights I am, man. Especially compared to the useless hicks and jackoffs around this fucked-up place."

Dr. Schlagger and his assistant Doris completed another concussive act of sex outside Dixie's Diner. Jesus, if only my wife Eva could screw like this, mused the world's authority on tropical fish reproduction in closed habitats.

Anticipating his assistant's decibel level, he'd parked the double-tanker-trailer in a secluded area behind the eatery rather than in front of it. Insulated sleeper cab or no, young Doris celebrated her orgasms with Babylonian whoopings more robust than air-driven alpenhorns. And in all fairness, Herr Professor Schlagger was no Whispering Pete himself. In the afterglow, both concurred that humping was a devil of a good way to work up an appetite.

While ordering breakfast, Doris asked if she could drive the mammoth tanker truck, filled with this season's third and final shipment of tropical fish. "I know truck driving isn't a chick thing," she'd demurred, "but I just have a fascination with driving something that large."

Of course Herr Professor agreed. Doris was a cautious, thoughtful girl. Yes, and soon, he knew he'd have to sign off on her dissertation. Then, she'd become a very gone, thoughtful girl.

With this assistant—this marvelous Doris—his Frau Eva wasn't even suspicious. Yet.

Years before, he'd discovered that the homelier the assistant, the less likely his statuesque Bavarian wife was to become suspicious.

Gott,'he mused, how easy it vas to play into a woman's vanity. He was thus occupied when he looked up and saw the high-speed chase caught by Action 10 News. Racing beneath the choppers, a bone-white limo, already damaged in the chase, disappeared into the trees—and out of view. Doris pointed at the television with a spoon.

"Oh! I think that's happening close to here."

Herr Professor kept one eye on the set, but couldn't help returning his mind to business: This was the third massive delivery of tropical fish, and this one was pure profit. All profit.

What a crafty devil he'd been—both calculating the right market mix of tropical fish, and persuading Eva to stay at the farm in Florida.

"You know, my dear Eva, how traveling disagrees with you?"

And she'd agreed. "Oh, Helmut, you are so right. I'm no trucker."

33

"Thing is, they'll have the fuckin' bridge blocked."

The limo driver, perhaps as an afterthought, revealed his strategical thinking to Wagner just prior to his dramatic move.

"Bridge?"

"Steenman's Bridge, between South and North Carolina. It goes over a little piss-creek. But no matter—not to this old tank."

The driver, without such a conservative measure, say, as deceleration, swerved from the highway as casually as he might a two-degree turn across the Bonneville salt flats. Wagner's great bulk shifted portside, but when he clutched at the courtesy handle above the door, it uprooted, leaving him staring at its pearl countenance. This bit of kinetic razzle-dazzle served notice that fast maneuvers had now begun.

They smoked across a road surfaced with shell, traveled mostly by farm tractors or lolly-gagging school buses. Their passing created sounds similar to that of buckshot being shaken inside a tin can.

The driver grimaced.

"Fuckin' oyster shells will pit-hell outta' the paint job. It'll cost you, goddamnit!"

Wagner stuffed another pastry into his mouth, not wanting to negotiate financial intricacies of the escape at that moment. The driver shook his head confidently, keeping the limo just under ninety even on the small, frail road. He fell into a mood autobiographical.

"I drove for the Capracelli's when they did business in Atlantic City: Two-way Charlie and his fuckin' kid Lazy Angelo, the little fuck. In Jersey, man, you don't take chances. More heavyweight motherfuckers there than in Polermo."

Wagner was impressed with the driver's resume. He had become a different creature than the weeping sack of self-pity Wagner had oserved a few miles back. This man was sure, steady, and understanding of his abilities.

Wagner liked this, yet he felt somewhat better when after another hit from his inhalant the driver found it spent. Lowering his window, the driver tossed it. (Wagner felt that artistry—in this case the artistry of getaway driving—was best done clear-headed.) He scowled with disgust.

"I drove that overgrown gas-bag Woody here all the time to gamble and hump at the casino—it's just across the creek in South Carolina."

Wagner, as was his wont, began to see a dramatic pattern: A talented, dynamic driver being relegated to chauffeuring a worthless pile of shit like Woody about the Carolinas vs. shuttling Two-Way Charlie and his dimwitted kid Angelo along Atlantic City's ancient wooded pavilions.

Driving one-handed, he described the coming setup to Wagner—and a sly smile began to make itself at home. The chap was clearly a planner!

"It's like this: On this side of the border—which is the creek—is Dixie's Diner; on the other side is Indian Falls Casino. And dig this: The casino parking lot is ten feet lower than Dixie's lot."

Here he couldn't suppress a sardonic laugh—the expert getaway artist savoring a moment of creativity, knowing the moment was his. Actually, theirs.

At that instant, they emerged from the smallish road, and dropping his second hand onto the wheel—and pumping his foot several time against the brake pedal, the great limousine was sent into a semi-controlled ninety-degree right-wheelie. When they straightened, a true monolith of southern electric culture loomed directly off their bow: A twenty-foot-high neon sign depicting a sassy country girl (presumably, Ms. Dixie) complete with short sassy dress and shapely sassy legs. In an endless neon vaudeville, the gargantuan waitress twirled a platter of neon food and gave it a toss across a neon void of thirty feet where it landed before the second half of the sign: An eager, gapped-toothed customer, holding a fork high—set to dig Right Fucking In.

"Have you ever seen such a piece of shit?"

The driver's comment was made with all the calm of an art critic cruising a quiet museum. Yet his kinetically crazed vehicle sped along at over sixty miles per hour—first into and then through Dixie Diner's parking lot. They now maneuvered between pickups, cars and SUV's (with an odd tractor/trailer here and there) in something not much smaller than a M-1 class tank.

Wagner froze in mid-munch, rare for Wagner.

As this array of vehicles whipped by, the masticated pastry turned to a cud of tasteless cardboard. Transfixed, he looked on as this escape assumed dimensions heretofore unimagined.

Directly under the neon skirts of Ms. Dixie, the driver again multi-stroked the brake and once more directed his metal bomb into another, more dramatic ninety-degree turn. Now, the spirit of the escape took over, and he allowed a war cry, "EEEEY-OOOOWHOOOOW, Motherfuckers! Now watch power: pure, simple, with no holds fucking barred!"

Wagner, in shocked freezeframe, clutched half of an uneaten delicacy, forcing its doughy core to ooze through fingers.

"What in fuck are we doing?!"

"The creek, man! We'll jump it."

"Jump it!?"

Milepost 188.2
Watch for Elephants on Bridge

Lorena watched the new girl make a mess of prepping three platters of Dixie's Breakfast Specials. She forgot entirely the sprigs of parsley, put the cantelope between the pancakes and grits, and when hooking together the three platters, put her finger into the edge of one order's scrambled eggs.

"She ain't gonna' do, McGee."

"For Christ's sakes, Lorena, give the girl a chance. Learn her!"

Scotty, whom she always called "McGee," was a pushover for a new girl—always willing to put a favorable spin on poor help.

"I hain't no school teacher, McGee."

And Lorena headed out with her own four platters of breakfasts. As she strode into the dining room, she noticed everyone's gaze was locked on either one of the two giant projection televisions—one of McGee's innovations. ("Just like the Sports Bars, Lorena. It's the thing.") For Lorena, it was okay if customers wanted to be hammered by the tube—this a.m. she was running two waitresses short, and the ones she had weren't worth a damn.

But when three regulars let out a whoop, and identified the location on the television to be—well, right outside Dixie's, even Lorena paused momentarily after sliding platters of pancakes, eggs, and whatever, unnoticed, before them.

Now that was different. These regulars were straight-out hogs when it came to their breakfasts; usually, Lorena was lucky to escape with her arms unbitten.

She looked up at the closest screen in time to see a speeding white limo—barely kept in view by the camera—burst into a parking lot.

And when she saw their Dixie Diner sign—a State Historic Landmark of itself—her mouth dropped when the vehicle spun into yet another demolition-derby-style turn. One of the regulars exploded,

"Hot damn! Why Jee'Sus, Mary, an' Jeff Fuckin'Davis! That sokker's right outside!"

And right about then—when the limo had straightened out—Lorena felt and heard the choppers whirling and churning above the diner, and she tried to make sense out of what HAD to be one of the worst mornings on record.

And just at that moment, a customer to her right—scaring Lorena so bad she almost peed herself—shot to his feet, shouting, "OH GOTTENHIMMEL. MEIN TRUCK! MEIN FISH!"

34

Wagner always realized there was much nonsense promulgated concerning Fateful Moments. During times when people are faced with infamy, confronted with their immediate demise, movie, television, and supermarket pulp allow such moments to be graced with witty fateful lines. But Wagner always knew these for what they were—grist molded for halfwits.

Now, as they sped towards the creek to make an archetypal leap into South Carolina, this conviction was confirmed. Before them—within one unparalleledly calamitous second—loomed their end.

Wagner's end.

The driver had indeed made a correct call regards the layout of their jump. Though such obstacles as stout, mature oak trees arrayed themselves along the bank of the creek, let's assume, generously, he'd planned to simply avoid them.

After all, consider the vehicle: There was the speed; there was the power; there was the favorable disposition of their take-off versus landing platform.

But behind Dixie's Diner, along the bank of the creek, was parked, length-wise, a combination tractor/double-tanker-trailer. Probably the truck driver—a polite sort—wanted to park out of the way, so as not to inconvenience anyone.

So upon completing the second spectacular turning maneuver, and just after stomping on the accelerator to give them that needed burst of power to launch them from North Carolina to South Carolina, they found themselves hurtling towards this massive, impossible obstacle.

Wagner said nothing—voiced nothing. The driver had no witty remarks, no poignant observations—nothing.

Nothing. Nothing.

In the last half-second before they hit the monster vehicle, he managed to brake—his great skill and uncanny reactions accomplishing that much. But it was too little—and way the hell too late.

Driver and rider looked from the windshield as the wall of tanker/truck became their total world-view.

Before they hit, there was silence. The silence of being utterly, absolutelyandprofoundly flat-fucked.

Milepost 190.0
A Band of Brothers

Colonel Younghusband had preceded Herself and company to Styton, North Carolina, where Wagner had finally met his comeuppance. The Colonel looked forward to this. Well, savored it was a more precise word.

Yet knowing Herself's feelings for her eldest, he felt guilty about secret wishes for a dramatic resolution to her "fat chap." He knew how immeasurably easier his job would be if Wagner's crash into that bloody lorry proved fatal. But, technology being what it was, he doubted this would happen.

In Styton, he'd located MEI's headquarters in the hall housing the Fraternal Order for The Knights of the Corinthians. And since MEI was paying the bills, county and state agencies slid right in behind their private benefactor. Inside, Younghusband found the mechanisms of chaos working smoothly: diverse police officers claimed jurisdiction everywhere; cell phones chirped like squads of randy leopard frogs; press people barged in, barged out——were shown in, thrown out. It stupefied one, in trying to sort who were being read rights versus who were reading rights—for in fact there seemed to be those doing both at once.

On two television monitors, knots of officials, semi-officials, and plain hangers-on leered at Live Action 10 News coverage of the "Cutters." This elite highway rescue brigade—like giant termites—cut and gnawed their way into what had been the limo—now imbedded up to its waistline in the empty tanker.

The hall itself was the stuff of the whispered Arcana inherent in hushed-up men's organizations. A grand inverted triangle in gold and silver—the logo of the Knights of Corinthians—adorned the entryway, which opened into the Grand Hall itself.

But Younghusband had no chance for reflection, for once his identity as MEI's bagman became clear, he became the centerpiece of lobbying efforts by the brawling knot of lawmen desirous of one or both rewards. Especially the gold coins! A large black man approached, "Name's Slenderberry. Undersheriff, Deal County. I blocked the bridge and was first on scene at the diner when they tried to jump the creek. And I have jurisdiction here."

"Like hell you were and do."

A State Trooper with lieutenant bars stepped around the Undersheriff chap, then both turned on one another. The State officer pointed north. "I have an injured officer that was in hot pursuit. He made the initial ID and contact, Slenderberry."

Younghusband raised a hand for peace—his voice assuming his best public school aplomb.

"Gentlemen, please. After all," Younghusband's eyebrows rose and he gestured outside—downstream towards the rescue effort, "the stipulation, on most of it, was that he be unharmed. So, until later. Until things clear a bit."

Younghusband left them quarreling. Of course, now that the messy stuff over money began, Herself's youngest—the sniveling Oswald—was nowhere to be seen. "Too busy, don't you know," Younghusband said under his breath, "buying firms on the verge of anarchy." Oh yes, that was how he worked. It was up to Younghusband to deal with these clamoring semi-rural renditions of Southern Law and Order.

Milepose 190.1
Peggy In Spartanburg

Peggy had just gotten out of the shower when she saw Wagner addressing the labor protest on the morning news. Flinging the towel aside, the panicked woman nearly bolted from the door naked. This would have blacklisted her, surely, at all Red Lion Inns.

Getting hold of herself, she dressed wildly—her bony limbs thrashing in all directions. She maintained steady, horrified witness on the rapidly degenerating events on television. Now a speeding limousine was pursued by the aircraft. A "Recorded Earlier" tag flashed on the screen.

Without doubt, the very bad was becoming worse.

How could—where could—why would...., well, just what had brought Mr. Wagner to be so conspicuously involved? This made it a certainty he would be collared by reward-crazed rednecks and dragged back to that medieval, albeit overpriced, Bedlam—probably in chains or fiber-taped to a picnic table.

In her frenzied state, she forgot about Lulu. And when she rushed from the room, Lulu bounded out—loped down the hall, scaring a room maid so badly she dived head-first into the janitor's closet. Then the feline sprang over the maid's cart, out an open exit door, and became very gone.

It had to be. It had to be, Peggy anguished.

All her life, Fate seemed to follow her with a shovel-full of black ashes, keeping her in everlasting supply. Things, for her, had never been bright. Now this. But she continued—though checking out the closet, to see if the maid was all right.

She must rent a car—Lulu or no Lulu, Moynahan or no Moynahan— and herself try and render assistance to Mr. Wagner. In the lobby—looking up at the viewing area TV set—she saw the desk clerk and security man staring at the scene unfolding. The clerk pointed at it, then looked to Peggy, "Well, Ma'am, you missed the big crash."

On the screen was watery carnage—men laboring at a crash scene, the limousine now embedded in the side of a mammoth truck. People worked; lights flashed; other camermen scurried around. Brightly colored words blinked, "ACTION NEWS: LIVE." Emitting a yelp, Peggy bolted from the lobby. As her grandfather, Bomber Rothstein, used to say in either Yiddish or English: "Shit oh dear. Shit oh dear. Is this the Devil's handiwork?"

35

The stuff of American Arcana always provided Colonel Younghusband and the Missus with splendid talking points during visits home to Sussex. They kept the in-laws in rapt attention for hours. And this morning provided a bonanza of such material for countless future sessions.

After overseeing that Herself's chartered medical team was put in order, one of his chaps excitedly informed Younghusband that Wagner and his driver had been extricated, more or less intact.

"Very good."

Yet he still experienced the same blend of relief and disappointment. Keeping up with minute-by-minute developments, though, did not distract him so much he'd miss the unfurling of diverse Yank peculiarities.

The first-ranked oddballs, easily, were the nature people—"Eco-kooks," as the local authorities referred to them. They wept and picked up hats-full of half-dead Spotted Puffers and Rummynose Tetras, pleading into cameras for volunteers to come help the rescue effort. Representatives from regional conservation groups maintained the Styton spill was an ecological disaster of the gravest order. "What if," one blinked into the television cameras, "these exotic species were to establish in local waterways? There's no telling what damage might come of it."

Locals considered these concerns pure Raleigh-Durham urban horsefeathers. They assured any who would listen not to worry: There were enough animal wastes from industrial hog farms in Styton Creek to dissolve even a twenty-five-foot alligator in a half hour. "Why hells bells," bragged one local to reporters, "them tiny leetle fish will shorely dissolve like seltzer tablets."

There were more wandering Fantastics: Field operatives from the Southeast Center To Counteract Animal Wrongs focused not on the environmental impact of the spill but instead on the pervasive inhumanity of it. They appealed into other cameras, explaining that innocent creatures, flopping about helplessly—dying a slow, oxygenless death—were the result and responsibility of heartless businessmen.

They raised such animals in cold, dimly lighted hatcheries where, packed pectoral to pectoral, they endured the trauma of their early lives. After this, they were transported like apple or orange juice, sold on the open market. After amusing consumers for a few weeks, the best they might expect was being flushed down a toilet.

"All for profit! Such a business is a 21st-century version of slave trafficking."

Public sensitivities, they demanded, had to be elevated: One of the survivors from Dixie's Diner, still half dazed from near-drowning, was discovered bailing out neon tetras from the bed of his pickup onto the parking lot, and was pummeled and shoved to the side by two rescuers.

The secretive Knights of Corinthians' Hall itself, without help from events outside, was no small contributor to the ambiance of Offbeat Americana: The stalwart brotherhood had festooned the walls, north and south, with head mounts—now quite moldy—of every regional creature—fur and foul. This was no meeting place for those easily cowed by contemporary trends.

Younghusband picked his way through and around knots of people, passing into the inner sanctum of the building leading from the Grand Hall. Smaller, but far more lavishly designed, this was the lodge's "Sacred Induction Altar," cloaked in drapes and the mediaeval gobbledygook of secret fraternal organizations.

This was the birthplace of secret handshakes and male discussions concerning penis dimensions. And it was appropriate that this area was the most secure, hidden from public view, from the eyes of the non-anointed (and certainly all females and non-Christians, of course). Here, the medical team had set up and was now laboring to receive their extra-dimensioned patient and his clearly delusional driver.

Younghusband needed to steel himself before facing Wagner, and remembering the smell of coffee in the hall, turned. He'd prefer a stout cup of tea, but out here, finding someone who knew how to brew tea, well, that would be like finding a Wagner who exercised modest speech to articulate his disapproval about events. And that was not going to happen.

Milepost 190.15
Livestock Crossing
Proceed with Trepidation

Heavenly Fur Angora Rabbitry attracted every sort of creature with an affinity for a rabbit repast. But a giant bobcat was a first. Doreen McAllister finished off feeding and changing the water bottles of the nursing does, checked the nests for activity, then returned to the house where husband Dexter read the morning Spartanburg Sentinel.

"I saw a giant bobcat."

Dexter lowered the paper, looked up and thought a minute.

"You sure?"

"It had big tufts on its ears, and big old long legs. Plus it was the size of Jeanette's husky, Missy Nootka."

"Then it must have been a cougar."

"It wasn't a cougar. Cougars are larger, and have long tails," Doreen allowed herself a shifty smile, "and don't wear collars."

"Collar?! Well, what was it doing?"

"Ogling the rabbits."

Dexter stood and looked out the window, as if expecting the marauding feline to be staring back at him.

"Collar or no, I better fetch the shotgun."

"No use. It saw me and tore off down the middle of the road towards Styton. Like if it was carrying a dispatch or something."

Dexter reasoned this out: A cat the size of their daughter's dog ogling their rabbits, wearing a collar, and heading off down road towards Styton.

"So, it had a sense of purpose?"

"Well, Dear, it seemed to."

Dexter returned to the paper but became irritated. He knew it was another sign of eccentrics. And this, Dexter knew, added another black mark against the new casino six miles down the road—which he'd adamantly opposed. It, of course, lured eccentrics to South Carolina.

And with eccentrics, you logically got exotic ideas and behavior. Of course, worse was behavior. If a person wanted, say, to eat sheep meat wrapped in a pancake, this was fine in the privacy of their kitchens—but not out before

God, heaven, and everybody.

"Multiculturalism."

Doreen poured herself coffee, and sat down at her spinning; she shook her head, reached over and patted him on the knee.

"Don't get lathered up, Dear."

Who else but an eccentric would put a collar on a giant bobcat and let it roam the country—brazenly using county and state highways for comings and goings. Dexter picked up his paper, but glowered at the page, not reading.

"Eccentrics."

It all led directly to strangeness, which was never good nor right.

36

Their labors complete and with belts of equipment clanking about their waist, the emergency brigade filed into the Hall. It was now a secure area, meaning free from press cameras, weeping fish lovers, and non-participants diverse. The emergency workers dug into coffee and rolls set up by the Corinth Sisterhood.

They were not a crew of happy rescuers.

Younghusband offered solace to them as they huddled around the serving area, lapping their wounds. They had not been prepared for Wagner's lack of gratitude.

"When we cut through enough to make voice contact, and, you know, we asked if he was all right, the son-of-a-bitch told us. . . ," the ranking EMT ducked a look at a Corinthian Sister serving beverages, and couched his reportorial duties, ". . .well, he wasn't very darned grateful, let's put it that way. He spit fish at us."

Younghusband knew the time had come to face his own brand of Wagner music, and leaving behind the hurt feelings of the rescue squad, marched to his fate.

Herself's doctors from John Hopkins University, along with county and state medicos, were working over an irate Wagner. Sitting on the next gurney was the limousine driver. He and Wagner argued bitterly, using the most profane and obscene language imaginable. The root of the argument was compensation for the obliterated limousine.

Noise level diminished when the driver, having the temerity to be relatively uninjured, was whisked off by state patrolmen to be booked on a list of charges rendering his driving days over until the next ice age. But before being escorted out, he shouted that HE— and no one else—should collect the reward. Clearly, new knowledge concerning his passenger was grist for opportunity.

"None of you sons-of-bitches would have him, if it weren't for me. Goddamnit! Me!"

When the door closed behind him, Younghusband, now braced for the meeting—approached Wagner, unsmiling. The two knew where each other stood in regards to mutual disdain and matters odious. It had been almost eight weeks since Younghusband's chaps had bagged Wagner *en flagrante* with Madam Crazy Sue, and "By Jove," admitted Younghusband, "that quack had sweat the weight off the boorish swine."

The temperature of Wagner's response was not slow in rising: A meaty Wagner arm was raised—a hateful index finger was thrust at Younghusband over the shoulders of nurses hooking him up to diverse meters.

"This is all your responsibility, Younghusband, you rotten no good, sister-selling, kipper-chewing limey sodomist. And goddamnit to hell, where's my fucking lawyer!!"

The cardiac monitor indicator leaped around like fleeing gazelles in full panic—a doctor implored him to be calm.

Younghusband watched the medical types labor away—yet he knew Herself would arrive within minutes. Invariably every greedy, Butter-My-Biscuits politician hungry for MEI's investment dollars would be clinging to the hems of her dress, so he must act fast. Younghusband drew as close to Wagner as he dared, and played a rare mean-spirited trump card. After the misery Wagner put him through of late, could Younghusband be blamed?

"Your lawyer, Sir, until a few hours ago, was occupied pursuing Miss Crazy Sue all over southeastern Florida. So at this moment I can't say precisely where he is, or, in point-of-fact, *if* he is."

Coming from Younghusband, the news caught Wagner square, silencing him at least long enough for Younghusband to return to the main lodge hall. Good! He had his moment, and Younghusband had only barely managed it. For at that point Herself entered with the Governor of North Carolina, Stromboli, the Commander of the State Patrol, and an odd Senator and Congressman taking up the rear.

Billions of investment dollars created an aroma unyielding to the vulture-like olfactories of politicoes. But predictably, Oswald, had elected to stay in the suite to deal with breaking legal actions, regarding Carolina Packing's labor shenanigans.

When Herself strode up to him, her arm through that of the Governor, her eyes articulated wordlessly the question with grand clarity, and Younghusband replied, "He's quite all right, Ma'rm. Airbag burns, numerous contusions, bruises. Your team is with him. They should have an overall report soon."

The poor woman noticeably sagged. Her eyes closed momentarily, then opened. She excused herself, and after entering the Sacred Induction Altar, all personnel filed out, including doctors and nurses.

She been given ten minutes alone with her oldest son.

Stromboli closed the double door labeled Sacred Portal to The Perpetual Induction Altar in mother-of-pearl inlay. He stood at a stiff parade-rest, arms crossed. He would see to it that they would stay alone. Yet Stromboli's backside was bumped hard—and turning he opened the Sacred Portal to allow Miss Rothstein to exit. Both men looked at each other—as surprised as Stromboli she was even inside. Indeed, they hadn't even known she was in the country. She tottered over to a nearby chair and sat, wringing her hands—clearly she had been weeping.

Looking up, her jaw set in anger, she declared, "I'm not sorry. It was a matter of life and death."

Though momentarily perplexed, Younghusband was just putting Miss Rothstein's comment into context when, from the opposite side of the shut Sacred Portals, Wagner's explosive roar penetrated through the entire hall, "O Most Foul Treachery!"

Wagner resolved that everything was fucked up, and—despite all his most strenuous efforts—it was apparently going to remain fucked up. Wagner knew that—like the Salmon King—the Salmon Queen never negotiated a decision once made. Only an act of the Olympian Gods would remove him from North Carolina. So, regards any thought of remonstrating his status with his mother, Wagner knew it was best to save time and breath.

The remorseless fact remained: His escape failed.

So there had been tears, hot accusations, and hotter counter-accusations, during which Leggy Peggy, who'd hidden from the odious Younghusband, abandoned ship—exiting the arcane hall in tears. For, truth to say, Wagner's temper flared.

But what was Wagner supposed to do, forgive her? After the wretched female's guilt-ridden disclosure that she—Peggy!—had perpetrated all this? After she'd confessed, his mother had tried to shield his assistant from primary responsibility. But Wagner ranted. And why not!

Peggy! that double-dealing . . . . But Wagner thought a moment: *Calm thyself, Wagner old man. Remember your iron hand regards mental discipline.* So—after the poop settled out, he and the Salmon Queen displaced wonderfully—reverting to their mutual act of peacemaking and morning ritual established when he was barely literate: Crosswords. From her handbag, she removed the D Section of the *Raleigh Courier*, which included the New York *Times* Sunday Crossword.

It was an amazing demonstration of getting-on-with life that she and her eldest son had perfected early. What was done was history. Only the Salmon King would have known the truth—words and wit were their way of touching. "Oh, you're a cold pair of birds," he would complain—for despite his harsh reputation, the Salmon King was a secret hug sharer.

So when the medical team returned, they were puzzled by this calm, the odd choice of activity. Yet, they found a Wagner far more composed.

Ultimately, Wagner decided, *What the hell*, and even allowed them to draw blood. Yet Wagner found bile returning when Younghusband put in a reappearance, and pausing in his contemplations over a fourteen-letter expression meaning 'measured joy,' Wagner resumed with some of his earlier bitterness. His eyes locked on his enemy.

"You, Sir, regards my friend and attorney, now have stooped to methods of a common slanderer. In a word, you are a shithook."

The Salmon Queen protested Wagner's abuse, reminding him that the Colonel was doing her bidding. Also, she reminded him of

Wagner's original accusation—that it was the Colonel who'd sniffed out his health problems, "When in truth, Son, you were very wrong."

Then, with a glance, realizing strangers were in the room, she took off her reading glasses, putting them away. Wagner smiled, appreciating the Salmon Queen's long indulgence to feminine vanity.

"I must go, son, really. A business crisis." Then she looked intently at him—and they locked eyes.

"And I meant it, son. You're much better, but I insist on more weight off. I remain adamant. I shall return this evening."

Then she kissed him, and strode out—and Wagner glared while Younghusband took in a most unusual development: For the first time since his employ, Stromboli did not accompany the Salmon Queen, but stayed with Wagner.

Wagner smirked.

"That's right, Younghusband, you Anglican doorstop. Stromboli will make sure your lot of North Carolina pederasts and necrophiliacs don't finish me off while I'm unable to defend myself—seeing's they did everything but kill my ass for those fucking rewards," and when Younghusband, with a polite and controlled nod, began to exit, Wagner added, "Oh, about rewards: Tell Brother Boy, I'm personally going to purchase a million dollars of gold kruggerands and shove them down his throat, one at a fucking time, the little capitalist worm."

Despite the good healthy feel of heaping abuse on those who so plagued him, Wagner fell into a pout while the team worked: Doctors prodded; little, wicked machines blinked away after being fed his blood; curtains were drawn around him, then repeated requests to pee into this, that, and every goddamned thing.

His life was not his own and he missed his offices in Eagle River, and the hands-on work of the journal and foundation. Working by laptop and modem from St. Finny's, well, it just was not the same.

And when an escape goes as cattiwompus as this one did, psychologically it was like finding oneself abandoned on a rocky, hostile coast.

Wagner was marooned.

Milepost 190.2
Caution: Similes Crossing
Flagperson Ahead

He appeared like Mephistopheles, suddenly erupting from out of the dark, fiery earth;

Or, was it—he appeared like a great tiger, who suddenly charges into a clearing, surprising grazing young deer—their death-day at hand;

Then again he might have appeared like the deadliest of falcons, dropping unseen from the sky, latching onto a dove, the hunter's talons powerful, and unmerciful;

Or, not to deal with second-raters, go straight to the ancient source itself, the Ionian poet and mystic, Homer:

"As when some stalled horse who has been corn-fed at the manger/breaking free of his rope gallops over the plain in thunder/to his accustomed bathing place in a sweet running river/and in the pride of his strength holds high his head, and the mane floats/over his shoulders; sure of his glorious strength, the quick knees/carry him to the loved places and the pasture of horses…"

So from the uttermost Florida battlefield came Moynahan, striding into the International Knights of the Corinthians Hall (Styton, North Carolina Branch) holding a writ aloft, intoning to all, "I have a court order enjoining any and all actions to remove, transport, or otherwise convey my client, Einar Innokenty Wagner, from the legal bounds of the municipality of Styton, North Carolina, until conduct of fair-hearing, at Court 11-A, County seat, Polk County, of self-same state."

And somehow knowing the Officer-of-Jurisdiction, Moynahan walked over to a bewildered Undersheriff, gave him the order, turned and, taking the briefest of pauses (looking to his right at Peggy Rothstein, who burned an angry look at him), entered the Sacred Portal to the Perpetual Altar.

37

Wagner glared at his childhood friend and visibly choked up. Then looking to Stromboli, he said, "I need to be alone with my lawyer, Stromboli."

For in truth Younghusband was not a conjurer of facts, and Wagner had been shaken by his information, however ill-intended it might be.

Wagner was blessed with few friends, and to be so betrayed by his closest and most trusted? Well, it hurt. Shaking his head, Wagner raised his hand before his face, as if blocking from view the sight of a demon. Moynahan, knowing his cover had been blown, managed to keep his chin high, but stayed his distance.

As Stromboli conveyed all others out, the two men confronted one another.

"Moynahan," Wagner's voice sank to one of despondency. "My mother's action I can understand—she's my mother, and believes these fucking quacks and 21st-century quasi-alchemists. And Peggy, too. She's a rattlehead. But you?! But you? You were my friend," and Wagner, remembering the Salmon King's admonition at men weeping, steeled himself. He gestured outside to what might have been freedom, justice, and a helluva fast plane ride back to Alaska.

"Moynahan, I got within fifty fucking feet of getting out of this accursed state. I needed you. Now you tell me face to face, goddamnit: Was that vile Younghusband telling me the truth? Were you in Florida chasing Crazy Sue—that odious, double-dealing, abject harlot? You. Who so roundly condemned her, always. Of all people. You?"

Moynahan fell back a pace, dropped his briefcase to the floor; though struck to near silence, he struggled for voice.

"You would believe a mercenary over a friend of forty years!?" Moynahan raised a finger—jabbing it at the ceiling. "Well fuck you! When people told me you bedded my mother, asshole, wasn't I at least friend enough to ask you—man to man, if it were true?"

This aged bit of bad highway, Wagner knew, was a well-crafted grounder between first and second base. Wagner always denied it, of course, for in spirit he had not—she'd seduced him specifically to ruin their friendship. (When choice was denied, could moral responsibility be assigned?) So Wagner's denials were, at their center, an essential truth.

And anyway, to raise this business now, well it was pure Moynahan artifice.

"Don't divert, Moynahan! You base lizard. Were you chasing Crazy Sue around Florida while all the capitalist evils so plagued me? Yes or No, and don't fuck around."

Moynahan picked up his briefcase, walked up to Wagner—almost chin to chest—and said, "You're fucking rights I was, always with you in mind, you pigheaded asshole!"

With a grand, practiced flourish, he opened the briefcase, brought out a set of papers, dangling them before Wagner's eyes, "For these are your passport out of North Carolina. Here. You're goddamned rights I was chasing her around, because I needed a woman crazy, heartless, and mercenary enough to marry you. Because, therein—marriage to your worthless frame—lies freedom. But even that duplicitous slattern bolted at the idea."

"Marriage!"

"That's correct, *mi amigo*, Marriage. A wife trumps a mother, commitment-wise, in North Carolina, and you're home free. But **only** as long as you and the woman have 'previous, and demonstrated association' (Funk vs. Wolfenspach, 1922). And in the case of an acid-mouthed tyrant like you, that's a helluva tall order. So! I'm working on it—and I think I have a solution. Now, it's OK by me, if you go ahead and feel like an abject shithead for so doubting me."

Wagner's mind was turning on an axis of shame and gratitude, and he was just about ready to embrace his friend—so terribly wronged by himself—when a grand clatter and outcry came from outside. A cry of fear and outrage dominated. "Holy shit! Watch out!

Look at the size of that cat!!"

Outside was the sound of people scrambling for cover. The Sacred Portal burst open, and along the west side of the room, Wagner and Moynahan watched the floor-to-ceiling drapes ripple as something struggled to find its way through.

"Close that goddamned door!"

Which someone did—with a heavy BANG! Wagner's faith in friendship and truth was raised even more when slipping beneath the drapery trotted Lulu. She spotted Wagner, and, bounding past Moynahan, jumped up on the gurney next to her long-absent master. Knowing Lulu's less-than-appealing personality, Moynahan jumped aside.

"That goddamn thing is a menace."

But the physicians and nurses of the medical team looked on with professional interest, though a distant, hands-off variety.

So secured, Lulu leaned against him, purring.

Wagner stroked her and inspected right, left and underneath—a true, proud cat owner.

"Lulu, you little shit, you are badly in need of a trim and shampoo. But, it's hard, getting groomers."

It was true: Lulu's ear tufts had completely grown out, and her pelage had reverted to its deep arctic texture—a rich off-white, with small chocolate-dark checkerings everywhere.

Yet, as Mottled Macedonians go, Lulu was perfect.

Milepost 190.25
No Transmitters; Explosives in Use, next .15 miles

The lawyers for Carolina Packing knew Mrs. Wagner and son hadn't a bit of law behind them, yet General Harris—CEO of Carolina Packing—was not a strong man. And Mrs. Wagner was a very strong woman—a different, more tireless opponent than Oswald Wagner.

(Didn't the name say it all about him?! They would chuckle, in private!)

And, of course, the MEI lawyers made it appear there was law behind the Wagners, for they were good, loyal sorts. And possibly General Harris might have held his mark, if an incredible thing hadn't happened:

Oswald Wagner sprang to his feet and burst into a fury, screaming, "If you continue General, THIS is what will remain of Carolina Packing's reputation and financial portfolios!"

And with a scream, whoop, and banshee cry, he jumped into the air and did a classic Bruce Lee into the suite's wall, caving it in. Then, landing on his two's, he reached out, and with the same effort one might expend tearing a hunk of cake loose, ripped the drywall off, and tossed it into the center of the room.

Then he passed out.

Without pause, Mrs. Wagner eyed General Harris, and said icily how wronged Oswald had been, and clearly, this led to his nervous collapse.

"He took you at your word, General," she concluded, shaking her head, "then, to find out there were major labor problems, scattered across national television. It crushed him."

When the Carolina Packing people left, defeated—signed by the General into renewed legal territory—the MEI lawyers stayed behind as Mrs. Wagner and her maid Katrina helped Oswald into his room.

These MEI lawyers had worked with Oswald for seven years. What they'd seen was like witnessing a turtle dove suddenly flying up and taking out a tough old rooster with a Muhammed Ali combo shot.

And there really hadn't been a shred of law behind their reneging on the Carolina Packing deal. Truly, the Wagners were an extraordinary family. But, until a few moments ago, Oswald had seemed the least extraordinary of them all. Apparently, that assumption needed reappraisal.

38

Moynahan began to earn his $850 an hour plus expenses when the prospective bride and groom refused to be in one another's presence—and in fact, would negotiate only by note.

Note #1 presaged what was going to be a hard sell:

Leggy Peggy:
You scrawny, two-timing bitch. You do this thing, or you're fired!
Wagner
P.S. You should be honored I'd even entertain it.

"Wagner," observed Moynahan, "this is not the stuff of expert negotiation. I would revise."

And handed the notepad back.

The frustrated escapee labored over his composition, scratched out—rewrote, scratched out—sighed, then presented it to Moynahan with a *harrummph* and a mumbled, "What total compromising bullshit."

Leggy Peggy:
I forgive you for ratting me out to my mother. Now, you can redeem yourself by doing this thing. You got me in North Carolina, now you can fucking well get me out.
Wagner
P.S. Thank you for taking care of Lulu.

Moynahan decided this was an improvement, and since Peggy would not deal with the good attorney personally (taking umbrage with past days' tardiness), she recruited Stromboli as a Messenger Figure. In minutes, he returned with the response.

Mr. Wagner:
I never liked being addressed as "Leggy Peggy." It is demeaning.

And, I respectfully point out, there's no purpose served in a man of your highly developed intellect and compositional skills using obscenities.

Peggy

The immediate response was not good.

"By fucking Christ, I'll cut the turncoat's gullet!!"

With that, a quick fifteen-minute break was called by Moynahan when—well, in truth, the physician-in-charge feared immediate cardio-vascular catastrophe. He pointed out that accumulated walls of chicken fat and cooking grease allowed Wagner's great heart benefit of only twenty-five percent of its blood supply. "I fear such rages have life-threatening potential."

He insisted on at least mild sedation.

After the sedative took hold, almost a half hour had elapsed, and Wagner labored over his response, and finally, with his body visibly relaxed, he wrote,

Peggy:

I am now drugged. I've always had a high opinion of your abilities. If you were so negligent as to not communicate how you felt concerning my good-natured nickname, that is not my error. Now, I repeat: Your treachery got me IN North Carolina, and, by doing this thing, it seems you can get me out.

Wagner

Mr. Wagner:

Request how I might do this "thing" specifically, and I'll be more than happy to comply, for I agree—my good intentions foolishly contributed to your being in this situation. I do apologize for this.

Peggy

Peggy:

Don't be coy. You know damned well what "this thing" is. You've been married two—or is it three—times? You have a son the size of a goddamned polar bear.

Wagner

Mr. Wagner:

I've never been married. You just assumed I was. And Freddy is not the size of a polar bear.

Peggy

Peggy:

I didn't assume. You told me. Anyway, who was, or who was not—during your reproductive career—your husband(s), isn't central. Your response to the issue at hand is.

Wagner

Though Peggy ran out of the Hall weeping, retreating to the motel, Moynahan knew signs were favorable. He did remind himself to edit the notes a bit more heavily upon resumption of negotiations.

But fatigue had set in all the way around, and emotionalism was to be expected. Rest was needed.

As a veteran negotiator, Moynahan knew that with some sleep—plus tweaking Wagner's prose style here and there, eventually an agreement would be reached by court tomorrow afternoon.

"Listen Wagner, after we break bread, I've gotta haul ass. My driver is outside. There's much to do."

Wagner—at the mention of bread—turned his attentions away from Peggy. He listened intently when Moynahan ordered a six-cheese pizza smothered in black olives and Portuguese anchovy. But anticipating his request, Moynahan warned, "According to the doctors, there are hamsters who have more blood supplying their hearts than you do. You get a salad."

"By that, you hoggish prick, I assume you're not going to let me have any pizza."

Moynahan reflected on the last few days, and on his friend's recent near-death experience; and his resolve for better health weakened.

"Well, a slice wouldn't hurt, I suppose. To celebrate your upcoming marriage."

In the end, you see, they were friends.

Milepost 190.3
No County Maintenance Beyond this Point

Cops, newsmen—everyone—had seen the lawyer arrive at the Knights of Corinthians Hall in the gleaming scarlet Jaguar. It was a classic '65 with black, ornate pinstripes hand painted around the outside of each wheel well.

When he bounded into the hall, though, eyes remained on the Jag', but not because we had a group of automobile aficionados. From the driver's seat, two long, ebony white legs emerged; then, stepping onto the pavement, a woman appeared that seized every male's soul at once.

She was tall, with long auburn tresses that tumbled freely below her waist. Her attire could not have been more simple or primordial: Cut-offs, a bright yellow tank-top—barefooted, yet with one ankle sporting a thin, gold anklet and the other an encircling tattoo of laurel leaves.

Reaching into the Jag, she took out a purple hair squisher, and, reaching back, took hold of her hair, wrapping it quickly into an extraordinarily long pony tail with the gaily reddish ribbon. When she did this, all the men watched her full breasts move in sync beneath the tanktop, its thin material revealing perfect sculptured beauty.

The upper garment's lower edge rose sadistically—almost far enough.

Most prominent, though, were, first, her eyes and then her face. The eyes were green, and mobile—flashing tints of aquamarine as she looked about. Her face had high cheekbones—the cheekbones of some Scythian shepherdess. Then there was a wide, downward slanting mouth, a matchless emblem of beauty and utilitarianism. And when she smiled, she seemed to smile towards all—causing each male to greedily fantasize what it might be like, taking each one of those garments off and bringing that perfect body close against theirs. Then to know her absolutely.

Thus within their collective fantasies, they drew moral and civilized curtains around this secret erotic vision and got with the program, even if just mentally.

Fools! Destitute of good sense!

This was no simple beauty, whose critical ingredient depended on youth; not the frail material of fashion-magazine stick-girls or movie celebrities.

She was a perfect, mature woman who could screw any man into a heap—leaving him a virtual roadkill buck rabbit, ripening for the buzzards. Sexually, she rendered males down to their essence: A set of reproductive organs shuttled left and right atop a pair of willing legs.

No moral misgiving would ever find bottom in her azure waters.

Then she got back into the Jag (was there a suggestion of yet another smile—an invitation?) and drove off.

When—two hours later—the attorney left the hall, he looked to where his car had been—looked to where it might have gone—looked to the sky—looked to the earth. Then, shamelessly, he fell to his knees, and slowly raising his fist, thumped the stairs softly, repeating to the heavens, "Oh, God! She took the Jag. She's gone. Why did I do it? Oh, Sweet Mother of Mercy, is this the end of Moynahan?"

Milepost 190.35
Roadside Cenotaph Ahead

This memorializes Wagner who by all rights should be dead, but is not. But sooner or later he will be, which renders this a hopeful cenotaph.

Near this locale in the year XXXX , he departed the bounds of North Carolina a free man. A more ruthless, selfish and self-indulgent fiend never before traversed the soil of North Carolina. His joy in leaving is fully matched by the exultant, pure contentment regards the state of North Carolina, and its citizenry, knowing he is gone. God help the people and territory of any and all in the event Wagner ever visits. And God grant similar reprieve to the United States of America, its territories and holdings,

\#

OTHER BOOKS BY PLEASURE BOAT STUDIO: A LITERARY PRESS

Schilling, from a Study in Lost Time. TERRELL GUILLORY
  ISBN 1-939355-09-2, $16.95, 156 PAGES, FICTION
Rumours: A Memoir of a British POW in WWII, CHAS MAYHEAD
  ISBN 1-929355-06-8, $17.95, 201 PAGES, NONFICTION
The Immigrant's Table, MARY LOU SANELLI
  ISBN 1-929355-15-7, $13.95, POETRY
The Enduring Vision of Norman Mailer, BARRY H. LEEDS
  ISBN 1-929355-11-4, $18, LITERARY CRITICISM
Women in the Garden, MARY LOU SANELLI
  ISBN 1-929355-14-9, $13.95, POETRY
Pronoun Music, RICHARD COHEN
  ISBN1-929355-03-3, $16, SHORT STORIES
If You Were With Me Everything Would Be All Right, KEN HARVEY
  ISBN 1-929355-02-5, $16, SHORT STORIES
The 8th Day of the Week, AL KESSLER
  ISBN 1-929355-00-9, $16, FICTION
Another Life, and Other Stories, EDWIN WEIHE
  ISBN 1-929355-011-7, $16, SHORT STORIES
Saying the Necessary, EDWARD HARKNESS
  ISBN 0-9651413-7-3 (HARD), $22; 0-9651413-9-X (PAPER), $14, POETRY
Nature Lovers, CHARLES POTTS
  ISBN 1-929355-04-1, $10, POETRY
In Memory of Hawks, & Other Stories from Alaska, IRVING WARNER
  ISBN 0-9651413-4-9, $15, 210 PAGES, FICTION
The Politics of My Heart, WILLIAM SLAUGHTER
  ISBN 0-9651413-0-6, $12.95, 96 PAGES, POETRY
The Rape Poems, FRANCES DRISCOLL
  ISBN 0-9651413-1-4, $12.95, 88 PAGES, POETRY
When History Enters the House: Essays from Central Europe,
  MICHAEL BLUMENTHAL, ISBN 0-9651413-2-2, $15, 248 PAGES, NONFICTION
Setting Out: The Education of Li-li, TUNG NIEN, TRANSLATED FROM THE
  CHINESE BY MIKE O'CONNOR, ISBN 0-9651413-3-0, $15, 160 PAGES, FICTION

OUR CHAPBOOK SERIES:

No. 1: *The Handful of Seeds: Three and a Half Essays,* ANDREW SCHELLING
  ISBN 0-9651413-5-7, $7, 36 PAGES, NONFICTION
No. 2: *Original Sin,* MICHAEL DALEY ISBN 0-9651413-6-5, $8, 36 PAGES,
  POETRY
No. 3: *Too Small to Hold You,* KATE REAVEY, ISBN 1-929355-05-x, $8, POETRY
No. 4: *The Light on Our Faces: A Therapy Dialogue,* LEE MIRIAM WHITMAN-
  RAYMOND, ISBN 1-929355-12-2, $8, 36 PAGES, POETRY
No 5: *Eye,* WILLIAM BRIDGES, ISBN 1-929355-13-0, $8, 20 PAGES, POETRY

No.6: *The Work of Maria Rainer Rilke: Selected "New Poems" in Translation,* TRANSLATED BY ALICE DERRY, ISBN 1-929355-10-6, $10, 44 PAGES, POETRY

FROM OUR BACKLIST (IN LIMITED EDITIONS):

Desire, JODY ALIESAN
ISBN 0-912887-11-7, $14, POETRY (AN EMPTY BOWL BOOK)
Dreams of the Hand, SUSAN GOLDWITZ
ISBN 0-912887-12-5, $14, POETRY (AN EMPTY BOWL BOOK)
Lineage, MARY LOU SANELLI
No ISBN, $14, POETRY (AN EMPTY BOWL BOOK)
P'u Ming's Oxherding Tales, RED PINE
No ISBN, $10, TRANS FROM CHINESE WITH ILLUSTRATIONS, FICTION
(AN EMPTY BOWL BOOK)
The Basin: Poems from a Chinese Province, MIKE O'CONNOR
ISBN 0-912887-20-6, $10/$20, (PAPER/ HARDBOUND), POETRY (AN EMPTY BOWL BOOK)
The Straits, MICHAEL DALEY
ISBN 0-912887-04-4, $10, POETRY (AN EMPTY BOWL BOOK)
In Our Hearts and Minds: The Northwest and Central America,
ED. MICHAEL DALEY, ISBN 0-912887-18-4, $12, POETRY AND PROSE
(AN EMPTY BOWL BOOK)
The Rainshadow, MIKE O'CONNOR
No ISBN, $16, POETRY (AN EMPTY BOWL BOOK)
Untold Stories, WILLIAM SLAUGHTER
ISBN 1-91288724-9, $10/$20, (PAPER/HARDBOUND), POETRY (AN EMPTY BOWL BOOK)
In Blue Mountain Dusk, TIM MCNULTY
ISBN 0-9651413-8-1, $12.95, POETRY (A BROKEN MOON BOOK)

ORDERS:
Most Pleasure Boat Studio books are available directly from PBS or through any of the following:
SPD–Tel: 800-869-7553, Fax 510-524-0852
Partners/West–Tel: 425-227-8486, Fax: 425-204-2448
Baker & Taylor–Tel: 800-775-1100, Fax: 800-775-7480
Ingram–Tel: 615-793-5000, Fax: 615-287-5429
Amazon.com
Barnesandnoble.com

FOR PBS ORDERS:
Tel/Fax: 888-810-5308
Email: pleasboat@nyc.rr.com
Website: www.pbstudio.com

HOW WE GOT OUR NAME:

from *Pleasure Boat Studio*, an essay written by Ouyang Xiu, Song Dynasty poet, essayist, and scholar (January 25, 1043)

"If one is not anxious for profit, even at the risk of danger, or is not convicted of a crime and forced to embark; rather, if one has a favorable breeze and gentle seas and is able to rest comfortably on a pillow and mat, sailing several hundred miles in a single day, then is boat travel not enjoyable? Of course, I have no time for such diversions. But since 'pleasure boat' is the designation of boats used for such pastimes, I have now adopted it as the name of my studio. Is there anything wrong with that?"

- Translated by Ronald Egan